# Daydreams
# of a
# Country Boy

# Daydreams
# of a
# Country Boy

## Thomas McDonald

To order additional copies of this book, contact:
**Bookwhip**
1-855-339-3589
https://www.bookwhip.com

Then the cool night air hit their sweaty bodies, and they started to shiver. Quickly they dressed and got into the truck.

Mike opened his arms and she went into them. "I love you," he said quietly.

"I love you too," she responded.

"Someday, I'm going to make that dream come true."

"I know you will."

They both looked at the waterfall and dreamed. Linda giggled and Mike stared at her.

"What?"

"When are we going to make love in our own bed or any bed for that matter?"

"Very soon I hope." Mike laughed.

# Chapter 1

July 1, 1952

Mike lived fifteen miles from town. The last two miles was dirt road, running beside a prairie, then turned left into the woods.

Mike Love was fifteen years old, had brown eyes and brown hair, and was of medium build, just a plain old country boy. Bill Love was sixty-five years old and looked forty, six feet tall, black hair, and was strong as an ox, probably from all the hard work he did all his life. Elsie Love, his mother, was short and fat, with long black hair, and looked like she was in poor health, as she was fifty years old and looked older.

"Well, Son, we're home."

"All it needs is a little work and paint."

"You got to be kidding."

"No, I'm afraid not."

"Dad, I've seen barns that look better than this old house."

The truck pulled in front of the old frame house. It was set high off the ground. It needed paint and a lot of repairs. The house had a porch across the front and another porch across the back. There was a well beside the house for water. An old outhouse was back behind the house for personal use. There was a large barn further back for the livestock. It looked better than the old house.

Bill was a sharecropper. He moved from farm to farm searching for the best land for growing crops, but like most sharecroppers, he didn't have a pot to piss in or a window to throw it out.

Bill had hired a truck to move them, since he didn't own a vehicle and never had. He never learned to drive either. Horses and a wagon were all he ever knew all his life.

Elsie Love looked at the old house. "Let's go in and see what the old barn looks like."

"Mom, watch your step. The steps are busted."

Elsie glanced at her husband. "That's your first, honey. Do."

It had a large living room, a large bedroom, and a back-to-back fireplace for heat, and off the living room was another bedroom. In the back of the house was a kitchen with bare wood walls. It would be cold in the wintertime. The house wasn't too bad since it had electricity, a good wood floor, and a good tin roof. Bill planned to fix up the old house and give it a paint job.

There were trees around the house that would keep the house cool in the summer. It was nine in the morning, and it took the rest of the day to clean the house. It was dark by the time they had everything moved in.

The next day Bill and Mike went to move the horses, one old milk cow, and the chicken. Plans were made that evening for the work in the summer ahead.

"Mike, I'm not sharecropping anymore. Mr. Glover is going to pay me a salary to take care of the ranch and the farming. We can grow a garden for food, corn, and hay for all the livestock."

"It sure would be better than sharecropping."

"Mr. Glover said he would pay you to work also."

"Great, I sure would like to earn money to buy a car."

"It will be hard work and cheap pay."

"I don't care. I just want to work and earn some money."

"I'm old enough to draw social security now, so things should be getting better."

Mrs. Love looked up from her ironing. "Bullshit, old man! You have been telling me that for years. You are not ever going to get us any better off. All I've ever done is work all my life, and we will always be dirt poor."

Mike got up and went outside, not wanting to hear his mom and dad fuss, as they had ever since he could remember. As Mike walked toward the barn, he looked up at the sky. The stars were so bright and pretty that he started to daydream. *I would work all summer to buy a new car, a red convertible, and some new clothes. Then when school starts, I will find myself a girlfriend and have some fun.*

"Son, come on to bed! You hear!"

"Mom, I'll be right in."

Bill was up early the next morning, milking the cow and feeding the chickens. Mrs. Love woke Mike up and started breakfast. They didn't have much in the way of food. They didn't buy much from town. They tried to get along by raising everything, but at times, it got hard to put food on the table. They had biscuits, cowboy gravy, and milk for breakfast.

After breakfast, Bill and Mike rounded up their tools and went to the woods. They would work from daylight until dark. That was a normal day for farmers and ranchers.

"Mike, did you get the water jug?"

They would clear the land of undergrowth and clear the brush from the fences. They would cut some of the trees and cut them up for posts. Splitting posts was a backbreaking job. They cut the post to the right length and used wedges and a sledgehammer to split the post.

Mike thought he would die by the second day; his hands were blistered, and his whole body ached.

"Dad, there must be an easier way to make money."

"Mike, why do you think I keep making you go to school?"

"I don't know."

"So you won't have to work hard all your life, like I have, and not have anything to show for it."

"Dad, I'm sorry for what you have had to go through."

"I only got ahead one time in my life. I had some cattle and horses. The big depression hit, and I lost everything."

"What did you do?"

"The only thing I could—dirt farming. I wasn't smart. I had only gone to the second grade."

After a few days, Mike's hands and body became hard, so the work didn't make him ache anymore. One morning, Mr. Glover, the owner of the ranch, brought a new Ford tractor to the ranch.

"Mike, would you help me unload the tractor off the trailer?"

"Yes, sir."

After the tractor was unloaded, Mike was looking the tractor over. "It sure is a pretty thing."

"Well, Mike, are you ready to drive the tractor? I got some work for you to do."

"But . . . but, Mr. Glover, I don't know how to drive a tractor."

"No problem. I'll show you how. It won't take long."

Mr. Glover told him to get in the seat and do exactly what he was told. Turn the key, set the gas throttle at two notches, foot on the clutch, gearshift out of gear, the N position. Now push the start button. Mike was a little nervous. He pushed the start button and the tractor roared to life. Next he showed him how to drive, pushing in the clutch, putting the gearshift in first position, and letting off the clutch. Mike was driving in a few minutes.

Mr. Glover spent the rest of the day, teaching Mike how to attach the mower and the rest of the attachments. By the end of the day, Mike could do it all.

All Mike talked about that night was driving the tractor till finally his mom said, "Go to bed, Mike."

"OK, Mom." He went to bed.

The next weekend Rex Johnson came to visit. Mike and Rex were best friends. They had known each other most of their life. Rex was fifteen years old, had black hair, was of slender build, and was a city boy. Rex loved to visit the country, while Mike loved to visit Rex in the city, so it worked out great for both of them.

Mike helped Rex carry his gun, knife, and other hunting equipment into the house.

"When will your dad be back to pick you up?"

"He said I could spend the night and he would pick me up tomorrow evening. Boy, we got a lot of catching up to do! How do you like the ranch? You sure are lucky to live out here. You can hunt, fish, and ride horses. It sure is neat."

"Well, look at the calluses on my hands. My face and arms are blistered, and my clothes are worn out. Do you still want to be a farm boy?"

"I guess not. Too much work for this city boy."

"Dad said since tomorrow was Saturday, he would let me off work, so we can go hunting."

"That sounds good to me."

Mrs. Love called, "You come in, wash your face and hands. Supper is ready. Come and eat, or I'll throw it out to the chickens."

"We're coming, Mom."

After supper, Mike and Rex sat outside on the front porch, talking over old times. Mike gazed up at the stars and daydreamed about the hunt tomorrow. He would get the first squirrel and the most squirrels for the day. He daydreamed a lot, hoping they would come true. He daydreamed about girls but really didn't know much about them. But he was going to learn as soon as he got a new car.

"Hello, hello, are you there?" Rex waved his hand in front of Mike's face.

"Sorry, I was thinking of something."

"It had to be girls or food."

"I was thinking, I could almost taste squirrel and dumplings."

Mrs. Love would cook squirrel and dumplings if they killed any. The family was lucky to have meat once a week. They were out on the porch.

"Mike! You boys come to bed."

"OK, Mom, we'll be right in."

The next morning, the sun was slowly rising, the rooster was crowing, and you could smell fresh bread baking in the oven. It was going to be a beautiful day. Mike sat in bed as the rooster started crowing again.

"One of these days, we are going to eat that rooster for Sunday dinner."

"Then what would you use for an alarm clock?"

"I don't care. I could get some sleep."

Rex jumped out of bed and began to dress. "Come on, let's eat and then go hunting for squirrels."

Mike finished eating first and went back to his room to get his guns and hunting knife. He took his belt with the holster and knife attached from the closet, and then he put the belt around his hips. He reached under his mattress and pulled out his .22-caliber pistol and checked to be sure it was loaded. He put it in his holster and tied the holster to his right leg, "fast draw" style.

He went into the living room to wait for Rex to finish eating. Elsie Love came into the living room and sat in an old rocker.

"Rex sure is a big eater, and if he stays long, he will eat us out of house and home."

Mike turned to face the fireplace. "At this rate, all the squirrels will be back in their nest by the time we get into the woods."

Rex entered the living room and sneaked up behind Mike. He pulled the pistol from Mike's holster and leveled the pistol. "Stick your hands up. I got you covered."

"Rex—" Mike spun around.

"Bang! I got you!"

The pistol sounded like a cannon confined in the living room. Rex stood staring at Mike and finally got his voice back. "I didn't know the gun was loaded."

"Well, it was."

"Honest, I didn't—didn't mean to do it! You got to believe me!"

Mrs. Love started crying hysterically and wringing her hands. "What are we going to do? What to do?"

Mike had felt the impact as the bullet passed through his shirtsleeve, at the left wrist, and slammed into his chest, almost knocking him to the floor. Mike regained his balance but felt a severe pain in his chest. It felt like a branding iron.

"Rex, go get Dad. I think I'm hurt bad."

"I'll be right back. Don't die."

Rex ran out of the house to find Mr. Love. Mike sat down in a chair and opened the front of his shirt to find a hole in his chest, and blood was flowing from the hole.

"Mom, I think I'm going to die, but I'm too young to die."

"Don't say things like that."

Mrs. Love sat with a blank look on her face and continued to cry. She just sat there in shock and didn't know what to do.

"Mom, get something to stop the bleeding."

Mrs. Love finally got up and left the room, searching for something to stop the bleeding. She returned with a towel. Mike covered the wound with the towel, applying a lot of pressure to stop the bleeding.

Mr. Love and Rex charged in from the front door, talking a mile a minute. They picked Mike up and carried him outside, where Mr. Glover was waiting with his car. Mrs. Love stayed at home, while the rest of them headed for town.

It was fifteen miles, so Mike was imagining he would be dead before they got to the doctor. Mr. Glover drove like the devil was after them.

"Son, don't be afraid. We'll be at the doctor's office in a few minutes."

"It hurts. Oh, it hurts!"

"I know it hurts, but hang in there. You're going to be fine."

His son's suffering hurt Mr. Love, and he prayed he would live. He was an only child, and he was afraid it would kill his wife if Mike didn't pull through. As they arrived at the doctor's office, Mr. Glover brought the car to a screeching stop.

Mr. Love and Rex quickly helped Mike out of the car. They carried him into the doctor's office.

Dr. Latham, a fat little man with a bald head, stood waiting until they were in the room.

"Put him on the examining table in the next room."

"My son has been shot," said Mr. Love.

"Let me remove your shirt so I can get a look."

The doctor removed Mike's shirt and the towel so he could examine the wound. The wound had stopped bleeding, but there was a large jagged hole.

"What size gun were you shot with?"

"It was a .22-caliber pistol."

"Well, that's a mighty big hole for a twenty-two."

The doctor used a probe to locate the bullet, but he couldn't find the bullet. He called for his nurse to take Mike for an x-ray. Nurse Marsh wheeled Mike down to x-ray room. She helped him onto the table, while positioning the x-ray machine next to Mike's chest.

"This thing is cold."

"Yes, it is, but you are a tough guy. I think you can handle a little cold. The x-rays won't take long." They were finished shortly. "See, that wasn't so bad."

Nurse Marsh wheeled him back to the examining room to wait for the x-rays. A short time later, she brought the x-rays to the doctor, and he examined them.

"I can't find the bullet on the x-rays."

He came over to the table and started using the probe again. He didn't understand why the bullet didn't show up on the x-rays.

"Oh, that hurts!" complained Mike.

"Are you sure it was a .22-caliber bullet?"

"Yes, it was a .22-caliber long rifle, fired from a .22-caliber pistol."

"Then I don't understand why the hole is so large. It looks like a .45-caliber hole."

Mr. Love moved Mike's shirt off the table, and everyone heard something hit the floor.

"Well, how about that?" the doctor said as he picked up the bullet off the floor and handed it to Mike. The bullet was bent into a "U" shape.

"I guess you'll live. Looks like the bullet must have hit a rib and came back out the same hole. That would explain why the hole was so large."

The doctor called his nurse over. He gave her directions to patch Mike up and give him a tetanus shot. That would fix him up.

Mr. Johnson came to pick Rex up and take him home.

While the nurse finished with Mike, Mr. Love paid the doctor bill and filled out a police report on the accident. Mr. Love thanked the doctor for his time.

"OK, Son, let's go home. Your mother is probably half-crazy worrying about you."

"Do you think we will ever have a telephone?"

"I don't know. They are so high priced."

Mr. Glover was waiting nervously in the car as Mike and Mr. Love returned to the car.

"Are you all right?" asked Mr. Glover.

"Yes, sir, let's go home."

"At least, I won't have to drive as fast home."

Mrs. Love was still crying when Mike and Mr. Love walked in the front door.

Mike explained, "It is OK, Mom. Please don't cry anymore. The nightmare is over, and after all the excitement, I'm hungry."

The long hot summer slowly moved closer to time for school to start. Mike worked long days and weekends trying to raise enough money to buy a car. It wasn't looking too good moneywise. He would be lucky to buy a piece of junk, but he still had hopes.

Mike's dream was to buy a cool car to impress the girls so he could make out. Mr. Glover let Mike practice driving his pickup all summer so he would know how to drive when he got his own car. If you don't have wheels in a small country school, you can forget about the girls.

Two weeks before school was going to start, Mike counted his money, hoping to have enough to buy that dream car. He had saved nine hundred dollars. That would have to be enough.

Mike approached Mr. Love. "Dad, I want to buy a car."

"No way. With you going to school, you can't work, and you will have no job, no money, and no driver's license. Just how do you expect to support a car and make payments?"

"I'll get a job in Booneville and work nights. I'll get a driver's license if you will sign for me. After I buy a car, we won't have to depend on Mr. Glover to loan us his pickup to get to town and other places."

"I don't like it."

"Dad, I have to have a car. If I don't have a car, I'm dead in the water."

"You will be broke all the time trying to keep up a car."

"Then I'll have to be broke, but I can take people with me to buy gas."

After two days of argument, Mr. Love agreed to give it a try.

"Saturday we'll go to town and buy a car, for better or worse. I don't like it, but we'll do it."

"Thanks, Dad. You won't be sorry."

"Mark my words, Son. After you buy a car, it will always keep you broke, trying to keep it running."

A few days later, Mike had to admit that his dad was right. He was always broke after buying that dream car, or should he say pile of junk?

Saturday morning, Mr. Glover came by and took Mike and his dad into town. He let them out on the square. Stores were built in a square around the courthouse, like most small Texas towns. Main highways ran through the town, and streets branched off from the square with more stores on the side streets.

Mike and his dad walked two blocks west from the square to Sherman Ford. After thirty minutes of talking to a salesman, Mike didn't want to face the fact that his dream was shattered. He would never be able to pay for a new car.

"Well, Son, what do you want to do?"

"Go find a used car lot, I guess."

"I think there's a used lot on the north side of the square."

"OK, let's see if we can find it."

They walked back to the square, the one block to Honest John Used Cars. Mike started looking over the cars. John looked outside and thought to himself, *I got myself a fish.* He rushed out of his office.

"Honest John, best cars, best deals, lowest prices in Texas. What can I do for you?"

"My son would like to buy a car, but we don't know anything about cars, and we don't have very much money to put down."

Honest John started his sales pitch, "I got just the car for you, with low mileage. This 1948 Ford is only three hundred down, plus tax, title, and license."

"Dad, what do you think?"

"I don't know anything about cars. It is pretty and shiny."

"That car belonged to a little old school teacher that hardly ever drove it."

"We'll take the car," said Mike.

Honest John had them hog-tied before they knew what was happening.

"Dad, we sure got a good deal."

"I'm not so sure about that."

Mike drove the car off the lot and headed for home. Five miles out, they pulled into a service station to get some gas, but when Mike put his foot on the brake to slow down, the pedal went all the way to the floor. The car barely missed the gas pumps. He pulled up the emergency brake, but the car kept going until it hit a ditch.

"Son, what happened?"

"We don't have any brakes."

Mike used the telephone in the service station to call Honest John. "My brakes went out on the way home. Can you send someone out to fix the car?"

"Young man, didn't you read your contract?"

"Not too good. It was too hard to understand."

"After you drive a used car off the lot, it's your problem now," said Honest John and hung up.

After buying the car and paying to get it fixed, and also a fill-up on gas, his money was going down fast. *Surely nothing else would happen today.* He knew he was going to hear from his dad.

"Well, Son, at this rate you will be broke before we get home."

"It hasn't been a good day so far, but maybe it will get better," he hoped.

"I doubt that."

Mike was mad. He burnt rubber in first and second gear while leaving the service station. Elsie Love came out to meet them as they pulled up in front of the house. She walked around the car and touched it.

"Son, it is a beautiful car. It's so bright and shiny. I can see myself in it."

"Mom, we got a real good deal."

Bill Love looked at his son and shook his head. As they went inside, Elsie Love said, "Supper is ready. Come and eat, or I'll throw it out to the chickens."

"I don't think the chickens would eat it," said Bill Love, laughing.

"Shut your mouth, old man."

Monday morning, Mike went to town to take his driver's license test. If he passed the test, then he would look for a job. He had a form signed by his father so he could get hardship driver's license, since he wasn't sixteen yet.

There were a lot of people at the Department of Public Safety taking their driver's license test.

"Young man, if you are here to get a license, put your name on the list."

"Yes, ma'am, I want to get a driver's license."

Mike put his name on the list to take the written test. He picked up a driver's handbook and sat down at a table to study. After an hour, his name was called to take the test. He made an eighty, which was a passing score, and was told to report back after lunch to take the driving portion of the test.

The Dairy Queen was a few blocks down the street, so he decided to go there for lunch. As Mike drove past the Dairy Queen, he saw a couple of fine good-looking chicks watching him. He turned around, squealing tires, and turned in front of the Dairy Queen. He got out of the car and combed his hair. His ducktail would never stay in place.

Mike was trying hard to be a cool cat and get the girls' attention. He got their attention when he dropped his Coke. The girls started to giggle as Mike got back in his car. He felt like an ass. *How could I have done such a stupid thing?* He backed out into the street and burnt rubber as he made a fast retreat.

After reporting back to the Department of Public Safety, Mike nervously waited his turn to drive. The ADPS officer told him to go to his car and wait. The officer came out and told Mike that his car had to be checked before he drove it.

"Get in and turn on your lights."

"Yes, sir."

"Blow your horn."

"Yes, sir."

"Turn on your right-turn signal."

"Yes, sir."

"Turn on your left-turn signal."

"Yes, sir."

The officer got in and looked the car over. "OK, start your engine, back out, and let's go driving."

Mike jerkily backed out and started to move forward.

The officer said, "Do not be nervous. Drive as if you were by yourself."

After a short time, Mike finally relaxed and drove normal. "How am I doing now?"

"Just fine. Just keep it up, and you'll get your license."

The test didn't take long, and Mike got his driver's license.

Mike was happy and singing as he drove to the edge of town, where a new drive-in theatre was under construction and was almost completed.

The Skyline Drive-in Theatre was small but nice. A sign was posted *Help Wanted,* so Mike drove down to the concession stand and went inside.

Mr. Jones was the manager, and he was a very friendly man. After a short interview, Mike was hired for ticket catcher on the coming in.

"As soon as we are ready to open, you will be notified by letter when to report for work."

"Thank you, Mr. Jones. I won't let you down."

Mike was on his way home a very happy young man, believing dreams do come true. He had a car, driver's license, and a job. It was good to be alive. He was daydreaming about having a good-looking chick sitting beside him, with her hand resting on his thigh, causing his manhood to rise. Mike was still a virgin, but with a car, he would soon take care of that problem and become a man that all the girls would be after.

# Chapter 2

School started on Wednesday of the following week. The little country school was located in a small hole in the road, called Casper Texas.

The school bus came early that day, and Mike almost missed it. As he walked down the island to find a seat, out the corner of his eye, he spied this sexy little thing. He wanted to say something to her, but the cat had his tongue. As Mike passed her, his manhood started to rise, and he had to hurry to find a seat so as not to embarrass himself.

The bus was noisy, and the dirt road had a lot of holes with deep ruts, causing everyone to bounce up and down on their seats, like on a trampoline. All the foliage along the side of the road was covered with red dust, until the bus turned onto the highway for the rest of the leg to school.

Shirley and Ann Link gossiped and giggled, both trying to glance around to watch the new boy that had gotten on the bus.

"I think he is cute," declared Shirley.

"Well, he looks like another country boy to me."

"I know he isn't queer."

"How do you know?"

"I saw him get a hard on when he passed us," replied Shirley, giggling.

Ann scolded Shirley, "You are so nasty. All you think about is sex."

"I guess that is because I'm still cherry."

"Well, I am too, but I don't talk about it."

"Ann, have you ever thought what it would feel like to have a guy stick it in you?"

"No, I didn't." Ann smiled. "Well, maybe one time while I was dreaming."

"Did it feel good in your dream?"

Ann blushed. "My panties were wet after the dream."

They both giggled. Shirley was outgoing, said what she thought, while Ann was the quiet one and very shy, even though she was the older sister.

Shirley was in the ninth grade and playing athletics, while Ann was in the tenth grade and was a bookworm.

The bus unloaded in front of the school. Shirley and Ann got off the bus and waited to see the new boy again. He walked by them, and they giggled but didn't say a word to him. No one said a word to Mike. He hated changing schools, especially the first day. The girls giggle, and the guys look you over, wondering how tough you are.

It was like having a new bull in the pasture. The guys wondered which girl he would try to take. They didn't want him messing around with their girlfriends. Last was the bully, or cock of the walk will try to put you down in a fight or abuse; either way was very effective if he put you down.

As the students went inside the school, Shirley lagged behind, and as Mike moved up, she stepped over just enough to cause a collision with him, making her books drop from her hands.

"I'm sorry," stammered Mike, as he picked up her books.

"That's all right. My name is Shirley Link. What's your name?"

"It's Mike, Mike Love."

"You aren't from around here, are you?"

"No, I moved here during the summer."

"I wondered why I never saw you."

"I worked all summer on a ranch."

Mike was staring into the most beautiful brown eyes he had ever seen. Shirley was about five feet five inches tall and had a nice suntan and a cute little nose with just a few freckles across it. Her long brown hair was in a ponytail, with a tiny bow on the end. She was dressed in a light-brown sweater, a full skirt, bobby socks, and loafers. The bell rang and Shirley broke eye contact.

"See you later, Mike."

"I sure hope so."

"You will." She smiled at him as she walked away down the hall.

Mike walked in a trance on the way to his first class. He was in love. The following days on the bus, Mike sat by Shirley to and from school, and in some of their classes they had sat together. He carried her books, and they held hands. Things were looking good for Mike.

A few days later, the school bully found Mike. Al was a senior and a basketball jock, as well as the school bully. In the lunchroom, Al stuck out his foot and tripped Mike, causing him to drop his tray of food. He would be pushed into a fight, but he didn't expect to be flat of his back so quick. He knew he didn't stand a chance of a snowball in hell, beating the guy, so he stayed down.

Al walked off laughing. "Well, another chicken to add to the chicken list."

Shirley was watching Mike as he got up off the floor. She asked, "Are you a chicken?"

"No, but I'm not a fool either."

"Well, you could have fooled me."

"No way. I could win with that gorilla. He would have beat me to a pulp."

"At least you would have been a man." Shirley walked off without a word.

When Mike got off the bus, he was in a very bad mood. Shirley was still mad at him for not defending himself. Mike decided not to get mad but get even. The question was how to do it, so he would have to think on it.

Mike had received his notice to report to work. Tonight would be his first night at work and the first night the Skyline Drive-in was open for business. Mike stopped on his way to work for gas. He hadn't been taking his car to school so he could save his gas to get to work. Counting his money, he sure was glad to receive a letter telling him to report to work, as money was getting low.

Grand opening signs were posted at the entrance. It was on the radio and in the local newspaper. Mike pulled in behind the ticket booth and parked. He came around to the front of the booth.

"Good evening, my name is Mike Love."

"Glad to meet you, Mike. My name is Alice Long, and you can call me Alice."

"I'm your ticket catcher."

"Nice to have you working with me. The job isn't hard at all."

Alice explained to Mike what his duties consisted of, which were very easy. He would take the money from the customer in the car and hand it to her. She would make change, then hand Mike the change and tickets, and he would hand it back to the customer. Not much to it, but at least Mike had a job and a paycheck.

"Mike, what do you think about your new job?"

"Yes, it looks easy enough to me."

"You can have free popcorn, Cokes, and a free pass for your car to see all the movies," explained Alice.

"How many can I bring in my car?"

"You can bring one guest."

Mike liked the job already. The movie had been full that night, which was a good opening night.

When the movie was over, Mike said, "Good night, Alice. It's been nice working with you."

"You too. See you tomorrow."

Mike got in his car and headed for home. As Mike drove home, he thought back. He didn't remember what was showed, only that John Wayne was the star of the movie. It took twenty minutes to drive home from work, and Mike daydreamed all the way home.

He had come up with a plan to get even with Al for embarrassing him in front of his girl. *Payback would be fun. I would make sure of that.*

For the next few days, Mike watched Al to figure out how to pull it off. He noticed that in history class no one sat down around Al until he was seated. Probably they were scared or showed respect. That was the clue for payback.

For the next few days, Mike watched the clock on the wall and timed how long from the first bell until Al was seated at his desk. It took an average of one minute and ten seconds until he was seated.

That evening, before Mike went to work, he worked on his surprise for Al. He removed the powder from a box of shotgun shells, wrapped a small amount in tissue paper, rolled it in a ball of candle wax, dipped a string in lighter fluid to use as a fuse, and installed the fuse in the ball of wax.

Mike lit the fuse, tossed it into the yard, and bang! It worked like a charm! Mike laid out more string and lit it, timing the burning time. He kept burning lengths of string until he had the burning time down to one minute and ten seconds.

Mrs. Love watched Mike. "What do think you are doing?"

"I was just having a little fun blowing up things."

"That's dangerous. I want you to stop it right now!"

"But, Mom, can't I just do one more time?"

"I said no, and I mean it!"

"Yes, ma'am."

He wanted to test his whole device, but he would have to settle with what he had done so far. Mike made up another ball and attached the long fuse. He went out in the cow pasture and found a ripe cow pie. He placed it on a piece of cardboard and brought it back to the house. He took the homemade firecracker and slipped it into the cow pie. He found a paper sack and put his creation in the trunk of his car.

Mike's car would smell like cow shit, but it would be worth it to pay back Al. He would do just about anything to get back at Al for embarrassing him in front of his girl.

The next day, Mike drove to school early. He took the sack out of his car and put it in his locker. Everything was ready, except waiting for the right moment. Everything had to be timed just right to make his plan work.

Between classes Mike took the sack out of his locker and slipped in through the door to the history classroom. The room was empty, so Mike's luck was still holding. He sat the sack on Al's desk and took the cow pie out, laying it on the desk.

Mike waited for the bell to ring. He was scared to death, and his heart was beating ninety miles an hour. If Al caught him, he was dead meat. The bell sounded to go to class. Mike lit the fuse, then ran like hell for the door, just as Al entered the classroom. Al walked over to his desk.

"What the hell?"

No one said a word. They only sat and stared at Al. The cow pie exploded, and cow shit flew all over Al, head to toe. Al rushed out of the classroom to the bathroom, cussing as he went. He was going to kill someone if he found out who did this to him. The classroom went wild, with everyone laughing. Not many people liked Al; they were afraid of him. When he came back in the classroom, he wanted to know who did it, but nobody knew.

"I'll give fifty dollars to the person who can tell me who did this."

They looked at one another, but nobody knew who did it. The teacher had the janitor come and clean up the mess, and he didn't like it.

Mike was told later what had happened to Al, the janitor cleaning up the mess, and Al offering fifty dollars to the person who could tell him who did it. Mike wasn't sure, but he didn't think anyone but a friend of Al's would turn him in anyway. But he wouldn't ever take the chance and tell anyone. The only thing wrong with getting even was that he could never tell anyone that he did it.

Al didn't know whom to blame, because he picked on everyone. He thought over all the people that might have done it, but he thought they were too chicken to do it. From that day on, Al got the nickname of shit head, behind his back, since no one was fool enough to say it to his face. Friday evening, on the way home, just before Mike got off the bus, he asked Shirley for a date Saturday night, and she accepted.

On the way to work, Mike stopped at a drugstore. He wanted to get some rubbers, just in case Shirley was willing. At least in his dreams she was, but by now, Mike relinquished the fact that dreams don't always come true.

As Mike opened the door to the drugstore and went in, he noticed the only one behind the counter was a little old lady.

"May I help you, young man?"

Mike became nervous. His face turned red, and he lost his voice. It was the first time he had ever tried to buy a box of condoms.

"May I help you, young man?" she said, with lack of patience.

"May I have a box of rubbers?"

"What size rubber bands?"

Mike was blushing from embarrassment. "The other kind of rubbers, you know, condoms."

She slowly reached under the counter and put something in a sack.

"That will be one dollar and twenty-five cents."

"Yes, ma'am."

Mike paid his bill, picked up the sack, and made a fast exit, as the little old lady glared at him. You would think he was going to screw her daughter, with the look she gave him. Mike jumped in his car and beat feet for the drive-in. It was time to go to work.

Ticket catching was a fun job, since a lot of good-looking girls came to the drive-in. It gave a guy time to look and flirt with the girls, but he had to take a lot of cold showers, because a lot of the girls forgot to or, on purpose, didn't pull their dress down when they stopped for a ticket. Boy, did he ever see a lot of skin! Mike realized he was becoming a man or just a horny boy.

Alice watched Mike while he worked and thought it was funny when he would get an erection while waiting on the girls. She smiled at him when he came to get tickets and change. He gave the girls their tickets and change while looking at the girls' black lace panties. He sure would like to see more. She giggled as she drove off. She probably left her dress up on purpose. Girls sure did like to tease. He walked back to the box window.

"What were you smiling at?"

She glanced down at the front of his pants. He turned around embarrassed. On the way home, it started to rain, and the road was slick. Mike ran over something in the road.

"Why me?" murmured Mike.

A few minutes later, he had a flat. His luck was the same as usual, all bad. The jack didn't work, and it was raining cats and dogs. But finally the tire was changed, and the jack finally started to work. Mike made it home, but he looked like a drowned rat.

Saturday evening rolled around, and Mike tried to make his appearance cool, that night being the night he dreamed of. He wanted everything to be right for a change. He had washed, waxed his car, and cleaned the inside.

As Mike pulled in front of Shirley's home, he was scared to death. It was his first time to pick up a girl. He wondered if he could just honk his horn but gave that up as a bad idea. It was also his first time to face a girl's parents. He finally parked his car and went to the door. Shirley was watching for him and opened the door.

"Mom, this is Mike."

"Good evening, Mrs. Link."

"Hello, Mike, I won't give you kids a lecture, but be home by eleven, and don't drive too fast."

"OK, Mom," replied Shirley.

She grabbed Mike's hand and pulled him through the door. As the car pulled out of the driveway, Shirley asked, "Where are we going?"

"To the Skyline Drive-in, where I work. Is it all right with you? We can get in free, and I get free Cokes and popcorn."

"Sounds good to me," Shirley lied. She had wanted to go to a house theatre. She didn't like a drive-in for a first date. She wanted to go someplace where they wouldn't be alone on their first date. When they arrived at the drive-in, Mike parked on the next to the last row.

Shirley sat close to Mike but not close enough to touch each other. As the movie started, Mike moved over until their thighs touched. He draped his arm around her neck until the tips of his fingers touched the rise of her breast. Shirley couldn't relax and control her body. Her breathing became ragged, and her nipples turned hard, straining to be released from the confinement of her bra. Her body was alive, wanting to be touched. She had to do something quick.

Shirley had never had an experience like this. She could feel the juices in her private part starting to flow. She had to get control of her body.

Mike wanted to tell Shirley that he was in love with her, but knowing her only a couple of months, he imagined that she would think that he was just a foolish country hick.

Shirley liked Mike, but she didn't want to get serious. He was fun, but he was a poor country boy. Shirley licked her lips as she turned her face toward Mike. Their lips were only a couple of inches apart. He sensually touched her lips with his own, gently at first, then more demanding, as he slipped his tongue into her warm mouth and started to explore. Mike was winging it, since he didn't have any experience with girls, except what he had heard or seen.

Shirley slipped her arms around Mike's neck and pressed her breasts against his chest. A soft moan escaped in her throat.

"I love you and want to make love to you," whispered Mike.

Mike realized too late that he should have kept his mouth shut, as the spell was broken and Shirley pulled away.

"We have to slow down," gasped Shirley. "Everything is happening too fast."

Slowly her brain was taking back control of her body. "Would you go get us some Cokes and popcorn, please?"

"OK, right away."

Mike reluctantly got out of the car and went to the concession stand. By the time he returned, Shirley was on the other side of the seat and in full control of her body. They watched the movie, ate popcorn, drank Cokes, and made small talk about school. Mike knew the spell was broken, and he didn't know how to get it started again, but he didn't have the experience with girls.

On the way home, Shirley sat close to him but without any body contact. She didn't want to lose control of her body again and didn't want Mike to know how much she had been roused by him.

"Mike, I had fun tonight."

"Me too, but I did something wrong. I guess I went too fast with you."

"I guess you did, but I should have stopped you sooner."

"Are you going on another date with me after what I did tonight?"

"Yes, but keep it cool next time."

When they arrived home, Mike walked her to her front door. Shirley let him kiss her good night but didn't invite him in the house.

On the way home, Mike pondered over what had gone wrong and how to correct it on the next date. Less talking and more necking and touching had to be the answer. Mike had sensed when Shirley had lost control of her body. He would have to plan how to control her body. He knew she was hot and wanted more but quit too soon. He knew now that he should have done more kissing and kept his mouth shut. He didn't know why it turned her off when he told her he loved her. He thought all girls liked to hear things like that, but maybe it was because he told her he wanted to make love.

But on the next date and following dates, Shirley maintained perfect control of her body, except on one occasion, when after a long period of necking, Mike eased his hand inside her blouse, cupping her firm breast, while sliding his other hand under her skirt and between her thighs.

"No, please don't do that," moaned Shirley, as she caught his Mike's hand before he could reach her private area.

"Why don't you want to? I know you want to."

"I'm too young. I'm only a freshman, and I don't want to get serious yet."

"But you're driving me crazy with wanting you."

"It's doing a number on me also, but I just can't do it."

Their relationship started to crumble after that night. It was never the same again. Shirley became cold, and they grew further and further apart.

A week before Christmas, Shirley approached Mike in the hall at school. "Mike, we need to talk."

Mike had a gut feeling what was about to happen. He didn't want it to happen, but he didn't know how to stop it.

"I don't want to date you anymore, but we can still be friends."

"But I love you, Shirley."

"Yes, but I don't love you. I'm sorry."

The bell rang for the next class. Shirley turned and walked away without looking back. Mike felt like he had a knife twisted in his gut. He left the school in a daze.

Mike had driven his car to school that morning. He left school, skipping his next class, and headed for home. Mike walked in slamming the front door and went straight to his bedroom.

"You're home early," called Elsie Love. "Are you sick?"

"Yes, Mom. I got a bad headache," Mike lied.

Mike ran out the back door and went to the outhouse. He sat over one of the holes with tears running down his cheeks, while looking at the Sears and Roebuck catalog.

*I'm nothing but a damn country boy.* Mike laughed. *I should have known it wouldn't last.*

That evening, as Mike sat on the front porch, Bill Love came out and sat beside him. He could tell something was wrong.

"Son, do you want to talk about what's wrong? I can see you are hurting."

"I lost my girl. She doesn't love me."

Bill studied his son for a few minutes. "It's time we had a father-to-son talk. I'm going to give you some advice. I know it hurts, but time will heal the pain. I know a few things that will help you. First of all, we are poor as church mice, and it wouldn't have lasted with her. She is out of your league, and you couldn't buy her the material things a girl wants. So don't worry about it. It was puppy love anyway. You aren't old enough for real love. When there's one girl going, there's two coming. Don't have sex with a girl unless you want to marry her. Don't buy the cow if you can get the milk free."

Quietly, Bill got up and went back into the house. "Some talk. I didn't understand a thing he said," murmured Mike. His luck went from bad to worse. In the next few months, his car had flat tires, blowouts, battery trouble, a blown transmission, and a tie rod fell off, causing him to have a wreck.

If he didn't have bad luck, he wouldn't have any luck at all. It took all the money he could earn to keep the old car running. What a piece of junk! His dad had been right about owning a car. He was having a hard time keeping the pile of junk running. Mike swore off girls and just worked.

"Dad, can I work on weekends in the daytime, on the ranch?"

"I don't see why not."

"You were right. I can't keep this old car running."

"Well, I won't tell you I told you so."

"We'll split post Saturday."

"Oh boy, just what I wanted to do!"

"Yeah, I bet you did." Laughed Bill.

Mike didn't date anymore the rest of the school year. He didn't have money to date.

All summer, Mike kept working at the drive-in, trying to get some money saved. He was slowly getting a little saved.

One night, Mike came home to find Mrs. Love wandering around outside the yard.

"Mom, what are you doing out of the house this time of night?"

"I don't know."

"Well, you had better come back inside."

Mrs. Love seemed like she was in a daze, and she didn't know where she was. Mike led his mother back into the house and woke his dad. They put Mrs. Love back to bed.

"Dad, what's wrong with her?"

"I don't have a clue."

"She was wandering around outside, and you know how scared of the dark she is."

"We'll have to take her to the doctor tomorrow."

Next day, Mike carried his mother to the doctor and was informed that she would have to go to Galveston. She would be emitted to John Sealy Hospital, where she would receive electric shock treatment for a nervous breakdown.

"Mike, would you take your mother to Galveston, while I stay here and work?"

"I guess I'll have to, but I have never driven that far before."

"Just read your map and follow it."

"OK, Dad, I'll make it."

Mr. Love stayed home and worked while Mike drove his mother to the hospital. Before they reached Houston, the old car blew a bottom water hose out in the middle of nowhere. Mike drove on into Houston, pouring water. The car ran out of water just as he pulled into a service station. He was lucky the engine didn't freeze up from being too hot.

After waiting for the repair on the car, they arrived at John Sealy Hospital in Galveston late that evening. After filling out the hospital forms, Mrs. Love was emitted to a ward. She was a charity case and would be put where they could find room for her. After she was put to bed and was sleeping, Mike decided it was too late to drive home, so he would have to find a room and spend the night, then start back in the morning. He leaned over and kissed his mother on the cheek and left the hospital.

Mike filled up his car with gas. He went looking for a motel to spend the night. He found a motel by the beach and rented a room for the night. Five dollars was sure high. Motels were two dollars back home.

Mike strolled along the beach, watching the girls. The water was a dark blue, the sand pure white, and the sun was slowly setting in the west. *What a beautiful sight to see!* Mike stopped and watched the waves splash upon the beach.

"Is this your first time to visit the beach?"

Mike turned to see a teenager about the same size and age as he. He was dressed in swim trunks and had a dark suntan.

"Yes, it is. I brought my mother to the hospital." They exchanged teenage experiences.

"Are you looking for some action?"

Mike looked puzzled. "Say what?"

"You know, wine, women, and song."

"Sure, why not? My name is Mike Love."

"Glad to meet you. Call me Ned. Have you got wheels?"

"Yes, I do."

"Good, because my car is broke down. See the bus stop over there? Well, I'll meet you there at eight tonight with the girls and booze."

"I'll be there."

Mike returned to the motel to get ready for his date. He showered, changed clothes, and put on some cheap cologne.

Promptly at eight, Mike parked his car close to the bus stop and waited. He started daydreaming about his blind date. She would be five feet two inches, and weigh one hundred and five pounds, with long black hair, and very sexy.

The bus stopped and the first one off was a girl with long black hair. Mike stared at her. She was stacked like a brick shit house, and he thought his dream was coming true. Next, Ned followed by a sexy blond holding his hand. Mike couldn't believe his luck. Maybe it was about to change for the good.

Mike stepped out of the car and waved to get their attention. They walked over to the car. "Hi," said Mike, "I see you made it."

"I had a little trouble rounding them up, but we made it."

"This is my date, Cindy, and this is Isabella, your date."

"I'm Mike and glad to meet you."

Isabella smiled. "I am glad to meet you too."

Ned got in the backseat with the blond, and the sexpot got in the front seat with Mike. No last names were mentioned.

"What do you want to do?" asked Mike.

"Let's go to a drive-in theatre," suggested Ned.

The girls agreed it was OK by them. They went to an old movie. Mike was the only one not smoking. Nobody was watching the movie, because it wasn't worth watching.

Isabella was a chain smoker and kept a beer in her hand continuously. Mike put his arm around Isabella's waist, pulling her into his arms with the intention of kissing her, but she held back.

"Not so fast. You'll make me spill my beer or burn myself with my cigarette."

"Sorry about that."

Mike heard a soft moan from the backseat and glanced in the rearview mirror as Ned ran his hand up Cindy's dress while engaging in a deep passionate kiss. Mike was thinking, *Some guys have all the luck.* He and Isabella sat and watched the movie and listened to the sounds from the backseat. The car started to bounce, and it drove Mike crazy. Cindy screamed when she reached a climax.

After Isabella finished her beer and lit another cigarette, Mike tried again to steal a kiss. As their lips touched, Mike almost gagged. Her mouth was cold and tasted like an old ashtray left over from a party. After a couple more kisses, Mike was totally turned off.

They began to talk about nothing of any importance, and Mike started drinking heavily the rest of the movie. He wasn't used to drinking and was becoming drunk.

"How long have you smoked?"

"I have been smoking since I was twelve."

"You know, smoking is bad for your health."

"I don't care."

"Isabella, aren't you going to give Mike a little piece? I thought you liked to screw."

"I'm not in the mood."

Ned had to drive back to the motel, as Mike was too drunk to drive. They were in the motel only a short time before Mike passed out. The last thing he remembered was staring at Isabella's big tits and wanting to suck on one of them.

The sunlight coming through the window woke Mike up. He raised his throbbing head and thought it would fall off any minute.

The room looked like a tornado went through it; cans and bottles were everywhere. Mike spotted his wallet on the floor, picked it up, and found what little money he had left was gone. He checked his pants and found less than a dollar in change in them. What a mess he was in! But at least he had filled up his car with gas. He could make it home. He might get a little hungry on the way home, but he had been hungry before.

After checking out of the motel, Mike went by the hospital to check on his mother and find out how long she would be in the hospital. She was awake and sitting up in bed.

"Good morning, Mom. You look good this morning."

"What am I doing here?"

"Mom, the doctors say you had a nervous breakdown."

"Well, I don't feel sick."

"I'm going to have to leave you for a few days so they can treat you."

"Well, if you say so, but I don't feel sick."

After his short visit, he headed home. As Mike left Galveston and headed toward Houston, he mulled over his experience in Galveston. It appeared he had learned another hard lesson in life. He stopped in Houston long enough to get a Coke and then continued on to Booneville. He arrived home at two o'clock in the afternoon.

"How is my wife, and how long will she be in the hospital?"

"Mom will be in the hospital at least two weeks, but she is doing fine."

"I guess you will have to eat my cooking, and I can't cook."

"Great! I can't cook either."

For the next two weeks, Mike worked every night at the drive-in. A little over two weeks, the hospital called to tell us Mrs. Love could come home. Mike had left a neighbor's number for the hospital to call.

Mike made a fast trip down and back. Mrs. Love sure was glad to be home. She had made a complete recovery from her breakdown. Now things could get back to normal. It sure was nice to have a cook again.

Dewayne Carter lived a half-mile down the road from Mike. He stopped by one afternoon to visit. Dewayne and Mike exchanged summer experiences, hitting it off real fine. Dewayne especially liked the Galveston tale. It was funny to Dewayne but not to Mike. The rest of the time before school started, every chance they got, they went fishing, hunting, or swimming. They became the best of friends by the time school started.

School started, but Mike wished the summer had lasted longer so he could have made more money. Dewayne and Mike double-dated a lot, pooling their money together to buy gas. This way they could go on more dates. Mike was determined to make out before school was out again, but the best of plans fell apart, and his daydreams turned to nightmares.

There was Rita, who played basketball, had muscles like a boy, lips as hard as bricks, and cheap perfume from a five-and-dime store, that would drive off any flying insect. Then there was good-looking Betty, with a mouth that never stopped flapping long enough to be kissed, and last but not least, Nickie, who thought she was God's gift to men but couldn't be touched with a ten-foot pole. Mike was about ready to give up on girls with the luck he had been having. He was still a virgin.

It was the last of April, with the school year slowly coming to an end. Mike turned seventeen years old and no love life to brag about. He was still cherry.

Friday morning, Dewayne waited at the lockers for Mike with a big grin on his face. He had talked Shirley Link into a date for Saturday night.

"Mike, I got a date with Shirley."

"Good for you." He couldn't help but show his anger.

"I know you went out with her and liked her a lot. I hope it doesn't make you mad if I go out with her."

"No, help yourself, and good luck, because I couldn't make out with her."

"I still want to double-date. I'm short on money."

"I don't like the idea," Mike argued. "Besides, who would I date?"

"How about asking Shirley's sister for a date?"

"No way. Ann is very straitlaced, a year older than I am, a straight 'A' student, and attending church regularly. So what would we have in common?"

"You are a guy and she is a girl."

"So what does that have to do with anything?"

"If you don't know, I'm not going to tell you."

"I still don't like it."

"Come on, please do it for me, Mike. I'll owe you big-time."

"Shirley will talk her sister into going for safety in numbers."

"I still think it will be a very boring night."

"When we park, we will divide them up like the military, divide and conquer."

"Dewayne, you are crazy."

"Come on, do me this one favor."

"I will only if you set up the date for me."

"Pick me up at five tomorrow evening. I forgot to tell you that the only way I got Shirley to say yes was to double-date with her sister."

"You set me up."

"Yes, but it will be fun. Thanks, I owe you one."

Mike felt used, having been set up by his friend. Besides, he still liked Shirley. She had been his first love, and it hurt seeing her with someone else. Mike decided, *What the hell! Might as well go, since I don't have anything better to do, nothing ventured, nothing gained.*

Five in the evening the next day, Mike pulled into Dewayne's driveway, still not sure he wanted to go. Dewayne charged out to the car.

"I see you made it. I wasn't sure you would show up."

"Yes, I might as well. I didn't have anything else to do."

Dewayne got in and slammed the door. He was on cloud nine with a date with Shirley. The old car jerked on takeoff. It acted like it was on the last leg to the junkyard, and it may not make it there.

"Darn that slipping clutch!" complained Mike.

"Do you think we'll make it to the club?"

"Yeah, it just gets jerky at times."

Dewayne sang, "We're going to get laid tonight, we're going to get laid tonight, we're going to get laid tonight, and it's going to be so good."

"Shut up, you idiot," Mike said, as he turned on the radio.

"You don't appreciate good music when you hear it."

"Dewayne, you couldn't carry a tune in a bucket."

"You just follow my lead tonight. We'll make out."

Mike had the gut feeling that tonight, before it was over, would turn into a nightmare. He could feel it coming.

The girls met them at the door, so they didn't have to come in and face the parents. Ann sat next to the door, making plans. She wanted a date with Dewayne, but he asked Shirley. Dewayne was in her class, and they were the same age. Mike was a year younger than Shirley. Since Shirley had a date with Dewayne, she was stuck with Mike. How could she get him to notice her? Maybe she could get his attention before the night was over. Dewayne broke the silence.

"Let's go to the Alligator Club, down by the river."

"We don't have identification to get in," argued Mike.

"On Saturday nights, they don't check for identification. We can dance and have a few drinks or just listen to the band."

"We can't go," said Shirley. "We told Mom we were going to the movie."

"Who's going to tell?" argued Dewayne.

"Come on, Shirley, let's do it. You don't want to be a stick in the mud," teased Ann.

"Be like your sister," argued Dewayne. "Let's have some fun."

Ann had just made her first put-down of Shirley and gained her first point with Dewayne.

"OK, I give up. How about you, Mike?"

"I don't care, but I'm not too good at dancing."

Mike pulled off highway 287 onto a dirt road for the rest of the way to the club. The road was dusty and full of potholes. Mike pulled off the dirt road and parked in front of the club.

"Everybody out of the pool," said Mike.

"Put this in your purse." Dewayne handed Shirley an ear of corn with a string attached to it.

"I don't want that in my purse."

"I'll put it in my purse," responded Ann.

She had scored point number two with Dewayne. Shirley glanced at Ann, angry with her sister. She wondered what she was up to. *Why is she putting me down?*

Mike looked at Dewayne. "The old corn on a cob trick. We may get thrown out."

"True, but think of the fun we will have before they throw us out."

The girls didn't have a clue what they were talking about. Mike opened his door, and everyone followed him in the club. They didn't ask for identification, so they were home free. The club had a small dance floor filled with couples. A loud band was playing at the side of the dance floor, making the walls vibrate.

Smoke hung like fog over the room. A large stuffed alligator, with boots sticking out of his mouth, was mounted over the bar. They found a table for four and sat down. When the waitress came to their table, they ordered a round of beer. They sat and listened to the band, until suddenly with a gush of enthusiasm, Dewayne pulled Shirley out of her chair.

"Let's dance and have some fun."

"OK, let's do it." She wasn't giving her sister another chance at Dewayne.

Mike watched as Dewayne and Shirley danced every dance. When the band finally played a slow dance, Mike finally got up enough nerve to ask Ann to dance.

"May I have this dance?" Smiled Mike.

"Sure, why not?" She was tired of sitting.

Mike closed his arms around Ann's waist and guided her gracefully around the dance floor.

Ann sighed. "I thought you said you couldn't dance. Well, you dance divinely."

Ann laid her head on Mike's shoulder, moving as close as possible. Her breast was flat against his chest. Her nipples became hard as they rubbed against his chest. She could feel the crotch of his pants getting tighter and tighter as she rubbed against him, but she didn't move back.

Sparks were flying between them, and it felt so right. Ann decided she had the right date. She was having fun rubbing her body against Mike. She liked the effect she was having on him, but she realized he was having a rousing effect on her. Her heartbeat doubled, and her body was hot all over. They danced several dances until the band took a break, and they went back to their table.

"Mike, I'm glad you asked me for a date. It's been a lot of fun."

"I'm glad I asked you. It has been fun, and we dance great together."

"Yes, we are like one person while we are dancing. I dance better with you than anyone else that I have danced with." She didn't mention the effect he had on her.

After a while, Dewayne said, "It's time to have some fun. Give me the ear of corn."

"Here it is," Ann pulled the ear of corn out of her purse and gave it to Dewayne.

Dewayne tossed the ear of corn out on the dance floor and started pulling it back, just as two fat girls were returning from the bathroom. As Dewayne pulled the corn off the dance floor, the two fat girls walked up to the table.

"What are you doing?" they asked.

"Trolling for hogs, and it looks like I have caught a couple of fat ones," announced Dewayne.

The girls couldn't take a joke. They started screaming at Dewayne, something about God and somebody's mother. Mike had never heard such language spoken by a lady. Well, maybe she wasn't a lady after all.

The owner, a fat little man, came rushing over to the table.

"What is going on here?"

The fat girls explained how they had been insulted and wanted to know what was going to be done about it. The owner didn't have a sense of humor either, as he leaned over their table, shouting, "Get out of my club and don't ever come back!"

They had to get up and leave. A big bouncer came over to make sure they did. Their night was over at the club. They got in the car and headed in the direction of home. They laughed about the night's event.

"Did you see the look on their faces when I told them about the hogs?"

"Yes, it was fun, but we got thrown out of the club and can't come back."

Mike pulled off the highway onto the dirt road to the girls' house. Dewayne said, "Pull off at the dirt road on the right. It's too early to go home."

"OK." He followed the instructions.

"Go down the road for a little way and let's park for a little while."

Ann sat close to Mike with her hand on his thigh. "Things could get tacky."

"Yes, only if your mind is in the gutter."

"Mike, stop over there under the large trees."

There was a full moon, and it lit up the inside of the car. Grabbing a blanket on the backseat, Dewayne said, "Let's go for a walk and leave the two lovebirds alone."

Shirley wasn't sure she wanted to go off in the dark, but she did. Mike put his right arm behind Ann's head as she leaned closer and gazed intently into his eyes, seeing the desire in her eyes. She wet her lips with her tongue and waited for Mike to kiss her. Mike touched her lips lightly at first. Then he kissed her hard, as he unbuttoned the front of her dress with his left hand. He worked fast by completely unbuttoning her dress from top to bottom. He used his thumb and forefinger to unsnap her bra. Her breast fell free and pointed at him. He could see her nipples turn hard in the moonlight.

Ann unbuttoned the front of his shirt. Mike pulled her to him and kissed her, easing his tongue in her mouth as she opened to him. They touched tongues, as Mike cupped her small breast with his hand and pinched her nipple with his fingers until it hurt. Ann moaned deep in her throat as she realized her silk panties were sliding down her legs and were around her ankles. Her brain sent signals to her body to stop, but her body had a mind of its on and didn't pay any attention to the brain.

Mike gently pushed Ann onto her back. He unzipped his pants and guided his erect manhood to touch her moist, warm spot. He took a deep breath and started to enter her. He forgot to put a rubber on, but he couldn't stop now. He pushed and barely had the head in her folds.

Lights lit up the inside of the car as a pickup approached them. Ann screamed as she pushed Mike off her into the floorboard. She was trying to pull up her panties, snap on her bra, and button her dress.

"Damn, damn, damn! I'll kill that joker!" raved Mike.

"Who is it?"

"I don't know. I don't recognize the truck."

"We got to get out of here," whined Ann.


Dewayne and Shirley buttoned and zipped clothes as they ran for the car. The pickup was filled with coon hunters, dogs, and guns. Mike decided it was time to go home. They couldn't ever get the girls in the mood again anyway. They were nervous about getting caught with their pants down.

The girls were quiet the rest of the way home. They both were embarrassed that they almost had sex. Ann could feel her wet pants from when she was hot and ready. Would she have let Mike go all the way? Yes, she probably would have and lost her cherry in the front seat of a car. How disgusting that would be!

They dropped the girls off without even a good-night kiss and headed toward Dewayne's house.

"Did you make out?" asked Mike.

"No, did you?"

"No, I had her primed and ready with her panties down, when that darn pickup showed up. I need a cold shower, but we don't have a bathroom or a shower."

"We can go to our swimming hole."

The creek ran across the road on the way to Dewayne's house. As Mike stopped the car, Dewayne jumped out, yelling. "Last one in is a rotten egg!"

The water was very cold. Mike gasped. "This cold water sure put out the fire, and now I can get some sleep tonight."

They got out of the creek, shaking like a leaf. They didn't have a towel to dry off with, so they put their clothes on their wet bodies. The next day at school, Mike approached Ann in the hall.

"I don't want to see you or date you again," said Ann.

"Why don't you want to date me again? I had fun, and I thought you did too."

"You took advantage of me last night after I had been drinking. I didn't have control of myself."

"Let's face it. You enjoyed it as much as I did."

"No, I didn't."

"You could have fooled me. You were hot to go until the pickup arrived."

"Don't you wish?"

Ann turned around and made a fast retreat down the hall. Mike didn't understand girls at all. This was one of those days Mike should have stayed home in bed. He would have played hooky from school the rest of the day, but he had an English test.

Mike did poorly on his English test and got bitched out in front of the class. When he tried to defend himself, he was sent to the principal's office. He thought the school day would never end.

As the bell rang, Mike rushed out to his car. *What a hell of a day it had been!* He turned on the ignition and pushed the start button. A loud piercing noise and smoke, followed by an explosion, came from under the hood. He raised the hood and found a smoke bomb, which was wired wrong, causing wires to melt together. It took Mike several hours to fix the wiring and get his car running again. It was too late to go to work at the drive-in. He stopped at a store and called his boss to explain. He begged off for the night and went on home. He sure would like to get his hands on the person who put the smoke bomb on his car. He knew nobody would tell, since they had damaged the car. If it had been wired right, it wouldn't have damaged his car. When Mike got home, the weather wasn't looking good.

He went to bed but didn't sleep too good. Mike woke up to a sound like a train coming through the house. Windows were breaking, and tin from the roof made a loud noise as it ripped away. He hid under the bed until the storm was over. Mike could hear his mother crying and Mr. Love trying to console her.

At first light, they looked outside and checked the area for damage. The house, barn, chicken house, and trees were heavily damaged. They had lived through a Texas tornado. The place wasn't worth fixing up. It would be best to hunt another place to live.

The next day was the last day of the school year. When Mike got home from school, Mr. Love told Mike they were moving to town. Mike would be close to his work, and his dad would hunt for a job.

Mr. Love sold off their livestock. They packed up their junk, borrowed a pickup from Mr. Glover, and moved to Booneville. They would be starting a new way of life, since they had lived in the country all their life.

# Chapter 3

The old house they moved into had running water, electricity, and gas for heat. The bathroom had a large bathtub with legs that held it off the floor. They had hot water. It was the first home they had lived in that was modern. They were used to a well for water, a washtub for a bath, an outhouse, and fireplace for heat.

Mr. Love was hired on at the sawmill. It would be hard work for an old man, but that was all he could find. Mike continued to work at the drive-in theatre. An old couple, Mrs. and Mr. Smith, lived next door to them. Mike cut their grass, repaired their fence, carried out the garbage, and did many other odd jobs for them, at no charge to them. They became the best of friends. Mrs. Smith baked a lot, always bringing cookies and cake over to his house.

One hot July afternoon, as Mike returned home after going for gas, he glanced in the Smith's yard next door and saw a sexy redhead, almost causing to miss the driveway. She was pushing an old lawn mower, and sweat was rolling off her body.

Mike watched her a few moments, while taking mental notes. She was about five feet six inches tall, with long red hair tied in a ponytail. She had a light suntan, dark green eyes, and large breasts. She must have stood in line twice when they were handing them out. Mike guessed her age at about twenty years old. She wore red short shorts with a white blouse, unbuttoned low at the top. It was tied in a knot below her ample breasts, with a lot of skin showing between her blouse and shorts. Her blouse was wet from sweating, and her dark nipples were visible through the thin material. He made it like he was doing something to his car while he stared at her. She was a fine-looking woman, not a girl.

April watched Mike out of the corner of her eye and knew he was watching her. She couldn't tell much about him in the car, but she liked to have men admire her. She knew she was pretty and had all the parts a man likes to see. She always used the saying, "If you got it, flaunt it."

She stretched her arms above her head and made her nipples strain to be free from the confines of her blouse. She bent over the mower with her butt toward him, like she was checking something. She then went around to the other side of the mower and bent over, facing Mike. Half of her tits were hanging out. He decided he would get out of the car.

Mike automatically had a hard-on. His pecker was like a radar, perking up when he saw a pretty girl.

Mike got out of the car and slammed the door. He looked down at his crotch while taking a deep breath and walked over to greet her. April watched him check his crotch, and her lips pursed in amusement. She looked him over like a prized bull as he approached her. He looked to be about seventeen or eighteen years old. He was built lean with lust in his eyes.

She looked down at the bulge in his crotch one more time before she spoke. She enjoyed the effect she was having on the young man. "Hi, I'm April Smith."

"I'm Mike Love. I live next door."

"I'm visiting my grandparents for a couple of weeks. I came up from Houston this morning."

"It's so hot. Would you like to go to the Dairy Queen for a Coke?"

"Yes, I would love to go, but let me dry off first."

April removed a towel from the mower handle and gently wiped the sweat from her face, arms, belly, and legs. She unbuttoned her blouse down to the knot below her breasts and carefully wiped the sweat off each breast. She didn't turn her back as she dried off.

Mike got a bird's-eye view of her nipples and turned his head to keep from blushing. April noticed how shy he was. She decided that with this young stud around maybe her visit wouldn't be boring.

Mike opened the passenger door for April, and she slid in the car. Mike closed the door and went around to the driver's side. He started the car and pulled into the street. He drove to the Dairy Queen and parked at the front.

"April, do you want to go inside, where it's cool?"

"Sure, it's so hot and muggy out here."

Mike ordered two big Cokes, while April found a table. Mike paid for their drinks and came over to the table. April had picked one in the middle of the room. She liked to show off. While they sat drinking their drinks, Mike could feel eyes watching them. The girls were curious, while the guys were envious. Mike glanced at a girl in a booth, and she smiled at him. He wondered, *Why she would give me the time of day?* Then he realized that she wondered how he had such a beautiful woman with him.

It was good to be seen with a pretty girl before he started school again. Some of the girls would be curious enough to talk to him, and maybe he could pick up a girlfriend.

On the way back, Mike said, "I would like to take you out, but I work until midnight every night."

"That's OK. I think we can find a way around that."

"Then you will go out with me?"

"Sure, I would like it very much."

April smiled at him and moved her body so he could see a lot of her breasts. She fluttered her eyelashes at him.

"I think we can think of something fun to do."

The way she moved and said it, Mike wondered what the something would be.

That night, as Mike pulled into his driveway and got out of his car, a voice said, "Come over here, Mike."

"Be right there." He went over to the porch, where April was standing.

"Hi, Mike, how was your night?"

"Not bad, just long."

April wore only a thin silk nightgown. Mike lost his voice, and all he could do was stare at her body. April touched his lips with her fingertips.

"You'll never get anything unless you ask for it."

"I want you."

"Then take me."

Mike pulled her into his arms, pulling her tight against his chest. April tipped her head back as Mike covered her lips. Wild passion growing in her body, she drove her tongue deep into Mike's mouth. She could feel his throbbing erection pressing on the lower part of her belly. He slid his hand through the opening in her nightgown, cupping her breast and stroking her hard nipple. April moaned deep in her throat. For a young guy, Mike was pushing the right buttons. He pushed her nightgown open and lowered his head, taking a nipple in his mouth and sucking on it.

"April, I want to make love to you."

"I know you do, and you can. I'm hot for you too."

From the porch, Mr. Love called, "Is that you, Mike? I thought I heard a car door slam."

"Yes, sir, it's me."

"It's late. You can talk in the morning."

"I'll be there in a minute."

Mike kissed April one more time. "I'll see you tomorrow."

He went in the house, grumbling, "Just my luck! Every time I get a girl ready, something happens, and I don't make out." Would his luck ever change? At the way things were going, he would be an old man before he made love the first time.

Mike took a cold bath, but it didn't help. He went to bed and dreamed of April making love to him. He woke up with a wet dream. Dreams can be so real.

The next day, Mrs. Smith came over and asked Mike if he would mind taking April out into the country to a friend's house to pick up some things.

"No problem. I'll take her where she wants to go."

"She will be right out."

April came out to the car. "You all drive careful, you hear?"

"Grandma, we will."

As April got into the car beside Mike, she had a smile that reminded him of a cat that had swallowed the canary. Mike pulled out of the driveway and headed out of town. They made good time until they turned off the highway onto a dirt road. The road had deep ruts and lots of holes, making the going slow. Mike wasn't in a hurry anyway. He was enjoying April's company. She looked good enough to eat.

April had styled her hair in waves. It hung between her shoulder blades. She wore a white sweater and a light green skirt with pleats. The skirt was resting well above her kneecaps.

Mike glanced at her face, then slowly moved his gaze down to her large breast for a moment, before continuing on down her legs. She sure had a sexy body, made for loving. He had a big hard-on. He began to daydream of pulling off April's clothes and making wild, passionate love to her.

A smile crossed April's lips as she watched Mike. She could see the desire in his eyes and the swelling of his crotch. She enjoyed the effect her body always had on men.

"A penny for your thoughts," teased April.

Mike's face turned red as he gazed into April's eyes. "Do you know what I was thinking?"

"That's easy. You were thinking of making love to me."

"You read my mind. I was thinking of making love to you."

"Was I good?"

"I don't know, because I had only got as far as taking your clothes off in my dream. When I finish the dream, I'll let you know." Laughed Mike.

"Turn in at the next driveway on the right and park in front of the old house."

Mike stopped the car, and April got out of the car. "I'll be right back. I only got a few things to collect."

She waved bye and went into the house. Mike watched her cute rear end bounce back and forth as she walked to the house. This gave him another hard-on. He needed a cold shower; he was so hard it ached.

After a while, April returned, carrying some clothes on one arm and a large feather pillow on the other arm. She hung the clothes over the front seat and put the pillow between them. She got in the car with a big smile.

"I've got everything. Let's go."

"Your wish is my command," Mike spoke out.

"I sure hope so," April teased. She was ready to have some fun with Mike.

After they were back on the highway heading back to town, Mike referred to the pillow on the seat between them. "Is that pillow for our use?"

"I told you before you wouldn't get anything unless you ask for it."

"I want to make love to you."

"That's the way to go! Sometimes a girl wants it just as bad as you do, so don't be afraid to ask, because all she can do is say no."

Daytime or not, Mike wasn't going to miss out this time. He turned off the highway at the next dirt road and headed into the woods. After a few minutes, he turned off the road and parked under a large oak tree.

April opened the front door and got out. She opened the back door and got in the backseat.

"Come on back here where we have more room and bring the pillow."

"I'm coming."

"Make it quick, or I may start without you," she teased.

Mike scrambled out of the car and into the backseat. He sat across from April, watching her large breasts rise and fall, while her hard nipples showed through her sweater.

April was going to enjoy teaching Mike the art of making love. This trick would be a free one. She slowly pulled her sweater off over her head, while holding the sweater in front playing the teasing game. She slowly dropped the sweater over the front seat. April wasn't wearing a bra.

"Touch them, Mike. They won't bite."

"Like this?" He cupped a breast in each hand.

"Good, now touch my nipples with your tongue."

"Like this?" He took a nipple in his mouth, sucked on it, then moved to the other one and sucked on it.

"Yes, that feels so good," April moaned, putting her hands on his head and pulling him tight against her.

Mike wasn't going to mess this up. He would play "follow the leader." He would follow April's lead. April leaned back, unbuttoning her skirt, and raised her hips up, letting the skirt drop to the floorboard. All Mike could do was stare with his mouth open. Next she removed her shoes and stockings. She sat with a big smile on her face as she watched Mike. This had to be his first time.

"Help me take my panties off."

He slid her panties off as she raised her hips. He was so nervous he was shaking like a leaf. Mike sat speechless, staring at the red patch of hair and folds. It was his first time to see it all.

"OK, Mike, are you going to play, or do I start without you?"

"Don't start without me."

"Then take off your clothes."

Mike quickly removed his clothes. He already had a hard-on and was a little embarrassed. His pulse quickened, and he drew a deep breath as April reached for him. Her lips were warm and moist as she French-kissed him.

April kissed Mike's face all over, before moving down to touch his nipple with her tongue. She reached down and stroked his penis as she kissed her way down his body. Mike felt he was ready to explode as April circled his manhood with her tongue and then consumed all of it in her warm mouth. She moved her head up and down while sucking, and it was driving Mike crazy.

"Now lie flat on your back," instructed April.

April rose up and straddled Mike, slowly lowering onto his erect shaft, which sank into the warmth of her. She rocked back and forth, moving her hips in a circle, while she increased her speed. They went over the edge together as Mike exploded deep in her hot passion. April moaned as her body shook with her long climax. She collapsed on his chest, her nipples digging into his body. He was still inside her, throbbing.

"OK, love, when we are rested, it will be your turn to perform," cooed April.

"You mean, make love again?"

"Sure, you'll be ready to go again in a few minutes."

April was still on top, with Mike's manhood still inside her. She could feel him growing and filling her. She got off and lay back for Mike to cover her. He followed the same routine April used on him. He kissed her face all over before moving down to her erect nipples and sucking each nipple. He moved down her body to the red patch of hair. He stuck his tongue deep into the warmth of her, hoping to please her.

"That feels so good," moaned April. She arched her hips and grabbed his head, pulling him hard against her.

He sucked her until he could feel her throbbing. Mike raised himself above her and drove his shaft home. She bucked under him like a bronco, sending both of them into a spasm. Mike collapsed on April's chest, flattening her breasts, both of them out of breath. Mike caught his breath. He felt April using her inner muscles to milk him dry. He had nothing left to give.

"Poor boy, you are all played out."

"You can say that again. I think I'm going to die."

"You had enough fun?"

"Yes, I think I have for one day."

"Mike, you are now experienced in making love. Don't be shy anymore. Go for a score every chance you get because most girls like sex. The trick is to catch them when they are horny. Any girl can be made at the right time and the right place," explained April.

"How do I know when is the right time to hit on a girl?"

"They usually are nervous and swing their legs back and forth. They are different from their usual self. Watch for the change."

That was one lesson Mike would never forget. While Mike drove home, Mike thought, *Dreams do come true sometimes and today had been the day.*

It was late in the evening when they arrived back home. Mike unloaded the car and carried her belongings into the house.

"Thanks for taking me to get my things today. I had fun, and we need to do it again." She smiled at him.

"That was the greatest time I ever had in my whole life," said Mike, with his face flushed.

"Yes, I know. It was your first time to have sex."

"How did you know?"

"It's my business to know. I am a fifty-dollar-a-night call girl."

"You are kidding."

"I work for a dating service in Houston, where the customer can get anything the customer is willing to pay for. Don't ever tell anyone what I told you. It would break my grandparents' heart if they found out."

"I won't ever tell anyone. You can count on it."

"One last piece of advice—don't brag to the guys about your conquest, because if the girls find out, you won't ever make out again."

"I won't tell anyone."

"Also don't forget to use a rubber to protect the girl."

"April, we didn't use a rubber."

"It's all right. I use my own form of protection."

April lightly touched Mike with her fingertips as she traced his lips with her tongue.

"Good-bye, lover, sweet dreams."

Mike went home to get ready for work. He was on cloud nine all night. He couldn't believe he had finally scored.

The next morning, April received a call from her dating service and had to leave early for Houston. Mike never saw April again, but he never forgot her and the good time they had together.

Punky Wilson started to work at the drive-in theatre that summer in the concession stand. Mike and Punky became friends and started to hang out together. Punky was a couple inches shorter than Mike. He cut his hair in a short flat top and had a pug nose. Punky liked to play pranks. You could see the mischief in his eyes.

"Mike, how about we go to the Dairy Queen?"

"Sure. You want to take my car or yours?"

As they were driving to the Dairy Queen in Punky's car, a cop was cruising in front of them, and his partner was drinking a cup of coffee.

"Watch this," said Punky.

Punky's car bumped the cop car in the rear end, causing the cop to spill his coffee. Punky slammed on his brakes, turning the wheels to cause a spin, and his car ended up heading back in the opposite direction. The cop car turned around and gave chase, but Punky had too much of a lead on him. He turned a corner and pulled off the street into a garage. The cop car turned the corner. He flew by with his lights flashing and siren wailing.

"What are you trying to do? Get us killed?"

"No, just shaking up our local cops."

"Punky, you are a crazy bastard. What makes you do stupid things like that?"

"Oh, come on, Mike. Wasn't that fun?"

"That's not my idea of fun."

"What is your idea of fun?"

"Wine, women, and sex, but I don't care which one comes first as long as I get all three."

Punky said, "Next time my cousin comes up from Houston, I'll get you a date with her. She has a perfect body, and she is built for sex. She always wants me to get her a date when she comes to visit."

"I don't like blind dates. The last time I had a blind date, it was a hell. I got robbed."

"We'll wait until she comes to visit, and then you can make up your mind, but right now, you need to take me back to pick up my car."

Mike told Punky about his trip to Galveston and how he had been robbed. That was why he was off blind dates, and he didn't know if the girl would be ugly. Knowing how much Punky liked to play jokes on people, he didn't trust him.

"You said she had a perfect body, but what about her face?"

"She is real pretty."

"So you say."

"Would I lie to you?"

"I'm not sure."

"You hurt my feelings."

Mike drove home, thinking over going on a blind date again. The last blind date had been for the birds. He still remembered what happened to him in Galveston. Then he remembered what April had told him about going for it every chance he got. He decided to forget it for the time being.

The next night, while Mike was leaving work, Punky drove up beside him.

"Some of the guys are going to the airport for drag race. Let's go with them."

"It's too late to go, and we might get caught using the runway to race."

"Come on, chicken, let's go," teased Punky.

"I'm not chicken. Let's go."

Mike was mad. He burnt rubber out the exit of drive-in while heading for the airport. He pulled off the road and headed for three cars parked at the beginning of the runway. He pulled in beside them as Punky pulled in on the other side of him. Everyone got out of the cars to talk.

Punky started introducing everyone to Mike.

"Mike, this is Leroy Cooper with the red Ford Thunderbird."

"Nice car."

"Gary Mitchell was driving a white Ford."

"Hi, glad to meet you."

"Rex, you know with the old Nash."

"How are you?"

Punky bragged that he was going to win, because his Ford had a souped-up engine to increase the power. "All you will see is my smoke."

Mike hoped someone would wax the bragger, but he knew it wouldn't be him. Leroy was tall with hair combed in a ducktail. Gary was also tall and had his hair in a ducktail. He had a mean look about him. Mike decided this was one dude not to mess with. Ducktails and flat tops were the way boys wore their hair in the fifties.

Punky waved everyone up to the starting line.

"We'll start at the zero marker and finish at the three-thousand foot marker. We will race in pairs. Leroy and Gary will race first. Rex and Mike will go next. The winners of the two races will go third. Then I will take on the winner of the third race. I'll be the starter of the races until it comes my turn to race."

Leroy and Gary started their engines, while Punky stood out to the side with his arm in the air. He dropped his arm, and both cars shot off the starting line. Both cars burnt rubber in the first and second gear. It was a close race, but Leroy won in his Thunderbird. Rex and Mike started their engines and pulled up to the starting line. Mike was thinking, *I should be able to beat Rex's old Nash.* Punky raised his arm and dropped it. Mike got the lead in first gear, but as he popped his clutch, he missed second gear and jammed his shift linkage. The old Nash won the race. Rex turned around and came back to help Mike.

"What happened to your car?"

"The shift linkage jammed."

"I'll push you back to the starting line."

"Thanks."

Rex pushed Mike back to the starting line. Mike got out and worked on his shift linkage, while the next two cars pulled up to the starting line. Punky raised his arm and dropped it. Leroy and Rex burnt rubber off the starting line, but it was an easy win for Leroy against the old Nash.

Punky got in his car and started his engine, while waiting for Leroy to return to the starting line.

"Mike, do you want to be the starter?"

"Yes, I guess I can."

Mike had finished fixing his gear linkage. He stepped up to the starting line to start the last race. Leroy pulled up beside Punky. Mike raised his arm and dropped it. Both cars burnt rubber off the starting line. Punky was in the lead but missed third gear, and the Thunderbird passed him to win the race. Punky would have won the race, except for driver error. He almost came back to win, but the track was too small. Punky was mad at himself for missing a gear.

Punky and Leroy returned to the starting line. Everybody got out of their cars to talk or brag about their win.

Then Punky came up with an idea. "Guess what the losers get to do?"

"What dumb thing do you have in mind?" asked Mike.

"I'll let you know when I find them."

Punky fumbled around in his car and pulled out two rocket bombs. He handed one to Mike and the other one to Gary.

The losers get to set these babies off downtown on the square. Both guys protested but were called chicken, so they decided to do it.

"If we get caught and get put in jail, you guys had better bail us out," Mike said.

Punky laughed. "Sure, we will."

Mike and Gary glared at Punky. They didn't trust him as far as they could throw him. Leroy, Rex, and Punky drove off, heading for their homes. The bombs would go off high enough in the air, so they could watch them from their homes.

Mike and Gary made plans to pull off the caper.

"Gary, we have to time everything just right, or one of us will probably get caught by the police. Their office is in the courthouse."

"Why did we let Punky talk us into this?"

"We were stupid, and now we can't back out."

"Kick me the next time Punky comes up with a stupid idea."

"We'll pull it off. Gary, you drive up on one side of the square, and I'll drive up on the other side. I will use my arm as a signal. When I stick my arm out the window, that means get ready. When I pull my arm back in the car, light your fuse, open your door, and set the rocket bomb out on the pavement. Then drive like hell and go straight home. We don't want to be caught on the street by the police. Well, how does my plan sound?"

"Good as any, I guess. Let's get it over with. We may be in jail before the night is over."

"We'll pull it off. Don't worry."

"OK, let's do it."

Gary and Mike drove into town at a normal speed. They didn't want to attract any attention to them. They had to circle the square three times before all the traffic cleared off the square.

Mike stopped on his side of the square and stuck his arm out the window. As he pulled his arm inside the car, he saw Gary light the fuse. He did the same at the same time. Their plan worked perfect.

They waved to each other as they passed each other on their way home. Gary yelled out his window, "We did it!"

"Yes, we did."

Mike and Gary were two blocks off the square when the rockets went off. The rockets went fifty feet in the air before going off. They made two big explosions.

Mike pulled into his driveway and turned off his lights while listening to the police siren. He smiled. *We got away with it and didn't get caught.* Punky almost got him in trouble again. *I'm going to have to watch that guy.*

Mike got out of his car and went into the house. His mom and dad were sleeping as usual, so he went to bed. The next few days, Mike lay low, just in case the police spotted his car. At night, he went straight to work and when he got off work, came straight home. During the day, he hung around the house and helped his mother. He even did a little yard work.

"Mike, are you sick?"

"No, I thought it was time I started helping out around the house."

Mrs. Love didn't believe a word of it, but she let it drop. Mr. Love was working at the sawmill. It was hard work for a man his age, or even a young one, but at least they had cash coming in, and times were much better. Mrs. Love didn't bitch at her husband half as much.

Friday night after work, Punky approached Mike.

"My cousin Paula Spinks is coming up from Houston tomorrow. She is the one I was telling you about. She is bringing a girlfriend for me to date while visiting."

"Lucky you! Poor girl!" teased Mike.

"Do you want to double-date?"

"I don't know. The last time I double-dated, it was a disaster."

"I told my cousin I would find her a date. Remember, I told you a while back, I would get you a date with her."

"I'm not sure I want to do it."

"If it will make you feel any better, I haven't seen my date either. We will both have a blind date."

Mike laughed. "I'll go just to see what you end up with for a date. I hope she is as ugly as homemade soap!"

"Thanks a lot, buddy. With a friend like you, who need enemies?"

"Well, at least we will start even."

"If they are ugly, I guess we could cover their face with a paper sack."

"I'll pick you up at seven tomorrow evening."

"Punky, what are we going to do on our date?"

"I know what I would like to do—go to lover's lane and make."

"Dream on, these are first dates."

"Well, maybe it's the time of the month when the girls are horny."

"Could be." Mike remembered what April had told him.

As Mike drove home, he mulled over the date for tomorrow night. He had a gut feeling that Punky would try and put something over on him. One thing for sure—it was never a dull moment when you were with Punky.

The window was up beside Mike's bed, but it was still hot in his bedroom. Mike wished his family had some fans, but they were too poor to own any fans. It was the end of July, and school would be starting soon. He was under a sheet and playing with his lizard. He was dreaming about making out tomorrow night. Finally, he dozed off but woke up having a wet dream. Mike wondered if all teenage boys had wet dreams.

He slept late the next day. The rest of the day dragged by, and he thought it would never end, but finally it was six o'clock in the evening. It was time to get ready for his date. Mike took a long hot bath and dressed for his date. When he was ready, he went outside and sat on the porch to wait.

Punky and the girls arrived at seven o'clock to pick him up. Mike got in the backseat, and Punky made the introductions.

"Paula, this is Mike Love. He is your date for the evening, and in the front seat is my date, Joy."

"Glad to meet you all."

Punky didn't lie about his cousin's body. She was about five feet four inches tall and very petite. Paula had a perfect body, but Punky forgot to mention what her face would look like. She had a protruding jaw, a slightly drooping nose, large red lips, and a wild hairdo. Paula looked like when God was making her, he took a break and when he came back, he forgot where he left off.

Mike thought, *I had better get a conversation going.* "Paula, how do you like a small town as compared to Houston?"

"I really like to come here, and I would like to live here, but my parents have good jobs in Houston. Mother is a school teacher, and Dad is a lawyer."

"How about you, Joy? Do you like small towns?"

"I don't know. This is the first time I have been out of Houston."

Mike looked at Paula and smiled. Paula smiled back at him. He was thinking, *God must have used leftover parts to finish Paula. How could she have such a beautiful body but such an ugly face?* He forgot to bring a paper bag. *Well, turn them all upside down and they are sisters.*

Paula wore a full skirt and a very low-cut blouse. The skirt was dark green, and the blouse was white.

Joy was a little plump but nice looking. She wore a brown skirt with a tan sweater, showing off her nice set of tits, and Punky already had his eyes on them.

"Why don't we ride around and show the girls the town?" suggested Punky.

"I have already seen it," said Joy.

"But Paula hasn't. We'll take a quick tour."

"I know there's not much to see or do, but Mike and I will try to entertain you."

Punky drove around the main drag a couple of times before stopping at the Dairy Queen. They ordered hamburgers, fries, and drinks. Mike paid for the food and drinks since Punky drove his car. When they had finished eating, Punky suggested, "Let's drive out to the park."

"OK by us," said Paula.

"OK, let's go," said Mike.

Punky backed out into the street and headed in the direction of the park. The park was attractive with green grass and lots of large trees. Punky pulled in under a large oak tree. There was a full moon shining, which lit up the inside of the car. They talked awhile, but it became quiet as each couple began to get intimate.

Paula lay down on her back with her head resting in his lap. She turned her head and smiled an invitation for Mike to kiss her. He turned his head and covered her lips with his own. She opened her mouth to him and he slid his tongue inside her warm mouth, exploring until she touched his tongue with her own. That sent a shock wave through his body. Paula moaned as she sucked his tongue deep into her mouth.

With her low-cut blouse, Mike could see a large portion of her breast. He eased his hand down the front of her blouse, pushing her bra down, and fondled her nipples. She arched her back toward his hand.

"You like that?" Mike whispered.

"Yes," she moaned.

Paula spread her legs and pulled them up close to her rear, causing her skirt to ride well above her knees. To Mike, with her legs spread, it was an invitation to go further. He thought he had a live one, so he might as well keep exploring her body. He removed his hand from her blouse and eased it between her thighs. Paula arched up again toward his hand. He slid his hand down the front of her panties until he touched her hot spot. She hunched his hand like a bitch in heat. He pushed two fingers into her folds.

"You like that?" whispered Mike.

"Oh yes! Don't stop."

"I would like to be inside you."

"OK." She turned around and pulled her skirt up.

Meanwhile, Punky hadn't lost any time in the front seat. He had Joy on her back with her skirt up and her panties pulled down. Joy let out a moan as Punky touched her fuzzy spot. All of sudden, Punky turned on the overhead light.

"I thought I saw a beaver. I did see a beaver. I had to see what I was playing with."

"Punky, you are a crazy bastard!" Joy slapped Punky hard across the face, as she pulled up her panties and pulled down her skirt. She was so embarrassed.

Paula had put her clothes back on when the light came on. Mike could kill Punky for that stunt.

Mike and Paula burst out laughing. Finally, Joy and Punky joined in. Punky was the only one Mike knew that could pull a stunt like that and get away with it. The girls were out of the mood for loving. They had their clothes back on.

"Let's go skinny-dipping at the lake," announced Punky. He wanted them naked again.

"I have never been skinny-dipping before. What if we get caught?" asked Joy.

"We get out of the water, put our clothes on, and go home."

"I would like to go, since I have never done it before. I'll do it if Paula will."

"I won't hold up the party. Let's go do it."

Punky drove out of the park and headed south. The lake was about five miles south of Booneville as the crow flies. It was a private lake for the wealthy. There were houses all around the lake with private boat docks.

When Punky pulled off the highway into a private road, he cut off his lights.

"Why did you cut off your lights?" asked Joy.

"I'm not a member of the country club, and we are sneaking in."

Punky pulled the car into the swimming area and parked. They got out of the car and walked out on a platform that extended out into the lake. It had a diving board attached and a ladder to climb out of the water. There were houses all around the lake. Trees extended down to the water and were good for shade on hot days. Mike walked to the edge of the water and tested it.

"The water is warm, just right for swimming."

"We can undress here on the platform and leave our clothes here," Punky said.

"In your dreams, Punky. We'll undress in the car," replied Paula.

"Suit yourself. Mike and I will undress on the platform."

The girls went back to the car to undress, while Mike and Punky undressed on the platform.

"Mike, I tried to get them naked on the platform."

"Do you think they will undress and come in?"

"I think so, but we will find out shortly."

"You girls, hurry up. Mike and I will be in the water waiting for you."

"As soon as the boys are in the water, slide over and start the car. We'll drive off and leave them." Giggled Paula. They heard Mike and Punky dive off the platform with a splash.

Joy looked at the steering column. "Punky may be crazy, but he's not stupid. He took the keys with him. What do we do now?"

"I guess we go swimming." Giggled Paula.

"What if the guys try something?"

"Joy, we have two choices. We can drown them or lie back and enjoy it."

They undressed while the guys called for them to hurry up. The guys wanted to see the girls naked.

"If I had a bar of soap, I could take my Saturday-night bath," declared Punky.

"Punky, you are so stupid."

Paula finished undressing. "Are you ready for this?"

"Yes, but I'm going to get even with that jerk, Punky."

"How are you going to do that?"

"I'm not going to let him touch me the rest of the night. I'll teach him a lesson he won't ever forget. He had me ready and willing to have sex, but he blew it.

"Mike had me ready also, but Punky spoiled it, so sock it to him."

"Are you ready?"

"I guess so. Let's do it."

The girls got out of the car and ran down to the platform, quickly dropping off the platform into the water, careful not to get their hair wet. Immediately, Punky swam after Joy, trying to touch her naked body, but she remained out of reach.

"Come back here, you little devil."

"Not on your life! You had your chance and blew it, so leave me alone."

Joy was on the swimming team at school, so she didn't have a problem keeping Punky from catching her. Mike was hanging onto the ladder, laughing and watching the chase, while Paula swam close by. She watched Mike, her red lips pursed in amusement. She wanted to continue where they left off in the park, when Punky turned the overhead light on. Paula wanted Mike to make the first move, but he was shy. He hung on to the ladder like it was a lifeline.

Paula swam over to Mike and put her arms around his neck, while pressing her hard nipples into his back.

"Let's take up where we left off in the park," she whispered in his ear.

Mike felt the full length of her firm body pressed against his. She nibbled on his neck and stuck her tongue in his ear.

Mike decided it was time for him to take action. He turned around to face her. Paula put her arms around his neck, while clasping her legs around his waist.

"Mike, I want you to make love to me."

"Are you sure?" He gave her a chance to back out.

"Yes, do it now."

She covered his lips with her own, pushing her tongue deep into his mouth. Mike, with his arms around her waist, slowly lowered her until she made contact with his erect manhood. With one hand, he guided his manhood into her folds. He eased her down until she consumed all of it. He was thinking, *I didn't have to guide my manhood in. She must be the football team playmate.*

Paula slowly moved up and down on his erection. She whispered, "Take it slow so Punky and Joy won't realize what we are doing."

"That's going to be hard. It's feels so good."

"Oh boy," she moaned, "that sure does feel good. Just keep on doing it."

Mike couldn't stand the slow pace any longer. He grabbed her buttocks with both hands, punching her faster and deeper. Paula moved with him, going down on his erection as he slammed up into her. She met him stroke for stroke.

"I'm coming! Oh, I'm coming!" moaned Paula.

"I am too."

Mike felt his manhood jerking deep within her. They hung onto each other in total exhaustion.

Punky swam close by. "That was quite an exhibition."

"What are you talking about?" asked Paula.

"I may be crazy, but I'm not stupid. I know what you two were doing. How was it?"

"That's none of your business." She splashed water in Punky's face.

Joy was swimming about twenty yards out in the lake and swam back to the platform to see what was happening.

"What's going on?"

"Mike and Paula had been making love, right there, holding onto the ladder."

"Well, good for them. You could have too, but you blew your chance."

Joy swam out about ten yards from the platform.

"Come on, we came out here to swim, so let's swim across the lake to that boat dock over there."

"I don't think I can swim that far," complained Punky.

"Well, stay here then."

Joy swam toward the other side of the lake. Punky, Mike, and Paula followed behind her. Punky was the last to make it to the boat dock. Everybody hung onto the boat dock to rest, but they didn't get out of the water.

After resting a short time, Paula said, "I'm starting back."

"I'm right behind you," Joy said.

Mike rested a couple more minutes and then headed back, but Punky hung onto the dock and rested a little while longer. He was the slowest swimmer of the bunch.

Paula reached the platform first. She climbed up the ladder and went to the car to get dressed. Joy reached the ladder next, but she hesitated, waiting for Mike. She started up the ladder, but as Mike reached the ladder, Joy turned her back to the ladder.

Joy lowered herself down between Mike and the ladder. She put her arms around his neck and her legs around his waist.

"I want to make love but not with Punky. Make love to me."

"You aren't my date. It wouldn't be right."

"Come on, Mike, do it. Paula is in the car, and Punky is halfway across the lake."

Mike hesitated a moment before he decided to do it. The girls would go back to Houston, and who would know they had sex?

Mike had a hard-on, and it was pushing into Joy's belly. She could feel Mike throbbing against her belly.

"Mike, I want you inside me now."

"OK, I'll do it."

Mike reached down and guided his erect penis into her tight opening. He thrust deep inside her, nailing her to the ladder, while her hard nipples dug into his chest.

"Honey, you are so tight, and it feels so good."

"I haven't made love but one other time."

"Then hang on for a wild ride."

"Give it to me. I want all of you."

Mike grabbed her buttocks with both hands and slammed into her as hard as he could. She was really good, being so tight. Joy jerked with a spasm.

"I'm coming! I'm coming! It's so good!"

Having a climax, her inner muscles squeezed his manhood. It exploded deep in her body. Joy covered Mike's lips with her own as she felt him throbbing deep in her body. She continued the kiss and hung on until she felt Mike go limp.

"Thank you. It was wonderful. You must have a lot of experience."

"Not a lot, just a good teacher."

Joy climbed up the ladder and went to the car to get dressed. Mike hung onto the ladder and waited for Punky.

"You finally made it back."

"Yes, but I feel like a drowned rat. I can't swim that good."

They climbed up the ladder and got dressed on the platform. A car turned off the road and headed toward the lake. Punky looked toward the highway.

"We had better get out of here."

As the car approached, they recognized the red Thunderbird, belonging to Leroy Cooper. They stopped side by side. Punky stuck his head out the window.

"What are you doing out here?"

"Rex and I were riding around and thought somebody might be swimming."

"We were, but we are on our way home now. See you later, alligator."

Punky drove out to the highway and headed back toward Booneville. Leroy turned around and followed him. He pulled up beside Punky. They were on a straight way.

"What are you looking for? Another race?"

"I thought I would give you a chance to get even."

"I can't race. I got girls in the car."

"Well, give them a thrill."

Punky wanted to race. The only reason he lost last time was because he missed a gear when shifting. It wouldn't happen again.

"OK, you're on."

Punky glanced over at the Thunderbird, raised his hand, and dropped it. The race was on. Both drivers slammed their gas pedals to the floor. The girls screamed, "Stop the car and let us out!"

"Shut up. It'll be over in a minute."

Punky reached for high gear, but Joy grabbed his leg, and he missed high gear. She was scared to death. Leroy and his Thunderbird won the race again.

"Damn, girl, what did you grab my leg for?"

"I was scared. I've never been in a race before." She was still clutching Punky's leg.

"Well, hell! We just lost the race, and Leroy will never buy why."

"I'm sorry I made you lose the race."

"Don't worry about it. There will be another time."

Leroy slowed down when he passed the "City Limit" sign and waited on Punky to catch up. They drove upon the square and parked.

"What happened to your hot car?"

"You wouldn't believe me if I told you."

"You ran off and left me at the start. What do you have under the hood?"

"A few little tricks. It's not a stock engine."

"It's my fault Punky lost. I grabbed his leg while he was shifting, and he missed a gear."

"Well, good luck next time." Leroy laughed. "Maybe you won't have a girl to blame next time. Did you know that watermelons are ripe?" asked Leroy.

"No, I forgot about them."

"I know where a watermelon patch is located. It's about five miles north of town, down a farm to market road. Do you want to go pick some?"

"Not tonight. I have to get my cousin and her girlfriend home, or my mother will ground me. We'll get together sometime next week and make a raid. We can have a watermelon party.

"I'll see you later."

Punky drove Mike home. As Mike got out of the car, he turned and kissed Paula good night.

"It sure was fun. The next time you come to visit, we'll have to do it again."

"Do what again?" teased Paula.

Mike's face turned red. "You know, skinny-dipping and, well, you know."

"Yeah, we know." Laughed Punky.

Joy smiled. *If Punky only knew, and I may tell Paula one of these days.*

Punky drove off, and Mike watched them until they were out of sight. He stood for a few minutes, daydreaming about his experience tonight. *It hadn't been too bad. If only Paula had a good-looking face to match her perfect body!* He dreamed about his extra benefit he received from Joy. It was the first time he had made love to two girls in one night, especially on the same date. Mike was growing more confident in his lovemaking each time, but he decided that from now on, he had better use a rubber for his protection, before he got a girl pregnant. He broke the rules tonight and hoped he didn't get a girl pregnant.

Latching the screen door behind him, Mike undressed down to his shorts and crawled into bed. He slept on top of the covers. It was hot, even with the window up and the door open. Finally, he dozed off into dreamland.

A noise woke Mike from his dreams. He turned on his side, facing the door, opening his eyes. He noticed a large man trying to jiggle the latch on the screen door with a knife.

Mike was scared, but he realized he would have to act fast before the man got the screen door open.

Mike rolled over and reached for his 12-gauge shotgun standing in the corner. He rolled back over with the shotgun leveled on the screen door. The man opened the door and saw the shotgun. He turned and fled with Mike in hot pursuit. Mike raised the shotgun to fire, but all he got was a click. He checked his shotgun and found it wasn't loaded. He felt like a dumb ass as he watched the man run off down the road. He turned and went back into the house.

Mike stepped upon the porch, and his mom came to the door.

"What's going on out there? Son, are you all right?"

"Go on back to bed, Mom. I thought I saw a stray dog on the back porch, but he ran off," he lied. He didn't want to frighten his mother.

Mike stood his shotgun back in the corner and lay down again. He had a .22-caliber pistol under the mattress fully loaded, but he was scared and forgot it was there. He pulled the pistol out and laid it on the mattress beside him, but he still had a hard time going back to sleep; after all it had been quite a night.

He slept until noon the next day and stayed around the house until time to go to work. His mother gave him another lecture about coming home late.

"There isn't anything to do that late at night except get in trouble."

"I don't get off work until late."

"I want you to start coming home sooner."

"All right, Mom, but I never know when the movie will be over. Sometimes they have a late show."

"Well, you come home as soon as it's over."

"OK, Mom."

That answer seemed to satisfy her. She went back inside to finish her chores. After getting dressed, Mike left for work. He drove up to the ticket booth. Rex was standing out front.

"Mr. Jones wants to see you down at the concession stand."

"What does he want?"

"I don't know. He didn't tell me."

Mike drove on, thinking, *What does he want?* He thought he had always tried to do a good job. *Am I going to get fired? Maybe I am going to get a promotion or a raise in pay.* He didn't have the foggiest idea what was going on.

After parking his car in back of the concession stand, Mike slowly went inside to face his boss. He entered the back door, and Mr. Jones waved him to come over to a booth to sit down.

"Mike, you have been catching tickets for a long time and have done a good job, so I think it's time for a promotion."

"What kind of a promotion, sir?"

"My other projectionist is off for a few days. I'm going to teach you how to operate the projectors."

"That would be great." Mike couldn't believe what was happening.

"You will get a raise in pay also. I am going to raise your pay one dollar per night while you are in training and three more when you complete your training. Well, what do you say?"

"Thank you, sir. I would like very much to become a projectionist."

"Good, let's go over to the booth and get ready to start the movie."

As they entered the booth, Mr. Jones told Mike, "Watch closely and listen carefully to my instructions, because if you forget what to do, you will have a blackout."

"Yes, sir, I'll try not to miss anything."

"OK, here we go. The movies are stored in cans, labeled 1 up to the number of reels in the movie, with the coming attractions and a cartoon on the first reel. The second reel will be the first reel of the movie. Does that make sense?"

"Yes, sir, I got it."

Mr. Jones removed the reel marked number 1 and moved around to the number 1 machine. Mike followed and stood over to the side to watch.

"Watch closely while I thread."

"Yes, sir."

"To thread the machine, raise the bell, put the reel on the top spindle, make a loop at the top sprocket, frame it like this, make a loop at the next sprocket, run it across the sound drum, and lock it. Make as loop on the last sprocket and continue on down to the lower spindle. That completes the threading of the machine. Do you have any questions?"

"What size film is it?"

"It's thirty-five millimeter."

"Would you show me how to make the right size loops again?"

"The film is safety film. If you have a fire, get away from the film. The fumes will make you sick."

Mr. Jones walked over to a large box mounted on the wall. "This is your sound amplifier. Turn it on with this switch, and these lights will light up, showing it is operating properly."

Walking back over to the projector, he raised the side door to the lamp house. "This is where you make your light for the film. When you strike these two carbons together, you get an arc. It produces light that is reflected off the reflector behind the carbons through the film to the screen. This large switch down here turns on the power for the lamp house. Make sure you have three inches of carbons to run a full reel."

"It sure is a lot to remember."

"Yes, it is, but I think you can do it."

"I don't know. I have never done anything like it before."

"It just takes practice."

"Well, I'll give it my best shot."

"This projector is ready to run. OK, now it is your turn. Get reel number 2 and thread the second projector."

Mike took reel number 2, placing it on the top spindle and threading the film as instructed. He had trouble with the sound gate.

"I can't get the sound gate to lock."

"Just close it until you feel a click and test it to see if it is locked."

"Like this?"

"That's right. Now you got it."

Mike finished threading. "How does it look?"

"You need a little more loop on the last sprocket."

"Like this?"

"You got it. Now check your carbons."

Mike checked his carbons for proper length, leaving the door up.

"Be sure to close the door before you strike the carbons. It will blind you."

Mr. Jones showed him how to play the record player into the sound system while waiting for time to start the movie. He showed him how to page someone if needed. The only time someone was paged was for an emergency.

"I got to make a phone call. We'll start the movie when I get back. You can play records until I return."

Mike walked around the booth, trying to understand everything and how each item worked. It sure looked like a lot to learn. He sure hoped he could learn it. He was playing with the film, trying to figure out how to splice it, when Mr. Jones returned.

Walking over to number 1 projector, Mr. Jones explained, "OK, here we go, time to start the movie. Strike your carbons and adjust for an even burn. Start your projector with this switch, open the dozer, and turn on the sound with this switch, stomping the foot switch on the floor at the same time, which opens the shutter. You now have a picture on the screen, with sound. Do you have any questions?"

"You make it look so easy."

"You will too, after a while."

"I sure hope so."

Mike touched each switch, repeating what they were used for.

"Very good. I believe you have it. Now come over here, and I'll teach you how to splice film while we wait for the first reel to run out."

Mr. Jones instructed him how to splice film and let Mike splice several times until his splices were good. The bell on the first projector dropped. Mr. Jones went over to projector number 2 with Mike close behind him.

"It's changeover time."

Mike watched as Mr. Jones did a changeover.

"Turn on the power to the lamp house and strike your carbons. Now watch the right-hand corner of the screen for 'Q' marks. There will be two sets of 'Q' marks. Watch what I do with each set."

As the first set came up, Mr. Jones said, "Turn on the projector and open the dozer." As the second set came up, he said, "Now stomp your foot switch and switch on your sound. That completes your changeover." Mr. Jones moved over to projector number 1. "Now we have to shut projector number 1 down and get it ready for the next changeover. Shut off the power to the lamp house and power to the projector."

"What do we do next?"

"Pull the reel off the bottom spindle and rewind it."

"When the film is rewound, put it back in the number 1 storage can. That is a complete cycle."

After the reel had finished rewinding, Mike put it back in the storage can. Mr. Jones sat down in front of the window and started watching the movie.

"OK, it's all yours."

"You're not leaving me by myself?"

"I'll stay for here until you are confident in yourself."

Pulling reel number 3 from the storage can, Mike threaded the projector and checked the carbons. He was ready for the next changeover. The movie was a long one, *Gone with the Wind,* starring Clark Gable. He would get a lot of practice by the time the movie changed. It was running for the next three days.

Everything went like clockwork until the fifth reel, when the film broke. Mike didn't know what to do.

"What do I do?"

"Watch me and learn how to fix it."

Mr. Jones jumped up, closing the dozer, turned off the sound, and then turned off the projector. He treaded the projector, lapping the film on the take-up reel, turned the projector on, opened the dozer, and turned on the sound. The picture was back on the screen.

"That's all there is to it."

"You sure fixed it fast."

"There's no reason to shut down the lamp house on a break. Just be sure you close the dozer, or you will burn the film."

"Yes, sir."

"Do you think you can handle it now?"

"Yes, sir, I think I can handle it."

"When the broken reel is finished, rewind it with the manual rewind and splice the bad place in the film. Be sure to frame the film when you splice it."

"Yes, sir."

"I'll be in the concession stand if you need me. Use the intercom to get me."

Mike operated the rest of the movie without any trouble. He liked the job and vowed to become a good projectionist.

After the movie was over, Mr. Jones came into the booth and showed Mike how to shut everything off. Locking the door, Mr. Jones handed Mike a key to the booth.

"I'm going to make you the relief operator for here and the Texas Theatre downtown. Do you think you can handle it?"

"I know I can."

"I believe you have missed only one day of work since you have been here."

"Yes, sir, somebody put a smoke bomb on my car and burned the wiring. By the time I got it fixed, it was too late to make it to work."

"Did you ever find out who put the smoke bomb on your car?"

"No, sir, I never did find out."

"I'll see you tomorrow night, and keep up the good work."

"Yes, sir, I will."

Mike drove to the exit where Rex was waiting on him. He pulled in beside Rex's car and got out.

"You bastard, you let me think I was being fired. You knew about the job, didn't you?"

"Yes, but you should have seen the look on your face when you drove up and saw me catching tickets. It was fun to watch you sweat."

"I owe you one, and I will collect sooner or later."

"You are a spoiled sport."

"I'll see you tomorrow night."

Leaving the drive-in theatre, Mike went straight home. It had been a long night, and he was tired. The next morning, after breakfast, Mike drove his mother to town to shop. He was still tired from the night before, but he was the only one that drove in the family.

"Mom, I got a new job at the drive-in. I am the relief operator for the drive-in and the Texas Theatre downtown. I'll be making more money."

"That's good. Now you can buy you some new clothes and shoes. You need them."

"Do you think Dad will sign for me to buy a new car?"

"I don't know."

"I'll be making more money, and I think I can make a car payment."

"Then I don't see why he wouldn't sign for you."

"I want to get rid of this pile of junk."

"If the old man gives you any trouble, I'll take care of him."

"Thanks, Mom. Would you like to look at cars while we are shopping?"

"No, I got to get back and finish my chores. I don't know anything about cars anyway."

After finding a parking space, Mrs. Love went about her shopping, while Mike stayed in the car. He watched the girls go by while daydreaming about buying a new car and meeting girls when he started school. It wouldn't be long before school started.

Jan Parker was walking down the sidewalk when she noticed Mike sitting in the car with his arm hanging out the window. She had heard he was going to work at the Texas Theatre. Punky had described him and his car to her. *This had to be him.*

She walked between the cars, bumping Mike's arm.

"Excuse me, I didn't mean to bump you."

"That's all right. I shouldn't have had my arm hanging out of the car."

"Is your name Mike Love?"

"Yes, it is."

"Punky described you and said you would be working at the Texas Theatre. I work there also, as an usher. I guess we will be working together. When do you start?"

"I don't know yet. I will probably start in a couple of weeks."

"It was nice meeting you, and I'll see you at the theatre."

Jan was about five feet four inches tall with a round face, surrounded by long curly brown hair. She was pleasingly plump but nice looking and dressed to show off her good points. She wore white short shorts, a deep V-neck blouse, exposing a lot of skin.

Mike watched her until she turned a corner, before going back to the girl-watching and daydreaming. Several more girls walked by, and some of them waved and giggled. He wondered if something was wrong with him. Mike came to a conclusion that there were a lot of fine-looking women in town, and he just needed one. Surely he could find one when school started.

Rex drove by and turned around and parked. He came over to talk. "What are you up to?"

"I am waiting on Mother. She is off shopping."

"And you weren't girl-watching?"

"It's a good pastime."

"Have fun. I got to go."

"See you later."

Mrs. Love returned from her shopping spree, loaded down with sacks. Mike got out and opened the back door for her.

"What did you do? Buy the store out?"

"No, but it has been a long time since I have gone shopping, and I needed a lot of things. I'm ready to go home now."

"OK, Mom," replied Mike.

He backed out into the street and headed for home. "I saw what you were doing while I was shopping. Did you find the one you wanted?"

"What are you talking about?" Mike played dumb.

"A girl. All boys do it." She laughed.

"I guess I was looking, but I didn't see the one I want."

"You will one day, and you will know it. It a feeling called love."

"How will I know?"

"You just will."

As they got out of the car, Mike unloaded the shopping bags and carried them into the house. He wanted to go shopping for a car.

"Mom, I'm going to look at cars this afternoon."

"I want to thank you for taking me shopping. Come and eat lunch before you go looking at cars."

"OK, Mom. I am hungry."

The Ford dealer had a poor selection of used cars, and the new ones were out of Mike's price range. He drove by Honest John's, but everything looked like it should be in the junkyard. He decided to give up for now and try again later. Mike went home to eat and get ready for work.

Mike went to work early and got his projectors ready to start the movie. He had a good night without any mis-frames or blackouts, but he would be glad when *Gone with the Wind* was transferred to another theatre, because it was so long. He got paid by the night. *The shorter the movie, I get off sooner.*

The movie was almost over when Punky came into the booth. "Rex, Leroy, and Gary will meet us on the square after the movie."

"What's happening?"

"It's time for a watermelon raid. We can have a party afterwards."

"OK, I'll be there."

"Good, I'll see you on the square. I'm going to check on Rex. He is cleaning the concession stand."

Everyone met on the square at one o'clock. After a short discussion about the raid, everyone piled into Punky's car.

Leroy said, "Spin out, man."

"You better cool it, or the cops will be after us," grumbled Rex.

Punky spun out, and sure enough, they heard a siren behind them. Punky drove around a corner, quickly turning into a driveway, and shut off the engine and its lights.

"Duck, everybody, until the cop car goes by."

The cop car came after them with lights flashing and the siren wailing. They didn't notice the parked car. They sat for a few minutes to make sure the coast was clear. Everybody laughed as Punky backed out. He eased off toward the watermelon patch.

"Why do always tease the cops and make them mad as a hornet?" asked Gary.

"It's fun to trick them, also the chase to see if you can out fox them."

"One of these days, they are going to catch you, put you in jail, and throw away the key."

"Catching is before skinning, and they haven't caught me yet," bragged Punky. Slamming on the brakes, he brought the car to a screeching halt, with dust flying everywhere.

"Everybody, out of the car! Each of you, pull only one watermelon, because it's late, and we won't have time to eat any more. We don't want to waste good watermelons."

Everybody bailed out to go pick a watermelon, while Punky stayed in the car to keep the motor running, just in case they needed a fast getaway. Everyone came back with a nice, ripe watermelon, except Rex.

"That watermelon is small and green," explained Mike.

"How should I know? I'm a city boy."

"Well, bring it with you. If the farmer finds a green watermelon pulled and left to rot, it will make him mad as a wet hen."

Everybody piled in the car with the watermelons as Punky spun out. He headed back to town.

"I was talking to a truck driver today, and he told me about a whorehouse located in La Grange. They call it the Chicken Ranch," quoted Gary.

"Why is that?" asked Punky.

"It was in operation during the depression, and customers paid with chickens. The Chicken Ranch sold some and ate the rest for food. They also sold eggs and ate the rest."

"It sounds like a bullshit story to me."

"The truck driver swears it's true."

"I guess we will have to go to La Grange one night and check it out," declared Punky.

"Is everyone for it?" Everyone agreed to go to La Grange.

When they arrived back in town, Punky drove straight to the park. Everyone got out and took the watermelons and busted them on the concrete tables. They took their hands and pulled the heart out of each watermelon to eat, except for Rex. He pulled out his pocketknife to use, just like a city boy, afraid to get his hands messy. After the party was over, Punky took everyone back to the square to pick up their cars.

"You guys, take it easy when you leave. There's a cop on the other corner of the square, watching us," explained Punky, "and given the level of competence of the majority of our police, you may get caught if you try to outrun them."

Everybody laughed, getting out of Punky's car. They got into their own cars. Each one backed out and eased off in the direction of his home.

*Gone with the Wind* was finally shipped out to another theatre, and a *Roy Rogers* Western replaced it. It was a short film, which made Mike happy. He would finally get out early.

The rest of the week Mike ran perfect movies. He liked his job and tried to never have mis-frames or blackouts. The next night, Mike had a surprise. Someone knocked on the booth door. He had started the first reel of the movie. He answered the door. Jan was standing there with a big smile.

"Hi, I was watching the movie and thought maybe you would like some company."

"Sure, come on it."

"When are you going to operate the Texas Theatre?"

"I still don't know."

"May I stay and watch the movie from in here?"

"Sure. I would enjoy your company."

At the end of the week, Mr. Jones came into the booth. "You have done just fine all week. Meet me at the Texas Theatre tomorrow night. I will get you checked out there."

Mike walked in the Texas Theatre, and Gary met him in the lobby. He was surprised to see Gary.

"I'm off work tonight, and I heard you were going to be my relief operator."

"That's right. The boss is going to show me the ropes tonight. Gary, you never told me you worked at the theatre."

"I guess I forgot to tell you and just assumed you knew. Leroy works here part-time also."

"I guess all the guys I know work at the drive-in or here."

"See you later, Mike. I got a hot date."

"Who are you going out with? I didn't know you had a girlfriend."

"I'll never tell."

Jan walked in the front door with a big smile on her face. "I see you are going to be our operator for tonight."

"Yes, Mr. Jones is going to start with me, until I find everything."

"Have you met the other girls?"

"No, I haven't. I just walked in."

Jan reached and took his hand. "Come with me."

They entered the back of the ticket booth, "Mike, I would like you to meet Joy Cane."

There was only one word to describe her—gorgeous. "Forget it," warned Jan. "She goes out with the captain of the football team." Joy smiled, and Jan pulled Mike back out of the booth. "Don't feel so bad. All the men look at her that way."

"But she is so—"

"I know. Don't remind me. If only I had a little of her looks!"

"I'm sorry. I didn't mean you were—"

"Forget it. I know I'm plain compared to her."

"You look just fine." He didn't want to hurt her feelings.

"Look, who is coming," Jan said. "Artis, meet our new operator Mike."

"Hi, Mike."

Mike looked her over. *A little heavy but nice.* "I guess we will be working together."

Mr. Jones walked up. "You ready to go to the booth?"

"Yes, sir."

"Well, follow me. You will work two nights here and two nights at the drive-in. You can catch tickets one night at the drive-in. Are the nights satisfactory with you?"

"It's fine with me."

"That will give you two nights off."

Mr. Jones led the way up a small flight of stairs to the projection booth. The equipment was old and out-of-date. It looked like a disaster waiting to happen.

"Everything here is the same as the drive-in, except for the sound. You will have to adjust your sound, depending on the size of the audience, and the sound on each movie is different."

"Why is that?"

"People make noise and absorb sound. At the drive-in, everyone has their own speaker and volume control."

"I see the difference."

"If the house is full, turn up the sound a couple of notches to allow for the noise. If your sound is too high or too low, the usher will call you on the phone on the wall. Do you have any questions?"

"No, sir."

Mr. Jones paused at the door. "Call me if you need me."

The movie ran without any problems, so Mike sat back and daydreamed about buying a new car. He thought about starting the new school and maybe meeting a nice girl. When the movie was over, he was still trying to put a face on his daydream. He decided he would look for a new car on Monday.

Then if he could get the down payment low enough, if the payments were low enough, and if his dad would sign for him . . . He decided there were a lot of *ifs* in buying a new car.

For the next few days Mike looked at cars and worked. He was ready to give up, because there was no way he could afford a large down payment to get his payments small enough so he could make them.

Punky spotted Mike at a used car lot and pulled in. "What're you up to? Are you going to get a new car?"

"I wish I had enough money to buy a new car. I'll have to keep driving what I got. The car needs to go to the junkyard. It must be nice to be rich."

"Dad helped me get my car, or I wouldn't have a car."

"My dad can't help. He can barely pay the bills."

"Well, good luck. I'll see you later."

It was Sunday morning, and school would start the next day. Mike was in his bedroom, lying on his back, staring at the ceiling and very despondent, when a knock sounded at the front door. He got up to answer it and got a big surprise.

Honest John was standing there with a big smile. "You may want to run me off, but before you do, listen to what I have to say. I've come to put things right with you for giving you a bad deal on your car."

Mike shouted, "That wasn't a car! It was an escapee from a junkyard!"

"Well, I'm going to make it right if it's the last thing I do."

"All right, I'm listening."

"Get your car and follow me back to the car lot."

Mike pulled up in front of the car lot and saw a new building with a showroom full of new cars. Honest John must have found a lot of suckers, like himself. A sign read "Honest John Ford." He was the Ford dealer now.

John opened the door and let Mike in. Mike looked the cars over and saw their price. He knew he couldn't afford them. John knew he was depressed, and he smiled. He was young once, a long time ago, and wanted a new car. There was a blue Ford Two-Door in one corner of the showroom.

"Mike, over here. Look at this one."

Mike walked slowly over with his hands in his pocket.

"Do you like this car?"

"Yes, sir, but I can't afford it."

"Let me see what I can come up with."

John looked at Mike, his old Ford, and the new car. He knew he would take a loss, but for some reason, he didn't care. He wanted to see the young man happy and right the wrong he had done the young man.

"The new car will cost you eighteen hundred dollars. I'll give you nine hundred for your old car and pay the tax, title, and license fee. That will leave you owing about nine hundred at thirty-eight dollars. You will have twenty-four payments. I'll even carry the note at zero interest. What do you have to say to the deal?"

# Chapter 4

"I love the car, and I can make those payments."

"Your dad won't have to sign. I'll take care of it."

John handed Mike the keys. "I'll open the door so you can drive it home and drive it to school tomorrow."

"You really mean I got the car, don't you?"

"Yes, you do. Come in after school tomorrow and sign the papers."

"Yes, sir, I'll be here."

John knew the signature wasn't any good, because he was a minor, but he knew Mike would make the payments somehow.

As Mike drove off the lot in his new car, John smiled. He thought he made a young man very happy. He knew why Mike wanted a new car so bad. John remembered when he was that age and was hunting a girlfriend. He found her; they have been married for twenty years.

Mike arrived at school thirty minutes early to show off his new wheels. The first day at high school, girls watched as each boy arrived. The girls looked for a guy with good looks and a car. Sometimes just a car would do. In a small town, without wheels, you were dead. There wasn't any way to take a girl on a date without a car. In the big city, you could take a taxi, bus, or subway, but in a small town, the only other way was to talk a friend into taking you on a double date, which gave very little chance of making out.

Punky pulled in and parked next to Mike. "I see you managed to get the new car."

"Yes, Honest John made up for the bad deal he pulled on me last time."

"I can't believe it. He always gets to people."

"Well, I'm not complaining. He made up for what he pulled on me with the first car."

"Mike, it's showtime. Here we go! Let's show off to the girls! Time to circulate!"

"There's a cute number on the steps going in the side door."

"Her breasts are too small."

"Well, I think anything over a mouthful is wasted anyway." Laughed Mike.

"I like them big. I like to bury my face in them."

Mike scanned the rest of the girls as they walked by. "What about that one?"

"Her nose is too long. You would have a hard time kissing her."

"Well, how about the one looking your car over?"

"Her hair is too short. I like long hair."

"Tell you what, Punky old friend. Just send me all your rejects, and I'll be happy."

The bell rang, and everyone went inside. They had to find their homeroom and get their schedule of classes. Mike found his name on a list on one of the doors. He went inside and took a seat.

Mike saw Rex in the back of the room and waved to him, but there wasn't a seat near him, so Mike had to take a desk a couple of seats from the front of the room. He didn't like that close to the front, but he didn't have a choice.

An old lady entered the room and stood at the front of the class. "My name is Mrs. Maples, and I will be your homeroom teacher. You will have your first class in here, which will be English III, and then you will go to the rest of your classes in other rooms."

She passed a paper around for everyone to sign for seating assignments. The class was a little noisy.

"OK, class, let's keep it quiet. Put a star by your name if this is your first time to attend Booneville High School."

Mike always hated changing schools. He hadn't run into the school bully yet. Maybe they didn't have one. He could be so lucky. After everyone signed the paper, Mrs. Maples looked it over.

"Class, we have one new student. Mike Love, stand up so the class can get to know you."

Mike stood while the class stared at him. He hated to be put on display. Some of the kids remembered him from the Dairy Queen. The boys were curious about the chick he had been with.

One boy next to him whispered, "What happened to that chick you were with at the Dairy Queen?"

"She went back to Houston. She was just visiting."

"She sure looked like a hot number."

Mike smiled. "She was."

Mike noticed some of the girls looking his way and smiling. He sure would like to know what they were saying about him.

Mrs. Maples handed out each student's schedule. She watched Mike still standing. He looked like a nice young man.

"Mike, you can take a seat now."

Mike looked over his schedule to see that he got what he signed up for. He would have English III in homeroom, followed by distributor education. It was easy to make the class because he already had a job. It was required in order to take the class. He had Glee Club the third period. Only four boys signed up for the class, all with the same scheme—to find a girlfriend.

Fourth period was hard. Math had always given Mike trouble and general math wouldn't be an exception. First period after lunch, he had science. Mike liked science even if it was a hard subject. He left science class early to make it to the theatre to operate the afternoon movie. Kids taking distributor education got out early to go to their jobs.

After Mike's first day at school, he was disappointed. He rated girls on a scale of zero to ten. All the girls he met, which rated five or higher, already had a boyfriend. That was another problem with changing schools. His dreams had been shattered to pieces. There wasn't a girlfriend in sight and little chance of finding one.

That night Mike lay in bed and dreamed about a girl, but he could never put a face on his dream. Finally, he decided he would look in another town for a girlfriend or maybe try to take one away from someone. *Why couldn't there be one that wasn't already going steady?*

For the next few weeks, life was a drag: Go to school, go to work, go home and study, go to sleep, and then back to school. Mike's love life was zero. He needed something to break the cycle.

Friday night, Punky asked Mike to work for him. "I got a big date. You don't mind covering for me?"

"Sure, I'll work for you. I got nothing better to do, so I might as well make some extra money."

"Thanks, pal. I got a hot date, and I don't want to miss it."

"May I give you some free advice?" suggested Mike.

"Sure, what is it?"

"Don't turn the lights on in the car, like you did with Joy."

They both laughed. "Not this time. I would rate her at number ten, and you know how hard I am to please."

"Who is she?"

"I can't tell you, because she has a big boyfriend, and if he found out, he would kick my ass."

Mike was better off not knowing. Then he would never let it slip. Punky paid Mike for working for him.

"See you later. Don't work too hard."

"I'll try not to."

At the time, Mike didn't know the money would come in handy Saturday night. He had a good night without any problems but was tired and went straight home after work.

Mike slept late the next morning. He cleaned and waxed his car for most of the day, except for mowing the lawn for his mother. Saturday night was his night to work at the drive-in.

Mike watched the clock. He had only one hour to go before the movie was over. He cleaned the booth and checked all the equipment to be sure everything was oiled and working. After the movie let out, he locked the booth door and walked over to his car. Punky was waiting for him.

"Hi, Punky, what's up?"

"Gary and Leroy are waiting on the square for us. They want to go to La Grange tonight and check out that truck driver's story about the Chicken Ranch. Are you game?"

"Sure, sounds like fun. Tomorrow is Sunday, and I can sleep in until time to come back to work."

"See you on the square!" yelled Punky, as he ran to his car.

Mike got in his car and followed Punky out of the drive-in. As they turned onto the highway, Punky burned rubber and left Mike sitting still. He took his time and drove the speed limit. He didn't want to get a ticket.

Punky, Gary, and Leroy were waiting on Mike, when he drove on the square and parked.

"Where have you been, slowpoke?"

"Driving the speed limit, not like someone I know. I don't want a ticket. They cost money, and I don't have much money."

"We can take my car," offered Punky.

Everybody loaded into Punky's car.

"Which way are we going?" asked Leroy.

"We'll pick up Highway 21 west until we cross Highway 77 and then turn south on 77 straight to La Grange. It should take about three hours."

Everyone settled down for the long ride to La Grange. If the truck driver were blowing smoke, the whole trip would be for nothing. You couldn't even sightsee because it was too dark.

They stopped one time at a roadside park for a pit stop and stretched their legs. Punky drove the rest of the way to Bryan while the others slept. By the time they arrived in Bryan, the car needed gas.

Punky pulled into an all-night service station. "Everybody get out for a pit stop."

The service station filled the car while everyone used the bathroom and got Cokes from the Coke machine.

"That will be five dollars and fifty cents."

Everyone pooled money to pay for the gas.

"Thank you, come back again."

"Have you ever heard of the Chicken Ranch in La Grange?" asked Leroy.

"No, can't say that I have."

Punky pulled back out on the highway, and everyone settled down for the rest of the trip to La Grange. Gary was riding shotgun. His job was to keep Punky awake. Mike and Leroy went to sleep in the backseat.

"There's your turnoff ahead," instructed Gary, pointing to a highway sign.

"I see it."

Punky took the off-ramp, stopping at the stop sign, then turning left and going under Highway 21. He headed south on Highway 77.

"Only one more town to go through, Gidding I believe, before we get to La Grange," said Gary.

As Punky drove downtown La Grange, Gary woke up Mike and Leroy.

"Boy, this town is dead!" said Leroy.

"What did you expect at three o'clock in the morning?" teased Punky.

"They should have a cute chick with a welcome wagon for out-of-town customers."

"Well, they don't."

"Someone should be out that knows about the Chicken Ranch."

They drove around, looking the town over for any sign of life.

"Well, what do we do now?" asked Gary.

"Ask someone where it is," replied Punky.

"Who do we ask? There's isn't anyone out this time of night, not even a service station open."

They drove around some more but without any luck. The only traffic in La Grange was passing through going someplace else.

"We might as well go home," complained Punky.

He pulled out on the highway and headed north out of town. Punky stopped at a traffic light.

"There's a night watchman over there. Pull up beside him," instructed Gary.

Punky pulled his car over close to the night watchman and shut off his engine. "Sir, could we talk to you?"

"You sure can. What can I do for you boys?"

"We heard from a truck driver that there's a place called the Chicken Ranch here in La Grange. Do you know where it is located?"

"I have never heard of it."

"Sir, the driver was very sure it was here in La Grange. It's a whorehouse."

The old man ran his hand over his bald head and looked to be in deep thought. "I do believe I did hear some talk down at the police station about it. I don't know anything about the place, only what I heard."

"Tell us what you heard."

"Well, you go about a mile north, turn right, and just a little way down, you will see a road off to your left. It has a white fence on each side of the road that leads to a big house. They say that's the place, but I don't know nothing about the place. No, sir, not me."

"Thank you for the directions," said Gary.

"You're welcome. You drive safe, you hear?"

Punky started the car and started to pull away.

"Wait a minute, wait a minute!" yelled the night watchman.

Punky stopped the car while he walked up next to the car.

"I almost forgot to tell you something. There's a big pothole in the road just as you pull off the road and head up to the house. You could break a spring."

"Thank you again," said Gary.

Punky pulled out and headed in the direction the old man had told him. He was headed north on 77, just outside of town.

"He doesn't know nothing. I repeat, nothing about the Chicken Ranch." Laughed Gary.

Everybody started laughing.

"Well, we're on our way. Have any of you guys ever been to a whorehouse?" asked Punky.

It was very quiet in the car.

"I guess we will all learn together. There's a first time for everything."

Punky didn't ask how many were cherry. He didn't want to embarrass anyone. He turned right and drove just a little way before turning left between the white fences. Punky headed toward the house, dodging the large pothole in the road. Everybody laughed again. There was a light on at the side Punky parked on. They sat and stared at the house.

"What are we waiting for? Come on, you guys. Let's go have some fun," said Punky.

"What if this isn't a whorehouse?" asked Gary.

"We just say we got the wrong house and leave."

Everybody got out and walked up to the back door that had a light over it. They were still hesitant what to do.

"What do we do now?" asked Gary.

"Knock on the door, stupid," replied Punky, as he knocked on the door.

A heavy black lady opened the door. "Come on in, boys. You are a little late, aren't you?"

"We had a long drive to get here," replied Punky.

"You have a seat on the couch while I go fetch the girls."

Five minutes later, eight girls filed into the room. They were all young, good-looking, and dressed very sexy in skimpy silk robes, which left little to the imagination. They walked around the couch while the boys looked them over.

"There are more girls if you don't see what you want," declared the old black lady.

"Thank you, ma'am, but I think we have enough," replied Punky.

"What do we do now?" whispered Leroy.

"Pick the one you want, I guess."

Punky pointed to a redhead. She took his hand and led him down a hall. "You made a good choice. I'll show you a good time."

"We're ready for some fun, so don't be shy," said a girl with very large breasts.

"I pick you," said Gary. She took his hand and led him out of the room.

A gorgeous blond entered the room. Leroy stared at her, and she smiled back at him. He wanted her, and she knew it. He held out his hand, and she took it.

"I pick you."

"I know. I wanted you to pick me."

"See you later, Mike."

There were still six fine-looking women in the room for Mike to pick from. One girl was shy, unlike the rest of the girls. She was petite, only five foot one. Her skin was flawless, long black hair, and green eyes. She had small breasts, but they were firm and pointed. Mike stood up and walked over to her and held out his hand.

"I pick you."

"Thank you." She took his hand and led him down a hall to her room.

"My name is Mike. What's yours?"

"It's Cindy."

Mike glanced around the room. There was a double bed, dressing table, and a stuffed chair. A door led to the bathroom. Both were silent for a minute or two, each one not sure what to say or what to do next.

"Would you mind paying first?"

"How much money do you charge?" Mike didn't have any idea what it cost, since this was his first time in a whorehouse.

"That will be ten dollars cash. We don't take chickens anymore."

Mike pulled out a ten-dollar bill and put it on the dressing table, while looking at her with a dumb expression.

"I'm sorry. That was a joke, but you and I were just kids when this place took them as payment for services."

Mike and Cindy both laughed and began to relax. She was glad Mike chose her. She had some bad experiences in the past with customers.

"Why don't you take off your clothes? And I'll be right back."

Mike undressed and sat down in the chair with his hands covering his manhood. Cindy came out of the bathroom with a pan of water, soap, and a towel. She kneeled down on her knees in front of Mike. "This is required by the house before we can have sex."

Cindy sat the pan on the floor. Mike still covered his manhood with his hands.

"This must be your first time."

"Yes, just my first time where you pay and do it with a stranger."

"To be honest, this is only my second week to work here. I never have done this before. I ran out of money in my third year of college. I couldn't find a job that paid enough to live on and go to college." She was quiet.

"Here I am working my way through college." She laughed.

"I know what you are talking about. You do what you got to do."

Cindy moved Mike's hands and stroked him gently with one hand, while dipping the soap in the water with the other hand. She washed his manhood and after drying it off, gave it a complete inspection. Mike watched her with exciting curiosity.

"We have to do this. It is house rules, to be sure of a clean-run house."

Cindy took the pan, soap, and towel back to the bathroom. She came back and stood in front of him. She teased him as she slowly removed her robe and eased between his legs, running her hands around his neck, entwining her fingers in his hair, and pulling his head toward her small breasts.

Mike opened his mouth and covered her breast with his mouth, sucking until her nipple became hard and her body quivered. Her female scent teased Mike's senses, and his manhood stood at attention, ready for action; playtime was over. She pulled back from Mike and stared at his erection.

She smiled. "I think you're ready to make love."

"I think you are right."

"Then let's do it."

Cindy backed slowly over to the bed, pulling Mike with her, then falling back on the bed and pushing herself to the middle of the bed. She spread her legs and slowly pulled her feet up under her. She looked at Mike with a slow coaxing smile.

"Come and take me."

"Do you mind if I just look at you for a minute? You are beautiful to look at."

"Go ahead, we can take our time." She blushed under his scrutiny.

"Spread your folds for me."

"Like this?"

"Yes." He touched her folds with his fingers, and she moaned.

Mike was staring straight at her center of passion. Cindy held her arms open for him. Mike eased down on the bed between Cindy's thighs. He placed his hands on either side of her head to support his weight. Cindy's hand found his hard manhood and guided it to her center of heated passion. Mike entered her, slamming into her hard, filling her, as she took all of him. He thrust, and she arched to meet him each time, while rotating in a circular motion with her hips.

"Oh, Mike, you are good. I love doing it with you."

"I try to please."

"It feels so good."

"You do too. You are still tight."

Each time he thrust deeper, she tightened her grip on his throbbing penis. He was trying to make it last. It felt so good, but he knew he was running out of time. He gave one more final thrust and exploded deep in her body.

"Don't pull out yet."

"I won't. Take your time."

Cindy moved against Mike. He felt her throbbing muscles around his erection with her climax. She kept on squeezing his organ, and he thought she would pull it off his body. He bit his lip to keep from crying out.

Cindy put her arms around Mike's neck and pulled him to her. He quivered as her firm breasts pressed against his chest. They lay coupled together until their breathing returned to normal.

Mike rolled off her and eased out of bed. Cindy lay there with her legs spread. She was smiling up at him.

"That was marvelous."

"I bet you say that to all the girls."

"There hasn't been that many."

Cindy went to the bathroom to clean up. She cleaned up and came back out. "You can use the bathroom to clean up if you want to."

She put her robe on and waited on Mike to take his turn in the bathroom. He cleaned up and took a leak.

They walked back down the hall, hand in hand, like two lovers. "Mike, I enjoyed having sex with you."

"I enjoyed doing it with you too, but I came too fast."

They entered the room, and Mike realized he was the first one to return. A large-breasted girl named Judy asked, "Couldn't pace your lovemaking?"

"No, I don't know how to do it," explained a red-faced Mike.

"Would you care to try your luck again?"

Mike stared at her nipples trying to tear through her silk robe. He had a moment of hesitation before he made up his mind.

"Teach me to last."

"Come with me and learn how it's done."

Judy took his hand and led him down the hall to her room. Mike put ten dollars on the dressing table.

Without hesitation, they both undressed and got on the bed. Judy pushed him down and straddled him. Mike arched up, and Judy completed the union.

"Let me take control. You lie back and relax," instructed Judy.

"What are you going to do that is different?"

"I'm going to bring you close to a climax and back off several times."

Judy moved up and down while her breasts bounced. Mike wanted to do something, so he reached up and began softly stroking her nipples. She gave a sharp intake of breath and tightened her inner muscles on his erection. He felt that he was about to come. Judy backed off until he was barely inside her and stopped any motion. That gave Mike time to gain control again. She did this several times, bringing him almost to the peak and then backing off so he could gain control again. It was a kind of torture, but they had been doing it for a long time, and he hadn't had a climax.

Finally, Judy rolled over, pulling Mike on top, but never breaking the union. "Now," Judy said, "give it to me. Give me all you got."

They moved against one another until they both went over the edge together. "That's what I call having fun," responded Mike.

"I'm glad you enjoyed it."

"It was fantastic."

"Now you know how to make it last. A girl doesn't like *wham, wham, and thank you, ma'am.* She likes to enjoy making love also."

"I see what you mean. Make the girl enjoy making love."

"Now you got the picture."

They got cleaned up and walked hand in hand back to the front room. Leroy, Gary, and Punky were waiting on him.

"What took you so long?" inquired Punky. "Scared and couldn't get it up?"

Cindy and Judy smiled at Mike but didn't say a word. The guys thanked the girls for a good time and walked to the back door.

The black lady smiled. "Come back real soon and have a safe trip home, you hear?"

"Thank you, and we will be back," they said in unison.

All the way home, they laughed and talked about their experiences. This night would be something they would never forget—their first trip to a whorehouse.

"It was a long trip but well worth the trip," said Punky.

"We'll have to do it again." Sighed Leroy.

"Yeah, real soon," said Mike.

They stopped in Bryan on the way home for a needed pit stop. Punky drove, and Gary rode shotgun to keep him awake.

On arriving home, Mike slipped into his room and removed his clothes, then eased into bed to relax. It had been a very long day and a short night. He lay on his back and dreamed about his experience. He was ready to try out what he learned. Mike was relaxed by now and would sleep, and he did.

"Son, are you getting up anytime today?" She was standing in the doorway.

"Mom, there's not any school today, so I would like to sleep in."

"If you got home at a decent hour, you would be up and about, but young people nowadays stay out all hours. No good is sure to come of it."

"Mom, didn't you tell me you and Dad never got home before four in the morning when you went square-dancing?"

"Well, yes, but we went by a buggy, not a car."

"And didn't you say it took hours coming home, but the horse knew his way home and you could make out?"

Mrs. Love retreated to the kitchen without another word. Mike smiled, trying to picture what it would be like to go with a girl on a date in a horse-drawn buggy, taking all night to get there and back. It had to be some kind of fun.

"Boy, would I like to go on a date like that!"

The trip was always too fast by car. Mike believed the dates he went on were timed. He believed the girl's mother must use a stopwatch. That way, nothing could happen to their little girl. Mike finally got up, cleaned up, and dressed for the day. He ate lunch and decided to go to a movie at the Texas Theatre.

Joy was selling tickets, and Mike waved as he went inside. Gary was on the stairs to the booth, and Mike walked over to see him.

"What are you doing here? Don't you work at the drive-in tonight?"

"I thought I would take in a movie."

*The Thing* was showing and was to be a good horror movie. While Gary and Mike talked about the Chicken Ranch trip, the movie slowly filled up. Jan came over and let the chain down to allow people to go upstairs to the balcony.

Two girls came by, and Mike liked the looks of one of them. He stared at her, and it got her attention. She stopped at the door to the downstairs section and looked back.

"Do you see something you like, or do you see my slip showing?"

"Yes, I see something I like." His face turned red.

She turned and walked back over to where Mike was standing. He couldn't think of anything to say to her.

"Do you work here?"

"Yes, I'm one of the movie operators, but I don't work here today. I came to watch the movie."

"We came from Palestine to see the movie. Would you like to sit with us and tell us about the town of Booneville? This is our first time to come here."

"What is your name?"

"It's Mike."

"My name is Pam, and this is Dorothy."

"Let's go," said Dorothy. "The movie is about to start."

Mike followed the girls to their seats. They sat halfway down to the screen and against the right wall. The movie was good, and a couple of times Mike felt Pam dig her nails into his arm during a scary part of the movie.

By the time the movie was over, Mike knew Pam was a cheerleader for the football team, and he had a date for next Friday night. That was his only night off that week. Pam lived at the edge of Palestine. She gave him her phone number and directions.

"I'll see you next Friday night at seven," Mike said.

"I'll be ready."

Pam and Dorothy left the movie to go home. Mike climbed the stairs to the booth.

"Well, old buddy, what happened down there?"

"I got a date for next Friday night. She is a cheerleader and good looking."

"You must have a death wish."

"Why do you say that? It's just a date."

"If the football players see you making out with one of their girls, they will simply kill you."

"I have to take the chance. I got nothing here in Booneville."

As Mike drove home, he thought about what Gary had said, and Gary was right. He could get himself hurt, but nothing ventured, nothing gained.

Friday night, Mike dressed and left early for his date. He drove and looked in the rearview mirror. Looking at himself in the mirror, he thought this could be another disaster, but he wouldn't back out.

Pam was waiting on her front porch for Mike as he pulled into the driveway. She rushed out to the car and got in.

"Get out of here as fast as you can!"

"What's going on?" He took off at a high rate of speed.

"Bigmouthed Dorothy told the boys at school that I had a date with you. I tried to call you, but I couldn't get through to you. Someone may be watching the house."

"Do they control who you go out with?"

"Yes, in a way. Do you know what will happen if the boys at school catch you taking me out? I am a cheerleader, and they think I should only go out with them."

"Well, maybe we can break the school tradition just this once," argued Mike. He didn't feel as sure of himself as he sounded.

Pam moved over next to Mike and slid down in the seat, making it hard to see her. It was almost dark. She was fearsome of what might happen if they got caught.

"Maybe you had better take me back home and forget our date."

"Not on your life."

"But they might hurt you if we get caught."

"We got this far. You want to go to a house movie or a drive-in movie?"

"No, a movie is too easy for them to spot us. Let me take you on a tour of the Dogwood Trails by moonlight. I don't think anyone would see us there."

"Sounds like fun to me."

"Turn left at the next street heading out of town. That is North Link."

They drove in silence for a few minutes. "Turn left here and drive down the winding road."

The drive was fun, like being on a raceway with a lot of sharp curves. "Take the left curve ahead and go straight until you come to a dead end."

Mike did as he was instructed and ended up on a ledge protruding out in space. Looking down were the lights of Palestine, and looking up, the sky was filled with stars. Dogwood trees were in full bloom. The view was breathtaking. Mike opened his door and reached for Pam's hand. She got out, and they walked hand in hand to the edge of the ledge. Mike reached down and picked up a small stone, tossing it over the ledge. They listened for the contact with the ground.

"That's a long drop, a real long drop."

"Yes, it is. Some people call it 'lover's leap.'"

"Well, forget it. I'm not in the mood to jump."

"You wouldn't jump for little old me!" She giggled.

"I'm afraid not. I'm too chicken."

They both laughed and started to enjoy each other. Mike turned and faced Pam, taking her other hand. He looked her up and down and liked what he saw. She blushed at his scrutiny. It made her hot, him looking at her that way.

Pam had long brown hair, tied in a ponytail, a tight white sweater showing off her firm uplifted breasts, and a long blue skirt. Mike daydreamed about a very short skirt showing off her legs. He wished someone would design a skirt like that. "What?"

"I was thinking what you would look like in a short skirt."

"Who ever heard of anything so silly?"

"I hope someday the length of skirts and dresses go up."

"How far up?" Pam giggled.

"Let me think about it. How about three inches above your knees?"

She was shocked by the suggestion. "You got to be kidding."

"And while we are designing clothes, make a deep 'V' on the sweater to show off some skin."

"Mike, you are crazy. It will never happen."

"Well, a guy can dream, can't he?"

"You have some funny dreams."

Mike slowly pulled Pam into his arms. Their eyes locked, and she closed her eyes. Mike covered her red lips. He moved his tongue along her teeth, and she shyly opened to him. Mike slid his tongue in her mouth and touched her tongue. It excited her, and they started a duel of tongues. Mike sucked her tongue deep into his mouth, and then she did the same to him. Mike ran his hands up and down her back, pulling her tight against his body. Her breasts were flat against Mike's chest, and all her body was in flames with desire. Pam moaned as Mike moved against her. She could feel something hard pressing against her belly and realized Mike had a hard-on. She started to move against him.

"Let's go back to the car," whispered Mike.

She was ready. "Let's go."

He dreamed what would happen next. He had the experience to make this a night to remember. Mike opened the car door for her, and they got in. Mike pulled Pam into his arms and kissed her deeply. She moaned, and he slid a hand under her sweater. Her nipples were hard and waiting to be touched.

"What was that?" asked Pam.

"I don't hear anything."

Lights shined in the car. A car came down the road at a high rate of speed, heading straight for them.

"That's part of the football team, I think. I was warned not to go out with you."

"Just great. Let's get out of here."

Mike started his car and surveyed the area but didn't see any place to run or any place to hide. There was only one way out. Mike put the gas pedal to the floor and headed head-on with the approaching car.

A split second before they hit head-on, the approaching car turned. Pam screamed and covered her eyes with her hands as the two cars made contact. Mike's car took the back bumper off the other car, while only losing a side mirror. He didn't slow down until they were out of the Dogwood Trails and headed back to Palestine.

"Please take me home," whimpered Pam. "I'm scared."

"It's all over now."

"Please don't be mad at me. I went with you to show them I could do what I wanted to do. I wanted to make Bob, my boyfriend, jealous. I'm sorry. I feel lousy about what I did to you. I'm sorry, I'm sorry," Pam was babbling.

"Forget it, but why did you let me kiss you and you responded to me?"

"I wasn't going to, but you did something to me. I was enjoying it and didn't want to stop. You swept me off my feet."

"Thanks, I needed that. At least the night won't be a total loss."

Mike pulled into the driveway, leaving the engine running, and opened his car door to get out.

"You don't have to walk me to the door."

"Yes, I do. I want to kiss you good night and good-bye."

"I would like that very much."

Mike walked Pam to her door, hand in hand. They faced each other, and Mike pulled Pam into his arms and kissed her hard.

"Good night and good-bye. It has been fun."

Mike turned to walk back to his car.

"Look out!" screamed Pam.

Too late. Mike caught a fist to his stomach, and it doubled him over. Two big lugs picked him up.

"Hi, can't we talk this over? You must be Bob, the boyfriend."

"No, we can't! Hold the punk!"

Bob drew back and let go a fist aimed at Mike's face. He ducked, and Bob's friend caught it full in the face, knocking him flat. Mike brought a foot up, kicking Bob in the balls, putting him out of action. He swung his arm, his elbow catching the other lug in the face, smashing his nose.

Mike jumped in his car and put his gas pedal to the floor. Cutting a U-turn in Pam's nice green lawn, he went through a fence, hit the mailbox, and went into the street.

He left a patch of rubber as his car hit the second gear and a little more when he hit the high gear. He looked in his rearview mirror but didn't see anyone following him. They wouldn't catch him now.

"Wow, what a night!"

When Mike passed the "City Limit" sign, he slowed down for the trip home. What a night it had been! It had almost turned into a nightmare. He wouldn't go back to Palestine for a long, long time.

Monday morning, Mike pulled in beside Gary in the school parking lot. They got out of their cars to talk.

"Well, I see you made it back alive."

"Very funny. I almost didn't."

"What happened?"

"I got in a fight and kicked one in the balls. Then I ran like hell."

"You got to be kidding."

"I kid you not." Mike told Gary the rest of the story. They went into the school building together, laughing.

That evening, as Mike prepared to start the movie, Mr. Jones stuck his head in the door.

"You have a long-distance phone call in the concession stand."

Mike went next door and picked up the receiver, wondering who would be calling him long distance.

"Hello."

"This is Pam. I wanted to call you and talk."

"Fine, but I only got a couple of minutes before I have to start the movie. What have you got on your mind?"

"First of all, I want to apologize for what I did to you. You could have been hurt. I am sorry, but I applaud you for what you did."

"Say what, did I hear you correctly?"

"Dad and Mom wanted to kill you for messing up the yard. Bob wants to get his hands on you, but guess what?"

"I'll never guess," answered Mike as he drummed his fingers impatiently on the counter.

"Bob gave me his class ring and said he loves me. And guess what else?"

"He told you that you were the only girl in the world for him."

"No, silly boy, but several of the girls here like your style and gave me their phone numbers to give to you."

Mike wrote down their names and phone numbers.

He studied their names. There was a bunch of them. Mike couldn't believe all these girls wanted him to call them.

"This last name you gave me, is it—"

"Yes, it's Dorothy. She came down to Booneville with me," Pam finished for him.

"But I thought she couldn't stand me?"

"Now she thinks you are the greatest for running a big risk just for a date with me. Dorothy thought it was romantic the way you insisted on walking me to the door and kissing me good night."

"I liked that part myself." Laughed Mike.

He remembered standing out on the ledge with her firm breasts flat against his chest. His body heat started to rise.

"Thank you again," said Pam.

Mike glanced at the clock. "I got to go start the movie. I'll see you sometime."

He ran for the booth before Mr. Jones jumped him for starting the movie late. While the movie was running, Mike looked at the names and numbers Pam had given him. He may try again, but he wasn't a fool and would wait awhile until things cooled off. The next day at school, Mike went to the bathroom. He washed his hands and started to leave. Bobby and Jack, players for the football team, came in the door.

"Well, what do we have here?" taunted Bobby.

Jack backed Mike against the wall. "We don't like dirt farmer kids messing around with our girls."

"I'm not a dirt farmer anymore."

"Once a dirt farmer, always a dirt farmer," ribbed Jack.

"But I haven't gone out with any of your girls, so what's the problem?"

"The problem is you. You went out with a cheerleader from Palestine."

"So what does that have to do with you?"

"Going out with her is the same as going out with one here."

"I don't get it."

"Stupid, all football players stick together. So don't try it here, or we will take your head off and hand it to you. Get the picture?"

"I got it, no cheerleaders. They belong to you."

"You finally got it, stupid."

They turned around and left Mike standing against the wall. He was mad and hurt at the same time. People in small towns put you in a class and never let you out or forget your place. Mike would always be the country boy to people in Booneville. He had a common name and wasn't one of the rich or didn't have a famous name in the town.

Driving home from school, Mike felt very low. He thought what Jack had said. It echoed around in his head again and again. *Once a dirt farmer, always a dirt farmer, dirt farmer, dirt farmer . . .* There was only one way to break out, and that was to leave Booneville. For the first time he realized he hated living in a small town. He vowed to leave as soon as he finished high school, but in the coming months, he would just try to make the best of things.

The next day, Mike pulled into the school lot. Punky, Gary, and Leroy were waiting for him. He was still low from the day before, but at least he had a few good friends. He walked over to meet them.

"I say we vote on it," Punky said. "What about you, Mike?"

"Vote on what?"

"We want to call our little group, The Four Horsemen."

"Do you have any more suggestions?"

"Everybody had a different name to call, us the Four Aces or The Four Studs, after our trip to the Chicken Ranch."

That got a good laugh out of everyone. They started talking about their trip to the Chicken Ranch and when could they go again. It took gas to get there and ten dollars each for a girl. Ten dollars was a lot of money.

"I wonder if they ever give discounts," said Leroy.

"I doubt it. It's not a grocery store." Laughed Punky.

"Well, it pays to advertise."

"I don't think they need to advertise. They are good at what they do."

"Well, I will have to save a long time before I have enough money to go back to La Grange," replied Mike.

It was almost time for school to start. They started toward the door to go to school.

"Anyone for playing hooky from school?" asked Punky.

Punky was always the one to get everyone in trouble. It was like "Follow the leader." Everybody looked at each other and back to Punky.

"Well, are we going or not?"

Punky got in his car, followed by everybody right behind him, with Mike bringing up the rear. The bell rang for school, but they wouldn't be there today. Punky started his engine and pulled out into the street. He hit the second gear, burning rubber.

"Punky, you dumbbell! Now you will have the cops after us," warned Leroy. "Do you ever drive normal?"

"There just wouldn't be any fun driving normal."

"I give up. Forget it."

Punky drove upon the square, and as he drove around the square, he opened his car door. "Here, Leroy, since you don't like my driving, you drive," he said, and he stepped out of the car.

"You damn fool!" yelled Mike as he reached over the front seat and grabbed the steering wheel.

"Get the brakes, Leroy!"

"I have got the brakes." The car came to a stop.

Punky hit the pavement running, but the car was going faster than he had calculated. He fell flat on his backside. It hurt his pride, but he got back in the car, rubbing his rear.

"So it was a stupid thing to do, but it didn't seem like it at the time." It never did with Punky. "What do we do now before I kill myself?"

"Let's go to the Dairy Queen and get something to drink while planning what to do today," suggested Gary.

"Good idea," replied Leroy.

After ordering their drinks, they sat down to form a plan for the day. "How about fishing at the river?" suggested Punky.

"How about jackrabbit hunting?" asked Leroy.

"Let's go swimming at the Country Club," said Mike. He daydreamed about the night Punky took the girls and him swimming. It had been a fun time.

"We don't have swimsuits," complained Leroy.

"We can swim in our shorts," replied Punky.

"If the caretaker catches us, he will throw us out."

"If he catches us, he will throw us out. We don't belong to the Country Club."

"Then we don't care."

They were silent for a few moments. "Let's go, guys."

They were off, following Punky as usual.

They approached the lake. The sky was blue, and the sun was shining bright. The water looked so cool. They didn't see any caretaker in sight. Their luck was holding. Maybe he had a day off. There was a school bus parked by the bathhouse. Punky pulled in beside the school bus and parked.

"What's a school bus doing out here?" asked Punky.

"Who knows, dummy?" replied Leroy. "Maybe they came to swim."

They could hear loud laughter and shouting coming from the bathhouse. Everybody looked at each other, and all together said, "There are girls here."

"I think the senior class is having a swimming party," explained Leroy.

"Come on and let's see if that bathhouse has some knotholes in the walls." Laughed Punky.

They approached the bathhouse very quietly and moved around to the backside. They were in luck—it was full of knotholes. The girls had just arrived and were still in their school clothes. The boys looked at each other. They knew they were in time for the show, and what a show it would be!

The girls started to undress, and the boys started to sweat. Never had they seen so many naked girls in all their life. Some of the girls had large tits, some small tits, and some had a flat chest.

Punky looked over at Mike. "Why does Mary have one color at the top and a different color at the bottom?"

"She dyes the bottom, dumbbell."

"You're putting me down."

"Would I lie to you?" Laughed Mike.

Punky watched as Mary wiggled around, and her tits bounced up and down. "I sure would like to chew on those mounds."

"Dream on, Punky."

"I like Sherry with the small breasts," said Gary, "anything over a mouthful is wasted."

"Yeah, I like them small also," replied Leroy.

Leroy unzipped his pants and stuck his large manhood through a knothole.

"What are you doing?" asked Gary.

"Fishing. Maybe one of the girls will see it and know what to do with it."

"I doubt that."

"Maybe if I moved it a little, they would notice it."

The guys watched to see if they noticed his penis. Betty hung her panties and bra on his manhood. The guys started to laugh.

"She thinks it's a peg to hang clothes on!" Laughed Punky.

Leroy lost his hard-on; the *peg* lost the vigor and went limp. Betty's panties and bra fell to the floor, and Betty screamed.

"Now the fat's in the fire! Let's get out of here!" warned Mike.

They ran for the car. Mike, bringing up the rear, dove through the rear window as Punky spun out and headed for the highway.

"Do you think the girls know it was us?" asked Gary.

"No, we got away too fast for them to see us," replied Punky.

"Well, one of the girls may know who it was," said Leroy.

"What Leroy is saying is how many guys in our high school have hung like him, and one of the girls may know it was Leroy," explained Mike, "but she may not tell, because the other girls would want to know how she knew who it was. It's a catch-22. She may want to tell, but will she want to admit she had sex with Leroy?"

"Who is the girl, Leroy?" asked Punky.

"You know the rule, never show and tell."

"But we're your friends. Don't you trust us?"

"Punky, if you knew, you would hit on her, so forget it."

Punky drove back toward town. The boys laughed and compared the girls. "I thought Martha had big tits," said Mike.

Punky teased Mike, "If you like foam rubber, she has big tits, but without her thick-padded bra, she has nothing."

"Did you see Patsy? I thought she was cherry. Boy, she looked like she had been hit with an ax!" complained Leroy.

"She is a cheerleader and is probably the punchboard for the whole football team!" Laughed Gary.

Mike thought back to what Jack had told him in the bathroom about leaving cheerleaders alone. They belonged to the football players. Now he knew what he was telling him. *But why would a beautiful girl like Patsy let the football team use her like that? Maybe she just wanted to be the most popular girl in school.* He didn't understand girls.

"Well, what do we do now?" asked Punky. "We didn't get to go swimming, and if we go back to town, someone will turn us in to the school."

"We could drive to La Grange and go to the Chicken Ranch," suggested Leroy.

"Does everybody have ten dollars to pay for the girl? They don't take chickens anymore. I'm broke, and I only got below a half tank of gas."

"It was a good idea anyway, but too bad everybody is too broke to go. We got to think of something to do. We can't just waste the whole day doing nothing. Punky, you always come up with something, so how about it?"

They headed toward town with everybody in deep thought. They passed a large field of sugarcane, and Punky turned around and headed back. He pulled the car off the road beside a bridge.

"You guys wanted something to do. Who wants to go get some sugarcane?"

They looked at each other, but nobody volunteered to go. "I got to drive the getaway car, so that canceled me out."

"We can draw straws," suggested Gary.

"Forget it. I'll go," said Mike as he opened the back door of the car and got out. "Besides I'm the country boy, and you city boys wouldn't know what to cut or bring back anyway."

"Do you want me to go with you?" asked Leroy.

"I think I can bring all we can eat."

"Are you sure?"

"Yes, all we need is one stalk each."

Mike ran down a creek bed, dodging a small running stream of water. He stopped about a hundred yards down the creek bed. He eased up the bank and out into the sugarcane field. The farmhouse was located on the other side of the field. He figured he didn't have a problem at getting caught.

He looked the cane over, looking for some big juicy stalks of sugarcane. He was picky; he wanted the best.

He looked at the farmhouse one more time. He figured he had plenty of time even if the farmer did spot him getting out of the car. He took out his pocketknife and cut into a stalk of cane. It was nice and juicy. He cut into several more before he found what he was looking for.

He cut a couple of stalks and was about to cut the third stalk when all hell broke loose. The shotgun sounded like a cannon and then shot fell all around Mike.

"Oh shit!"

Mike threw down the sugarcane and ran for the creek bed. He tripped and fell headfirst down the embankment, rolling into the water. He was up and running as more shot hit the trees on the creek bank above his head. He reached the car and jumped in the back window as Punky shot off down the highway away from town.

"Wow, that was close!" said Mike. He tried to control his heart as it hammered against his ribs.

"We are being followed by a red pickup!" yelled Punky.

He enjoyed a good race, but he knew the pickup wasn't a match for his car. "Shall we slow down and let him catch up so it will be a fair race?"

"Punky, you fool, get us out of here! That man has a shotgun and will use it if he gets close enough!" yelled Mike.

"Never fear. Punky is here to save the day."

"Damn fool, get us out of here! I've been shot at enough. I'm wet and covered with mud."

"Maybe I should let you out, since you are messing up my backseat," teased Punky.

"Just get that guy off our tail."

"Your wish is my command."

They rounded a curve out of sight from the pickup. Punky pulled off the highway into a driveway straight into an open garage.

"Everybody duck down."

Everybody hit the floor. The pickup rounded the curve and shot by on down the highway.

"You saved our butts," said Mike.

"I told you not to worry. I got everything under control."

"I don't like being shot at with a shotgun. That guy was mad. I think he knocked down more sugarcane than I cut."

Punky backed out of the garage and started to leave. A lady came out the front door and walked over to the car.

"May I help you?"

"Sorry, lady, we have the wrong house," said Punky.

"Now wasn't that fun?" said Punky.

Punky had a problem. He liked to live on the edge, and someday he was going to get them in real trouble.

"What are we going to do now?" asked Gary.

"We could go south and get some beer," replied Punky.

"How do we buy beer? None of us is old enough to buy beer."

"Funny you should ask. I know a colored joint that will sell it to anyone with the money to buy it."

"Where is it located?"

"It's off the main highway, back in the woods, without any sign to point the way."

"Then how do you know where it is?"

"I have a friend who brings me beer when he makes a beer run. So do we go? Anybody have a better idea?"

"OK, let's go, but I'm going to take a back road until we get close, before driving out on the highway."

Punky knew every back road and pig trail in the area. After running the back roads, he pulled onto the highway, and it was only a couple of miles before time to turn off. Punky pulled off the highway to the right and went down a narrow dirt road. He followed the road for a short distance before coming out into a clearing.

"We're here. That's the joint," said Punky.

"Are you sure this is the place?" asked Leroy.

"It's the place, trust me."

"Every time we trust you we get in trouble."

It was a rundown old house with a sign over the door reading "Tomcat." It was noisy for that time of day. It was only two in the afternoon.

"They must party early around here," responded Mike.

"I guess they do," Punky answered.

"Just how many times have you gone in this place?"

"Well, I haven't. Not exactly," Punky hedged.

"What do you mean by that?"

"I would wait in the car while my colored friend went in and bought the beer."

"Just great. Now which one of us is going in to buy the beer?"

"I thought all of us would go in, you know, show of force."

"What kind of force?"

"Just the four of us against a full house."

"Do you call that force? I call it stupid."

"Well, what would you suggest?"

After a short hesitation, Mike explained, "Send one person in and keep a low profile."

"And who will go in?" Everybody looked at Mike.

"OK, my idea. I will go in."

As Mike approached the door, he was mumbling to himself, *When will I learn to keep my big mouth shut? If I think after the sugarcane patch, I will know better.*

Opening the door very slowly, Mike stepped inside and started slowly toward the bar. It got so quiet. He could hear every step he took. All eyes were on him.

"Hey you, white boy, go around to the back door if you want something," the owner said gruffly.

Mike didn't like being told to go to the back door, but what else could he do if he wanted some beer? He went out the front door, and everybody laughed. The white boy had been put in his place. The colored people were treated that way all the time.

Mike went around to the back door and placed his order for a case of Pearl beer. The owner returned with his case of Pearl and an extra six-pack.

"What's that? I only wanted a case of Pearl."

"This is for two reasons. First, it's for letting you buy beer underage, and, second, it's for the bragger in your group who thinks he can hold his booze."

Mike handed him twenty dollars. "This should take care of it."

"I'll just keep the change. You don't mind, do you?"

"Would it make any difference if I did?"

"No, take your beer and get off my property."

Mike was mad, but what could he do or say? He returned to the car with the beer. He handed the beer to Punky and got in the car.

Driving down the dirt road to the highway, Punky asked, "What happened to you back there?"

"I was robbed."

"You were robbed?"

"He took the whole twenty dollars we had for the case of beer and whatever this junk is."

Leroy looked at the six-pack and began to read. "Bulldog malt liquor. Guess I'll have one. I can drink anything. Time would tell." Everybody else popped a beer. They passed the "City Limit" sign.

"Pull over, Punky. I think I'm going to be sick." Leroy had drunk four Bulldogs. Punky pulled over and stopped the car but not fast enough. Leroy stuck his head out of the window and messed up the side of Punky's car.

"That's it. I'm taking everybody back to your cars."

They could smell the foul odor inside the car. Mike couldn't help but laugh, remembering what the colored owner had told him about the bragger. To make things worse, Punky ran over a skunk before he got them to their cars. Punky would never get all the smell off his car. It had been a crazy day, but in a strange kind of way, it had been an adventure.

It was getting close to the end of school, and Mike still didn't have a girlfriend. He kept taking out the Palestine girl's phone numbers and looking at them, but he knew it was luck he got out with his life last time. It would be stupid to try again. He wanted some female company for a change. He was tired of just hanging out with the guys, and they all had girlfriends.

What was the problem? He wasn't bad looking but not good looking either. He had a car, not the best, but not the worst. He had some money from working, but he wasn't a rich kid.

Then the fact hit him that was always there—he was a dirt farmer's son. Maybe girls didn't like being seen with him. He had lived in town for almost a year, but he was still labeled a dirt farmer's kid.

Why didn't they call him a movie operator? He had worked as one for over two years now. He drove back and forth from the country to work. Didn't that count for something? He wanted to be accepted by everybody, but kids in school could be so cruel. Mike had seen it many times, kids in clicks that shun anyone that was not in their group. They make fun of the other kids. And there was always a school bully that picked on kids that were scared of him. Mike was feeling sorry for himself.

Mike was getting ready for work. It was Wednesday, and he was working at the drive-in tonight. He was feeling very low as he went into the kitchen, where his mother was fixing supper. He sat down and sipped at his glass of tea.

"What's wrong, Son?"

She walked over closer to get a better look at her son. "You look down-in-the-mouth."

"Did you have a fight with your girlfriend?"

"That's the problem, Mom. I don't have a girlfriend to fight with, and I'm in my third year of high school."

"You will meet a nice girl one day, and there will be electricity between the two of you. Everything you do together will be magic."

"Mom, you have been reading too many love stories. It doesn't happen that way in real life."

"Yes, it does. Look deep into her eyes, and if she loves you, it will show in her eyes. Even if she says she doesn't, it will be there. Her eyes will show what you can't see in her heart."

"Now I know you have been reading too many love stories."

"Don't make fun of me, Son. When you meet the right girl, take my advice, and you will be happy for it."

"I'm not making fun of you, Mom, but how will I know it is the right girl?"

"You will know. Put your trust in your old mother."

"OK, Mom, I will."

"Eat your supper, or you will be late for work."

"But what about Dad?"

"He will be late. You go ahead and eat."

Mike finished supper and went to get ready for work. His head was spinning with thoughts. Life was hard being a teenager. If he were out of school and married, he wouldn't have all these problems.

Such is life. If you think you have problems, look around. There will be other people with bigger problems. Thinking about it made things seem a little easier. Maybe he should just give up on girls. He washed up and got dressed for work.

On the way to work, Mike thought about what his mother had said. Maybe she did know what she was talking about.

*For a woman who didn't finish school, she sure is smart. Maybe I will take her advice if that right girl does ever come into my life.*

Mike finished threading the first two reels and put some records on. He decided to go in the concession stand for a Coke. He was fixing his Coke when the phone rang, and he went over to answer it. There was a girl on the phone.

"May I speak to Mike Love, please?"

"You have him. What may I do for you?"

"This is Dorothy from Palestine, Pam's friend. Do you remember me?"

"Yes, I do, and I have been thinking about calling you."

"You have. Why didn't you?"

"I was waiting until school was out. Pam's boyfriend might have cooled off and not be looking to beat me up."

"I called to see if you would take me to the prom."

"Can't you get a date without having to call me from out of town?"

"Yes, I could without any trouble, but I would love to see Pam's face and the football player's face when I show up with you as my date."

"There'll be trouble, you know."

"Not with Coach Higgens in charge of the dance. He doesn't put up with any trouble, even from football players. Will you take me to the prom?"

"I don't think so."

"Please, will you do it? It will be fun, and you won't be sorry."

What did she mean by that? After a short hesitation, he agreed to take her to the prom. He thought it was a crazy thing to do, but he had done crazy things before. This time he may be in over his head.

"Pick me up at seven this coming Friday night."

"Do you have a couple of bodyguards that will go with us?"

"No, silly, and we couldn't have any fun with them with us." She giggled.

There she went again with that fun routine again. He still wanted to know what fun she was talking about. *Is it the part where I got beat up?*

Dorothy gave him directions to her home. "Bye, Mike. It will be fun. You can count on it," and she hung up.

"Well, for better or worse, I have made a date."

Back in the booth and the movie running, Mike had time to think about his date. He had to be crazy for making the date, but he would like to see the expression on Pam's and the football player's faces also, if he lived long enough.

The next day at school Mike met Gary in the parking lot. He told him about the date.

"You got to be crazy!"

"Thanks, that's what I decided about myself already, but I got to do it, and I don't know why."

"I know, you have a death wish."

"Be serious, Gary."

"I am very serious. Today is Thursday, and that leaves you only one day to back out."

"I just can't back out after I gave Dorothy my word I would take her to the prom."

"Nobody would call you chicken if you backed out."

"I would call myself chicken. I'm tired of being told what I can do and can't do. This is America, remember, the home of the free and the home of the brave."

"Good luck in telling those football players that. You made them look bad. They won't forget it until they get even with you."

"The bell just rang, got to go, see you later I hope."

All day Mike couldn't keep his mind on schoolwork. Next week school would be out, and he would be glad. It had been hard working and going to school.

That night he had a bad night also. The film broke twice, causing two blackouts. Nothing seemed to be going right. After work, Mike lay in bed, trying to sleep. He wondered if he was scared. He didn't think he was, but why was he sweating? And it wasn't hot. He finally drifted off to sleep.

The next morning, Mike got up, determined to get his act together. He thought about taking a knife for protection only but decided it would only get him in trouble.

Punky, Gary, and Leroy came to his house, and he went out to meet them. "Hi, what brings you over here?"

"You. We don't want to see you beat up."

"I'll be all right."

"We could follow you to the prom and wait for you in the parking lot."

It was nice to see his friends care about him, but he decided he would do this on his own. "Thanks anyway. I appreciate the offer."

When school was out, Mike went to a flower shop. He bought Dorothy a large orchid. It cost him a bundle, but if he was going through with this date, he was going to do it right. He went home to get ready for his date.

Mike finished shaving, put on some cologne, combed his hair, and looked himself over. Well, that would have to do. He did the best he could with what he had to work with.

He went into the bedroom to dress. He put on his best dress shirt, pants, and a tie, but he didn't have a jacket. That would have to do.

Driving to Palestine, Mike had second thoughts. He could picture himself in a fight and getting the worst of it. He could see his car being torn up. Maybe Dorothy was right, and there was no need to worry.

Suddenly, Mike turned around and headed back. He drove for a couple of miles and pulled over to the side of the road and stopped. It was hard going to a strange place and not knowing anyone. There wouldn't be any friends to help him if there was trouble. Finally, he turned around again and headed for Palestine.

Mike pulled into Dorothy's driveway and got out of his car, taking the orchid with him. He hoped she would like it. Maybe it was too big. He rang the doorbell and waited for an answer. Mr. Young opened the door.

"Come in, young man. Mike, I believe Dorothy said was your name."

"Yes, sir."

"Have a seat. Dorothy will be down shortly."

They sat in silence for a few minutes before Mr. Young broke the silence. "Where did you meet Dorothy?"

"I met her when she and Pam came to Booneville to see a movie where I work."

"So you're the one who caused the trouble here?"

*Well, I stuck my foot in my mouth,* thought Mike. *The fat is in the fire now but too late to take it back.*

"Yes, sir, I guess it was me."

"You tore up Pam's mother's yard making a getaway."

"Yes, sir."

"And ran over their mailbox."

"Yes, sir, but I hope she isn't still mad."

"I also heard gossip that you did a number on three of the football players."

"I hope they aren't still mad. I told Dorothy we might have trouble, but she said Coach Higgens wouldn't let anything happen."

"They better not give you trouble with my daughter with you."

"Sir, you don't mind Dorothy going to the prom with me?"

"No problem. If she wants to go with you, it's fine with me."

"Thank you, sir."

"Well, I think it was funny how you out foxed those football players. Dorothy goes out with a couple of them from time to time. I don't like it, because they are very rude. They pull their car in front of the house and honk for Dorothy. I don't like it one little bit. I see your father raised you right to show respect to your elders."

"Yes, sir. He told me to always go to door for a girl and take her back when the date was over."

"Dorothy said you would come to the door to get her, and I could look you over. Now I see how she knew you would. You walked Pam to her door. That's when you got in trouble with the football players."

"Yes, sir, I didn't see it coming."

Dorthy came down the hall with her mother following close behind. Mike found out fast that Dorothy wasn't bashful. She spun in a circle and stopped, facing him.

"How do I look?"

Her hair was long, flowing down her back, the color of gold. She wore a long flowing red gown trimmed in white. Her dress stood out like she was wearing a dozen crinolines, petticoats, or whatever they call them. She was smiling at Mike with a look of mischief in her eyes. Mike could only stare at her, because he had lost his voice.

"Do you see something you like, or is my slip showing?" teased Dorothy.

Mrs. and Mr. Young looked at her, then Mike, and then at each other. They didn't have a clue what Dorothy was talking about.

"It's a private joke, Mom and Dad."

After a short hesitation, Mike commented, "You look marvelous."

"Thank you, kind sir, for the compliment. Now shall we go?"

Mr. Young glanced at Mike. "You kids drive careful and try to stay out of trouble."

"Yes, sir, we will."

"Come on, Mike, let's stir up some excitement."

She took his arm and pulled him through the door. When they reached the car, Mike said, "I almost forgot. This is for you."

"I thought you were going to wear it." Giggled Dorothy.

She stepped close to Mike. Her female scent teased his senses, and his blood pressure went up.

"Pin it on me here." She put her finger on top of her left breast. Her gown was low, cut to a V-neck, showing a lot of skin.

"Go ahead," coached Dorothy. "I won't bite, not now anyway."

Mike eased his fingers down the front of her dress far enough to pin the orchid in place.

"Ease your fingers a little further down. Yes, like that." She quivered as he touched a hard nipple.

"What am I doing right here in front of your house?"

Mike pulled his hand out of her dress like it was burned. He fought to keep his tone normal.

"We better go, or we'll be late."

"OK, if we have to." Dorothy frowned. Then she laughed.

Mike opened the car door for Dorothy and then went around to the driver's side. He slid in and started the engine. Then they were off to the prom.

Dorothy rested her hand on Mike's inner thigh while driving to the prom. Her hand was only a couple inches from Mike's erection. Her hand felt like a hot poker on his leg. It was pure torture, her hand so close and yet so far away from his erection. He wondered if she knew what she was doing to him.

They arrived at the school and parked in the parking lot. The prom was being held in the Palestine High School gymnasium. Mike took a deep breath and let it out slowly. Dorothy squeezed Mike's leg and then pulled her hand away.

Mike got out and went around to the other side of the car. He opened the door for Dorothy. She gave him a dazzling smile as she got out. She was having fun with everything. *It is time to shake her up,* mused Mike.

He put his arm around her waist and walked slowly in the direction of the gymnasium door.

Mike leaned close enough for his lips to touch her ear as they walked in the door.

"When this prom is over," he said just above a whisper, "I want to make love to you."

"You do?" She giggled.

"I want to touch you, taste you, and give you sensuous pleasure."

Dorothy glanced at Mike blushing, and her face turned bright red. She agreed without hesitation.

"I'll look forward to it," she said, inviting further intimacies.

They smiled at each other and went into the gymnasium. Mike was wondering if she meant it or whether she was joking. He would find out later on tonight.

The gymnasium was filled with couples dancing to the first number played by the band. Dorothy and Mike eased over to a rest area and watched the couples as they danced to a fast jitterbug. Mike watched as dresses stood out and showed a lot of legs and more. Dorothy glanced at Mike and smiled. He was a typical American male. He liked to watch girls. Mike liked watching the girls. He thought, *The prom could be a lot of fun after all.*

The dance stopped, and the couples returned to their tables. Mike scanned the room, looking for football players. He didn't see any yet. "Where do you want to sit?" asked Mike.

"Let's just stand here a couple of minutes."

Suddenly, someone across the dance floor was waving at them. "Come on, Mike, it is showtime."

They walked across the dance floor, holding hands. As they approached the table, Mike didn't like what he saw. Pam and her boyfriend and also his two friends and their dates were at the table. *Talk about walking into the fire.* Mike wanted to run, but it was too late now.

"I don't believe it. You did get a date with Mike, you sly fox. Everybody thought he was chicken and wouldn't ever come back to Palestine."

"Well, he is, in the flesh."

"I still don't believe it."

"Believe it." Dorothy put her arm around Mike's waist, staking her claim.

Mike glanced at the three guys at the table. Pam's boyfriend smiled at him, but the other two looked like they wanted his blood. If looks could kill, he would be dead now. He smiled at them, but that didn't help.

Dorothy glanced at the guys. She put her arm around Mike's waist, giving him moral support. She was having a ball. All eyes were on her and Mike. She loved every minute of the attention. She and Mike would be the talk of the prom.

"Sit down and join us," invited Pam.

They sat down next to Pam and her boyfriend. Mike was very uncomfortable but tried not to let it show.

"I believe you know my boyfriend Bob." Pam grinned. "This is his friends that you had a brief encounter with, Bill and Frank and their dates, Betty and Joyce."

Mike thought back to the other two girls on the list from Palestine wanting to go out with him. He glanced at Pam, and she nodded her head.

Bill and Frank started to rise as they stared at Mike. Mike got up, getting ready to defend himself.

"It's over," said Bob. "Sit down now."

"But, Bob, we can't let him make fools out of us and get away with it."

"This time we will."

Bob pulled out a small box and put on the table in front of Pam. "Mike, you're the one that made me see what it would be like without Pam. I didn't like what I saw. I tried to tell myself it was school tradition, but it didn't work."

Bob looked deep into Pam's eyes. "I love you, and I want to marry you when we get out of school."

He took a ring from the box and took Pam's left hand, placing the ring on her finger. Bob was still holding eye contact with Pam.

"Everyone at this table knows that God is my witness. I love you and want to marry you."

Everyone held their breath and looked at Pam. They waited for her answer. *What would be her answer?* Without hesitation, Pam threw her arms around Bob's neck and kissed him hard.

"Is that a yes?" asked Bob.

"Yes, yes, yes!" Pam was crying.

"Why are you crying?"

"I'm so happy. These are happy tears."

"I love you, babe."

"I love you too. Don't you know that all I ever wanted was for us to be together? I didn't think you would ever ask me to marry you. That's why I let Mike take me out, to make you jealous. Are you mad at me now?"

"No, I could never be mad at you, because I love you too much."

Bob pulled Pam into his arms again and kissed her. Everybody at the table cheered and clapped. Some of the students at the other tables that had been eavesdropping joined in with the cheers and clapped.

Bob jumped to his feet. "Let's party! Everybody up and dance."

Mike looked at Dorothy. "Would you like to dance?"

"I thought you would never ask."

She got up and moved into Mike's arms. He guided her gracefully around the dance floor to a ballroom step.

"You dance great, Mike."

"I got a good partner."

Dorothy moved against him, running her fingers into his hair and touching his ear. He was making her hot.

"That's going to get you in trouble."

"I hope so," she teased.

Mike danced with all the girls at their table and some at the other tables when they asked him to dance. Dorothy didn't care because she was happy to be with a date that was so popular. She gave Mike a dazzling smile when still another girl approached and asked him to dance.

"Go ahead and dance. You have earned a good time."

"Are you sure you don't mind?"

"I don't mind. We'll be the talk of the campus tomorrow."

Mike was having the time of his life. Tonight he was not a farm boy but somebody special, and it felt so good. Girls were asking him to dance, and it felt so good for his ego. The prom started to slow down and thin out. Mike danced the last dance with Dorothy. He always liked to dance the first and last date with his date. He didn't want the night to come to an end.

"You were right, Dorothy. Things worked out just fine."

"I told you to trust me."

"I'm sure glad I did. It has been a blast."

"I'll be right back. Wait right here."

Dorothy took off across the dance floor and returned with a girlfriend.

"Would you mind taking Sandy, my girlfriend, home? I called my dad, and he said it was OK with him."

"I'll be glad to take her home."

"See I told you Mike wouldn't mind taking you home."

"Thanks, Mike, I didn't have a date. I would have to call my father to come get me."

"How come a beautiful girl like you didn't have a date?"

"I'm a country girl."

"I understand."

"How could you?"

"That's because I'm a country boy myself."

Walking out to the car, Mike's dream was shattered. He wanted to be alone with Dorothy, but she had chosen safety in numbers. Mike drove out of the parting lot while Dorothy gave him directions. He realized after a few minutes that they were headed in the direction of the Dogwood Trails. He glanced at Dorothy, and she was grinning from ear to ear. She moved closer to him and laid a hand on his leg, while drumming her fingers impatiently up and down his leg. The hand on his leg caused him to have a hard-on, and her fingers were coming close to touching it.

Sandy lived a couple of miles past the turnoff to the Dogwood Trails. When she got out, she thanked Mike for taking her home. He turned the car around and headed back toward Palestine. Approaching the cutoff to the Dogwood Trails, he glanced at Dorothy to get her reaction.

"Yes, turn in."

Mike turned off and headed to the same place he had taken Pam. He stopped on the ledge sticking out into space. The night was clear, and the moon was full. All the stars were out to make the place perfect.

They turned to face each other. Dorothy wrapped her arms around Mike's neck and pulled him close. Her eyes were dark with passion. Softly he began stroking her back. They kissed lightly and very slowly at first. She opened her mouth to receive his tongue. Mike explored her mouth with his tongue until she clamped down on his tongue and started sucking on it. She was getting hot, and Mike knew she wanted to do more than kiss. Dorothy broke the kiss and looked deep into Mike's eyes. She could see the desire and passion building in him.

"I have to tell you some things about myself."

"Do we have to talk now?"

"Yes, we do. I am a virgin."

"No problem. We'll take it slow."

"I am a senior and will be going to Norman Oklahoma to college next year. It would be foolish to get involved now, but I want you to make love to me. I don't want to be a virgin when I go to college. I made up my mind a couple weeks back that I wanted you to be the first one to make love to me."

"You got it anyway you want it. Tell me what you want."

"I want you to do exactly what you said as we entered the door to the prom."

"All of it?"

"Yes. All of it and more."

"We have a little problem."

"What's wrong?"

"Your dress is so tight, it's like a suit of armor, and your dress at the bottom stands out like a cyclone fence around you. How do we go about making love? How do you get out of that dress?"

"I can't take it off. Mom helped me put it on, and if I take it off, I would probably never get it back on."

Just great! He had a girl willing and able, but he couldn't get to her. That's one for the record book. *Well, where there is a will, there has to be a way.* He had the will, and now all he had to do was find a way.

Mike slid the seat back. She turned and lay back into his arms. He covered her lips with his own, and their tongues dueled. Dorothy quivered at the tickling touch as Mike nibbled his way down her neck to the top of her firm breast. Next was the problem of how to get to the nipple. He put his right hand under her breast and with his left hand pulled out on the top of the dress.

"Now take a deep breath and let it all the way out."

"Like this?"

"Yes, like that."

She let out her breath, while he pushed up. Her breast popped out the front of her dress.

"There, we got one out."

Dorothy giggled, but it turned to a low moan as Mike touched her nipple with his tongue and then began to gently suck on the nipple. She was on fire and could feel her juices gushing out into her panties.

Mike knew she was ready for him to fill her, but the next problem was how to do it. He raised her up and let her lie back full length of the seat with her legs slightly bent. Mike was in the floorboard. He ran his hands under her dress until he reached the top of her panties. Next, he slowly pulled them down as Dorothy arched up with her hips. He had her panties off. *Now what?* The dress was standing up like a barbed wire fence.

"Hurry up, Mike. I can't wait any longer. I want you in me now. I'm burning up."

"Give me time to think."

"Hurry up."

"OK, sit up. Now swap places with me."

Mike lay back on the seat, pulling down his pants and shorts. His manhood stood at attention, ready for some action. Dorothy started stroking him softly.

"Give me a rubber out of the glove compartment."

"No, I want to feel you in me and not a rubber. It will be all right. It's not the time to worry. I counted my days."

"OK then, let's make love. Get on top and straddle me. Now lower yourself slowly while I guide it in."

"Will it hurt much?"

"Not if we take it slowly."

Dorothy hesitated for a moment before lowering herself. She tensed as his manhood barely entered her folds.

"It hurts."

"When I arch my hips up, you push down. It will be over in a second, and then it will feel good."

"I can't do it. It hurts too much."

"Yes, you can. On the count of three push down until you have all of me in you. Here we go! One, two, three, and push! That's it."

She pushed down, and he pushed up. She was so tight he was having a hard time getting into her. "This is going to hurt."

With a tremendous lunge, Mike went all the way home.

"It still hurts."

"Now just sit still until it quits hurting and starts to feel good."

Dorothy giggled when she realized that Mike was completely covered with her dress. He had pulled the dress up under his neck. She was starting to relax.

"You want to hear a joke?"

"Sure, anything to get you relaxed."

"Why does a girl wear fur on the bottom of her nightgown?"

"I don't have a clue."

"To keep your neck warm." She giggled.

Her muscles tightened on his organ. It was time to make love. "It doesn't hurt anymore."

Mike arched his hips and thrust deep in her. Dorothy rotated her hips and pushed down to meet each thrust.

"Oh, Mike, it feels so good. Give it to me faster."

"You got it."

They picked up a fast rhythm. Mike held back until she tightened her muscles and started quivering in a spasm.

"Oh, I'm coming. I'm coming. Give me everything."

Mike gave her a couple hard lunges before his juices started gushing deep into her body. She moaned softly as her muscles throbbed around his erection. She squeezed his erection until it finally went limp. She wanted to lie on Mike's chest, but the dress was in the way. Mike sat up, and she lay back in his arms.

"How was it?"

"Oh, Mike, it was fantastic. How did you know what to do, at the right time?"

"I've had a little experience."

"I think you have had a lot."

After their breathing returned to normal, they talked of their dreams of the future. Dorothy was going to Norman Oklahoma to college. She didn't know what she wanted to major in yet. She was going to take her basic subjects first until she made up her mind.

"I want to watch the Sooner football team play. I don't know much about football, but I want to learn."

She was going to live on campus her first year. She wanted to meet some of the sailors at the naval preparatory school.

"I may even have a date with a sailor and see if what they say about sailors is true. They say there isn't anything a sailor won't do."

"I wouldn't know about that. I don't know any sailors."

Mike finally got his turn to talk. He had one more year in high school. He didn't like small towns or school tradition, where only football players could go out with cheerleaders. His parents were too poor to send him to college, so he would probably join the army or navy and try to get a school or some college. He wanted to meet a nice girl to share his life. So far, he hadn't found her. He told her the silly tale his mother had told him about what would happen when he met the right girl.

"Your mother is a smart lady. I thank she is right. I believe the same way myself."

Mike was content to argue. "I don't know. Maybe she could be right."

Besides, with Dorothy's hot body against him, his manhood was starting to rise again. Dorothy could feel his erection against her bottom.

She turned in his arms and gave Mike a slow sensuous kiss. She was hot again and ready. Mike thought she wanted to make love again.

"Do we have time to make love again?"

"We'll take the time, but I want to do it different this time."

"What's your pleasure?"

Dorothy moved forward on her hands and knees. "Now throw my dress over my head, out of the way. Now ride me. You are a stud, and I'll be your mare."

Mike moved up behind her, placing his hands on her hips.

"We have to do it fast because we don't have a lot of time. If I come in late, I'll be grounded for a week."

"If it is fast you want, it's fast you will get."

He pulled back on her hips and gave her a brutal stab. He started pounding home with every stroke. Dorothy arched back and gave Mike a tight squeeze with her muscles every time he hit bottom.

She moaned and cried out, "Faster, faster! Oh yes, faster!"

"You are so tight it's hard to go fast."

"But it feels so good when you go fast."

"I can't hold out much longer at this pace before I come."

"Hold on just a little longer. I think I'm almost ready to come."

Then suddenly, she tightened her muscles and started quivering. Mike gave one more hard thrust into her hot body. They both had a total orgasm. He remained in her, not wanting to ever stop. She didn't want it to be over either. She remained still, enjoying it to the very last.

Suddenly a car came down the road. They both sat up quickly. Somebody sure knew how to ruin a good night.

"Here we go again. It must be our football boys again."

"No, they wouldn't, not after the good time we had together."

Mike saw a red light on top of the car. "We're in trouble."

Dorothy spread her dress over Mike from the waist down and across the rest of the seat. Her dress was like a big tent. The sheriff's deputy got out and walked over to the car. He looked in and shined his flashlight around.

"You young people can't park up here at night. It's not safe to park here at night. Now get out of here before I run you in for something."

"Yes, sir, we're on our way."

Mike started the car and drove off. Dorothy started laughing and couldn't stop. She pulled her dress off Mike. His pants and shorts were still down around his ankles. His manhood was limp.

"Look what I found, a dead snake."

She kept on laughing and started stroking him softly. "It wasn't dead after all, only sleeping."

"Stop that, or you'll cause me to have a car wreck."

Dorothy giggled while increasing her stroking, until his manhood was throbbing and ready to explode.

"I can't drive with you doing that." He pulled over on the side of the road.

She kept stroking his erection faster and faster.

"You better stop before I come all over you."

"I am going to finish it." She was enjoying watching Mike squirm and buck.

"I'm going to come."

"OK, go for it." She bent over and took his erection in her mouth and sucked him off.

"Oh, that feels so good."

"You taste a little salty. I wondered what it would taste like."

Mike got out of the car and relieved himself and pulled up his shorts and pants. He got back in and started the car. They talked nonstop the rest of the way to Dorothy's house.

"Mike, I loved every minute of our time together."

"I can't believe you went down on me."

"I can't either, but at the time it seemed the thing to do."

"It was so funny when we were trying to make love and get that darn dress off."

"I know we aren't supposed to show and tell, but I have to tell Pam and some more of my girlfriends. It's so funny, and it was so good."

Mike pulled into her driveway, and they got out. Dorothy hung her dress on the steering wheel and ripped it.

"Well, my dress was good for something tonight."

"Yes, it kept us out of trouble." Laughed Mike.

When they got to the door, they turned and faced each other, holding hands.

"I had a wonderful time, Mike."

"Me too. I had the time of my life."

"I won't see you for a long time. I leave for Oklahoma next week after school is out, so I guess this is good-bye."

Mike opened his arms, and she moved into them. They kissed long and hard. Mike turned and went back to his car. As he drove off, he looked in the rearview mirror. He saw Dorothy touch the tips of her finger to her lips and wave. Mike became all choked up. The night had been like a wonderful dream, but all dreams come to an end and you wake up.

Mrs. Love stood in the doorway to Mike's room, watching him sleep. He had a big smile on his face and was mumbling something, but she couldn't understand what he was saying. He was having a good dream. She hated to wake him up, but she needed to go shopping.

"Mike, wake up. Are you going to sleep all day?"

He opened his eyes and stared at his mother. He wanted to scream but held his tongue.

"Son, I need you to take me shopping."

"All right, I'll be dressed in a few minutes."

Mike got dressed and grabbed a glass of milk. "OK, Mom, I'm ready to go."

"Do you want to eat some breakfast before we go? We got time."

They headed into town. Mrs. Love said, "What is that funky smell?"

"I probably ran over a skunk last night," Mike hedged.

"It doesn't smell like a skunk to me, but I can't place the smell. Did you have fun at the prom last night?"

Glad to change the subject, he told her all about the prom, but not all of it. Mike parked on the square. He glanced down into the floorboard and about had a heart attack. Dorothy left her panties in the car. He held his breath while his heart hammered against his ribs.

"Son, you sure are in an odd mood today. Do you feel all right?"

"I don't feel too good. Not enough sleep, I guess. I'll be all right."

"I'll be back in about an hour."

"Take your time. I'll wait in the car."

Mrs. Love walked down the sidewalk. Mike let out the breath he was holding. *Boy, was that close!*

Mike picked up the panties. They were red, trimmed in white lace to match Dorothy's dress. They brought back good memories.

Suddenly someone bumped his arm in the window. "I'm sorry. I'm always doing that." Jan Parker giggled.

He tried to hide the panties but was too late. She had already seen them. She would want to know about them.

"I don't think they are your size."

Mike's face turned deep red. "They aren't mine."

"I won't ask where you got them, but rumor has it, you went to Palestine to a prom last night. It must have been fun."

"It was."

"You want to tell me about it?"

"No."

"Rumor has it you would probably get beat up if you went. You look all right to me. What does the other guy look like?"

"Sorry to disappoint everybody, but there wasn't a fight and no blood spilled."

"Did you know the football team was taking bets five to one you would chicken out and not go?"

"How did they know I was going? Nobody knew I was going, except Gary."

"Oops, I guess I let the cat out of the bag!"

"I'll have his hide for telling."

"Don't be too hard on him. He let it slip because he wanted to rub it in that you weren't afraid of football players. I can't wait to tell the girls in school what happened."

Mike started to protest, but Jan was walking down the sidewalk. He opened the glove compartment and put Dorothy's panties inside. Well, now he would have to lie low until school was out. He would stay away from the football players until they had time to cool off. He didn't know if anyone was stupid enough to bet with him. It was like he had a death wish.

Saturday evening, before Mike went to work, he dropped by to see Gary at work. He confronted Gary about the betting.

"I'm sorry I told them about you going to the prom, but they were talking about you and what would happen if you ever went back to Palestine. I had to say something. I told them they didn't know what they were talking about."

"That should have got a rise out of them."

"That's when I told them you were going to the prom."

"What did they say to that?"

"They got mad, and then somebody said they bet you would chicken out. I told them I bet you wouldn't. Anyway, a lot of bets were placed for money."

"What happened after that?"

"Jan was the first to see you and told them everything."

"I didn't tell her anything."

"You didn't have to. She saw you with the panties, and one of the football players called the prom last night to see if you were there."

"What happened then?"

"The person that answered the phone said you were at a table with football players and their dates. They said you had a date with you and wanted to know if they wanted them to call you. They said no and hung up."

"Go on, what happened then?"

"I won fifty dollars and enjoyed every minute of it."

Gary started laughing, and Mike joined in. It was fun to have made a fool out of the football players.

"Are you going to the prom next week?"

"No, I don't have a date, and I have a car-payment due. I'm short on cash. I spent a lot on Friday night, so I'll just work and skip the prom this year."

"You should go. I'm sure you wouldn't have any trouble getting a date. All the girls will want to dance with you."

"I've had enough proms for one year. I don't think I will push my luck."

School was out the next Friday, and Mike was ready. He had only one more year to go. He couldn't wait to get out of school. His grades were average. He would have liked them to be better, but he worked almost every night. Maybe next year he would do better. Maybe he could study more.

Friday rolled around, and Mike went to pick up his report card. He turned in his books. He made a dash for his car and made his way through the traffic. Everybody was in a hurry to leave.

As Mike drove home, he dreamed about the events of the year and hoped next year would be better. At least he hoped it would be. Maybe he would even find a girl.

# Chapter 5

With school out, Mike decided to get a day job. He looked, but jobs were hard to find, with so many kids from school looking for a summer job. He finally found a part-time delivery job at the laundry. It didn't pay much, but it was better than nothing.

Mike worked three hours in the afternoon at the laundry and nights at the movies. He still worked at the drive-in and a couple nights downtown. He didn't like the delivery job. The old truck that he drove had bad brakes, leaked oil, and the steering wheel had a lot of slack in it. People were never home to receive their laundry and pay for it. There were several dogs that would bite if they got to you. He got where he hated dogs.

Mr. Williams called Mike into the office.

"I got another complaint about you kicking a lady's dog."

"What am I to do? Let the dog eat my leg off?"

"The customer is always right."

"They have a lease law in this town. Why don't they enforce it?"

"I don't have time to argue. If I get one more complaint on you, you're fired."

"Yes, sir."

Mike was mad and would quit, but he needed the job. He loaded the old truck and headed out to make his deliveries. He had worked at the laundry for eight weeks. He ran his butt off, but nobody cared.

He didn't get to see his friends very much. They worked too, but sometimes they met at the Dairy Queen.

It was his lunch break, and Mike waited on his friends to show up. Punky, Gary, Leroy, and Rex all showed up. This was the first time in a long time they had all been together.

"Mike, it's time you told us about that hot date you had in Palestine," said Punky.

"I usually don't show and tell, but I will probably never see her again. She was one hot chick, but I thought with those darn prom dresses, I thought we would never be able to have sex, but we did."

That brought a round of laughter. "How did you keep from getting beat up by the football players?"

"The funny part is Pam, the first girl I went with, did it to make her boyfriend jealous, and it did. He asked her to marry him. He said I made him realize how much he loved Pam, and didn't want to lose her."

"Well, I'll be damn!" Laughed Leroy.

"I'll see you guys. I got deliveries to make."

Two hours into his deliveries and the old truck had a flat. Another reason he hated the job was he didn't like riding on bald tires. The old jack didn't want to work, but he finally got the spare tire on and continued his deliveries.

Mike had just two more deliveries before he was done for the day. He looked at the next ticket and turned right, stopping at the second house. They had one bundle prepaid with a note to drop it inside the screen door. As Mike closed the screen door, he heard a dog bark and felt a stab of pain in his left leg. Mike jerked away and kicked the bulldog in the face. *What an ugly mug! Maybe it would improve his looks!* Mike ran as fast as he could to the truck, with the bulldog nipping at his heels. After driving a block, he pulled over to check his leg. The bulldog left teeth marks but didn't break the skin. It would be sore for a couple of days.

Mike checked the last delivery ticket. It was across town in the rich section. His luck wasn't changing. Now he would be late getting off work, and he bitched out for taking too long. After finding the street, he stopped in front of a large brick house.

Mike approached the house and saw a sign beside the door. It read "Bert Arnold, MD." He had delivered there a couple of times.

He thought back to the last delivery. Mrs. Arnold had met Mike at the door, wearing white short shorts and a red shirt with three top buttons unbuttoned. Mike saw two large cream-colored mounds and part of a brown peak. She was not wearing a bra.

Mike looked into her eyes and saw a smile form on her lips. He thought he saw desire in her eyes, but like a fool he dropped his head, breaking eye contact, and put the packages down.

"Would you bring the package to the bedroom?"

"Yes, ma'am." He picked up the packages and followed her.

"Just drop them on the bed."

"Yes, ma'am."

They left the bedroom and went back into the living room. She was leading the way, and Mike watched her fanny sway from side to side. It was a good view.

"My name is Jan Arnold. What's your name?"

"My name is Mike."

"Just call me Jan."

Mike couldn't think straight. He had seen girls before, but this was a full-grown woman, the likes he had never seen before.

"Would you like some iced tea?"

"No, thank you. I got to finish my deliveries," stuttered Mike. "Maybe next time I can stay longer."

He backed out the door, got in his truck, and drove off. *What a fool I have made of myself! But next time would be different, if I get the chance again.*

Mike walked up to the door and rang the doorbell. He waited for someone to answer. He thought to himself, *Well, this is the second chance, and if she showed signs like last time, I am going for it.*

Being a doctor's wife could be a very lonely life at times. Jan was bored to death. Bert was never at home, and when he was, he was too tired to make love. A woman has needs, and Jan loved to make love. It had been almost two weeks since they had tried to make love, and it had been bad news. Bert had finished first and left Jan still climbing the path to fulfillment. He had said he was sorry and had to get some sleep.

She got out of bed and took a cold shower. Wasn't that what men did when a girl said no? The cold shower did the trick.

Jan was doing her housework when she ran across a dry cleaning slip. She looked at the date and realized the delivery was today. It was late in the evening and knew it should arrive any time now.

She thought about the last delivery. Something about the shy young man sent a tingle up her spine. Her body started to get hot. It was hot that last time he delivered, and she had been working. She forgot to button her shirt.

Jan smiled. He must have got his eyes full. She hadn't realized she was showing so much of her body. But now that she thought about it, he must have seen almost all of her breasts and then some.

She didn't understand why her body was reacting to her thoughts. She went to the refrigerator and got a cold glass of water. It didn't help.

She remembered how he backed out the door. She laughed, and it put her in a good mood. What was his name? She finally remembered it was Mike. She hoped he would be the one to deliver today. Jan was twenty-eight years old. She realized she was older, but it would be fun to tease the young man.

What would she do if he made a pass at her? She suddenly became very warm. She remembered his eyes and the desire she had seen in them. She wished Bert still had the desire to make passionate love to her, but he was always tired. He should take more time off from work and pay some attention to her.

Jan decided to be a big tease and play it by ear. She was bored and wanted to have some fun. She went to the bedroom and pulled a short nightgown out of her dresser. She removed her shirt and shorts. She touched her bra with her hand. *What the heck!* She took it off. Jan slipped the nightgown over her head. It was split on both sides all the way to her waist. Any movement and you could see her thin panties. You could see her breasts and nipples through the thin lace netting. She took her robe out of the closet and put it on.

Jan went into the living room and retrieved a pack of cigarettes. She picked up her lighter and lit up. She smoked the cigarette, blowing smoke rings, and tried to relax. Her nerves were strung tight as a bowstring. Her hand was shaking so bad she put the cigarette out and started to pace back and forth.

Jan started to get up and put her clothes back on, when she heard a truck pull in the driveway. She heard him shut off the engine. She looked out the window and saw Mike approaching the front door. What was she going to do now?

She pulled her robe tight around her and headed for the front door, but before she reached the door, she made a decision. She pulled off her robe and dropped it on the floor. She went to answer the door in the thin nightgown. It left nothing to the imagination. If she stood in the light, you could see her whole body through the thin material.

She looked down and realized you could see her hard nipples pointing straight ahead and also the hair on her private part through her panties. Was she ready for this? Yes, she wanted to have fun.

Mike knocked on the door and waited. Jan took a deep breath and opened the door. She stood behind the door while Mike came in with her dry cleaning.

"Where would you like me to put your dry—"

Jan stepped out from behind the door, and Mike stared at her. She stared back with a big smile. She might as well be naked with what she had on. Mike stared at her nipples and then looked down at her panties. He saw hair through the panties.

"Where do you want me to put the dry cleaning?"

"Put it on the coffee table, and I will take care of it later."

Mike put her dry cleaning on the coffee table. He looked back at her and waited for her to make the next move. He wanted to be sure she wanted to fool around before he made a move on her.

"Would you like a Coke?"

"Yes, thank you."

Jan left the room, and Mike sat down on the couch and picked up the newspaper on the couch. He scanned the headlines while waiting for her to return. Jan came in and handed Mike a Coke. She turned and sat at an angle in a stuffed chair. Mike lay the newspaper down. He almost dropped his Coke, staring at her almost naked body.

"I'm sorry, I couldn't find my robe," she lied.

"That's all right. It doesn't bother me," he lied.

Mike was a little bewildered by her directness. *Is she giving me the come-on?* He sure hoped so. If she didn't want to fool around, he was about to make a fool out of himself. Jan was enjoying his shyness. She spread her legs, and Mike could see her thin panties and hair on her private area. Her nipples were hard and pointing at him. Jan was having fun teasing him. Mike continued staring at Jan wordlessly, and the silence were deafening, except for their pounding hearts and ragged breathing.

Mike had a big erection, and Jan could see it if she looked. He didn't try to hide it. Jan stared at his crouch and licked her lips. That was all the invitation he needed to make a pass.

He slowly slid off the couch on his knees and moved slowly toward Jan. His eyes locked with hers as he slid between her legs. She didn't slap him or move away. He continued to search her eyes. He saw desire and a little fear. He knew she wanted to make love, even if she said no. She held her breath as Mike ran his hand under her short nightgown and cupped her breast.

"Mike," she whispered, "we have to stop."

"Just one minute more and we will stop," he lied.

He massaged her nipple with his thumb and forefinger until her whole body trembled with desire. She knew it was too late to stop now. She was on fire with yearning. She knew she was wet down below and ready to make love.

"Raise your arms above your head."

"That's it." She raised her arms over her head while Mike pulled the nightgown off and tossed it on the floor. Jan gasped in delight when his warm lips covered her nipple. He sucked on one and then moved over to the other one. She pulled him closer. "Touch me! Oh yes, touch me!" she moaned.

Jan ran her fingers through his hair. Mike covered her mouth with his and slid his tongue deep into her mouth. She was burning up and wanted more. She reached for his belt and pulled it loose. She unzipped his pants, and his erection sprang free. She took it in her hand and massaged it.

"Let's go to the bedroom," Jan said.

"I'm ready. Let's go."

They stood up, and Jan took his hand, leading him down the hall to a large bedroom. Jan pulled down the covers as Mike pulled off his shirt and dropped it on the floor. She sat on the bed and watched him. He removed his pants, shoes, and socks. He walked around to the other side of the bed, turning his back, and slipped out of his shorts. He slid under the covers. He was still a little shy. She turned her back and removed her panties, while Mike watched her. She slid in under the covers, facing him.

Their eyes locked. Mike put his arm around her waist and pulled her against his hard lean body. Her lips parted in invitation. Mike kissed her, and she opened to him. Their tongues entwined and dueled. Jan could feel his large erection pressing against her folds.

Mike kissed her deeply and pulled her on top of him. She straddled him, spreading her wet folds. She rocked forward and back, taking all of Mike's erection. She bounced up and down, grinding her hips as she went down. She was on fire, but she tried to pace herself and make it last. She knew she shouldn't do this. It had been too long since she had been satisfied and relaxed after making love. She wanted it to be good.

"Oh, Mike, it feels so good."

"Slow down and stop if you have to. I want it to last as long as possible."

Jan knew she was close to a climax, so she slowed down and stopped. She leaned forward and kissed Mike.

"That's it. Now move slower and build to a climax again."

"Where did you learn to make love?"

"I had a good teacher."

"Oh, Mike, give it to me. I'm burning up."

Mike slammed into her hard. She trembled as she had an orgasm. She had never had one this good. She kept bouncing until she felt Mike throbbing inside her, and she squeezed him, milking every drop out of him. She fell forward on his chest. They were both breathing hard. Mike put his arms around her and crushed her breasts and nipples against his chest. It felt so good.

"Did you like our lovemaking?" asked Mike.

"I loved every minute of it. I loved the way you taught me to hold back and enjoy it longer."

Jan placed her hands on Mike's chest and raised herself above him. Their eyes locked, and Mike could see nothing but passion and desire. He placed his hands on her taut breasts and began to slowly massage her brown peaks. Jan softly moaned in delight.

She covered Mike's face with urgent warm kisses and moved down his neck. She continued lower and circled his nipples with her tongue. Jan explored lower to his navel, pausing for a brief moment before moving lower.

Mike lay back in delightful agony and ran his fingers through her hair. He looked down at her and realized she was going to give him a man's greatest delight. Mike gasped as she covered him with her warm lips and brought his body to a pitch just short of a spasm.

"It couldn't get any better than this."

"Yes, it could."

Jan raised herself over his erection and lowered herself for a perfect union. Slowly they rocked together, building toward a climax.

"No, not yet. Hold back," Mike whispered.

"I'm trying to, but it's hard. It feels so good."

He circled her waist with his hands and rolled her over on her back without breaking their union. She spread her legs wide so he could stab her deeper.

"It's my turn to pleasure you."

She began to trail her fingers through the fine hair on Mike's chest. He covered a nipple with his mouth and sucked on it. He then pulled away from her, moving lower. He kissed his way down her body until he was between her thighs. He ran his tongue up her thigh until he was close to his final destination. She gasped and moaned, begging him to give her the greatest delight for a woman.

"Tell me what you want," teased Mike.

"Touch me with your tongue." Jan was not bashful.

"Like this?"

"Oh yes." Jan arched her back, trying to drive his tongue deeper.

He gave it to her as she rocked and quivered, lost in space on a joyous journey.

"Touch me! Oh yes, like that! Don't stop." But he did just before they reached the point of no return. Mike rose above her and looked into deep pools of passion in Jan's eyes. He lowered himself to merge with her body.

She raised her hips to meet his thrust. Jan rolled her head from side to side and moaned as Mike picked up the pace. She felt a spasm coming and began to quiver.

"Now, Mike, give it to me fast and deep."

He thrust several more times, and with one final thrust, they both reached the final release. Jan quivered and moaned while Mike lay flat on top of her. Her breasts were squeezed flat with her nipples digging into his chest. They lay like that until their hearts quit pounding and returned to normal. Mike finally went limp. Reluctantly Mike rolled over and lay beside Jan.

"That was a wonderful experience, Mike. I'll never forget it."

"I won't either. You're the best."

"I try to be."

"You sure know how to please a man. Where did you learn to make love like that?"

"I read a lot. Where did you learn to make love like that, being so young?"

"I learned from a fifty-dollar-a-night call girl. She told me when I thought a girl wanted to make love, always go for it."

"She gave you good advice." Jan giggled.

Mike turned on his side and lay his hand possessively on her firm breast. They were content and drifted off into a light sleep.

Suddenly a car pulled into the driveway and a door slammed, waking Mike. "Oh my god, I'm going to get killed!" screamed Mike.

He bailed out of bed, searching the floor for his clothes. Jan reached in the closet and pulled out a robe to put on. She followed Mike down the hall into the living room. He got his clothes and shoes on just in time. The front door opened, and Dr. Arnold walked in.

"Honey, I'm home."

"What happened? Did the hospital burn down? You never are home early!" fumed Jan.

"Now, honey, don't be mad," begged the doctor.

"Excuse me, sir. Could I get my money?"

"Who the hell are you? What are you doing here in my house?"

"I-I delivered your dry cleaning, sir."

Dr. Arnold paid Mike, and he retreated out the front door. He pulled out into the street and headed back to the laundry. He daydreamed as he drove. *Boy, that almost turned into a nightmare!*

Mike could still feel her lips on his manhood. *Oh, but she was good, the best.* Mike pulled the truck in the back of the laundry and parked. Mr. Williams was standing in the door. He knew he was in trouble.

"Well, you came back late and got two complaints called in on you. A neighbor saw you kick a dog, and Dr. Arnold said he didn't want you to deliver at his house anymore."

"Did the doctor say why?"

"No, what did you do?"

"Nothing I'm aware of."

"Do you have anything to say?"

"Would it do any good to say anything on my behalf?"

"No, you have had it. I told you one more complaint and you were fired. Well, you got two this afternoon."

"I guess that means I'm fired."

"You're fired. I'll mail your check to you. Don't come back."

"Yes, sir, thank you."

Mr. Williams watched Mike leave. He still was curious why the doctor didn't want him to deliver there anymore.

Mike wanted to tell him to take the job and shove it. But what good would that do? He was already fired. He got in his car and drove home mad.

While Mike ate supper, his mother watched him. "What's wrong, Son?"

"Nothing, Mom," he lied.

"I know better. I can always tell when you are hurting."

Mike told her about getting fired for kicking dogs and having to deliver laundry in that pile of junk they called a truck.

"Don't worry about it, Son. You will find a better job."

"But, Mom, all the summer jobs are taken up by now."

"Trust me, Son, you will find a better job."

Mike got cleaned up and called to his mother, "I'm going to the Dairy Queen and hang out with the guys. I'll be back later."

*Later usually means midnight,* mused his mother, while she washed the supper dishes. Mr. Love was late coming home as usual. The sawmill never shut down when it was time to.

Mike walked in the Dairy Queen and saw Gary seated in a booth. Mike slid in the booth across from Gary.

"Mike, what are we going to do tonight for excitement?"

"I don't know, Gary, but it's got to be something different."

"Here comes Punky and Leroy. Maybe they got an idea."

"Hi, guys, what's happening?" Punky yelled at the girl behind the counter, "Beer all around!"

"You know we don't sell beer. Besides, you're too young to buy beer."

"Make it Cokes all around."

Punky was the usual nut, but when he was around, the noise and action would follow. Mike looked at Punky and remembered all the times that just by being near Punky had got him in trouble. *Well, here we go again.*

"Punky, we want something different to do tonight, something funny."

"Hey, guys, drink your Cokes and watch the girls. I'll dream up something to do."

Punky sat and stared at the ceiling with a blank face. As usual, Leroy was the first to notice two girls coming in the door.

"Boy, what a set of lungs on that girl!"

Mike looked and made a face. "Dummy, don't you ever look at the face first?"

"Why would I do that? I close my eyes when I'm making love anyway."

"What happens when you are done and open your eyes?"

"I put my clothes on and leave."

"Leroy, I give up on you."

Punky jumped up. "I got it. Let's rock and roll."

"You got what?" asked Leroy.

Everyone followed Punky out to the cars. "You guys remember the watermelon patch about five miles north of town that we raided last year?"

"We going to raid it again?" asked Leroy.

"Well, tonight we are going to do it again, but with a different twist."

"What's going to be different?"

"Mike and Leroy, do you have shotguns?"

"Yes, we both have one," replied Mike.

"This is what we're going to do. You and Leroy pick up your shotguns and head out to the watermelon patch. After you get there, pick a couple of good melons for later. Then hide in the bushes and wait. Gary and I will cruise back up to the show. As soon as it lets out, we will pick up some girls and head out to the watermelon patch. Mike and Leroy, you know what to do. All right, let's do it."

"Mike, what are we going to tell our folks when we go in to get our guns?"

"We'll tell them if they ask that we're going out to Punky's old home place and hunt armadillos."

Mike pulled his car in back of his house as quiet as possible. "See, Leroy, no problem. My folks have gone to bed, no lights, be right back."

He slipped in the back door and into his room. He slipped his gun out of the gun rack. From the next room, his mother asked, "Is that you, Son?"

"Yes, Mom, go back to sleep. I was just picking up something."

"Don't stay out too late."

"Yes, ma'am."

Mike made it back to the car. "Well, Mike, did you have any trouble?"

"No, Mom and Dad are old. They don't keep track of me very much."

"You're lucky. My parents keep a close watch on me."

"Yes, but they are young and take you places. My parents don't own a car or know how to drive. I got a hardship driver's license. We never go anyplace on vacation or anywhere else."

Mike pulled in front of Leroy's house. "Hey all right, they aren't home. I'll be right back."

Leroy returned with his shotgun. "Boy, these things will sure make a lot of noise!"

"It should scare their pants off." Laughed Mike.

"You mean their panties, don't you?"

"Whatever comes off should be interesting."

As they drove north out of town, both were quiet. They were wondering how their little gag would work out.

"Mike, there's the watermelon patch."

"I see it. I'll back into those bushes at the end of the patch."

Mike stopped the car and let Leroy out. "Pick a couple of big ripe melons while I hide the car."

"I got the melons in the trunk, and you got the car hid. Now what?"

"We wait for Punky to bring the girls."

"What if Punky can't get any girls to come with him?"

"Are you kidding? He can talk a coon out of a tree."

"But girls aren't the same."

"Sure they are. You just have to use different bait. Punky will have them here. Just wait and see."

Jan and Joy were working as ushers at the show, and it was a busy night with standing room only. Punky slipped his arms around Joy's waist from behind, touching her ear with his lips.

"Want to have some fun?"

"Not with you, Punky, and besides, if my boyfriend sees you do that, he would break both your legs."

"Joy, you aren't any fun anymore since you got that jock for a boyfriend."

"Depends what you call fun."

"You know what I mean."

"I know. I never go out with my friends anymore. Tell you what, if Jan goes with you, I'll go."

"Where are we going?" asked Jan.

"Let it be a surprise. My car is parked out front, so hurry out as soon as the show is over."

"Punky, get your hand out of that popcorn. If the boss catches you, he will fire both of us," Jan said.

"Joy said she would go out with us if you went."

"Not on your life, Punky. You're nothing but trouble."

"Right, Jan, but fun trouble, right?"

"OK, you crazy nut, I'll go one last time, but I'll probably regret it in the morning."

"It will put some excitement in your life."

"That's what I'm afraid of."

"Meet us out front when the movie is out."

Gary was watching for cops as he waited for Punky. Why did he always have to park in a no-parking zone? Why did he always have the cops as mad as wet hens? One day he was going to stop going with that nut, if he lived long enough. Punky ran out of the front of the theatre. Opening the car door, he said, "Move over, Gary, I'll drive. The girls will be out shortly."

Jan and Joy came out of the theatre and got in the backseat. Someone called from the front of the theatre, "Where are you going?"

Punky opened the door. "Come on, girls, and join the fun."

Artis jumped in. "Get in, Alice. Come with us. We are just going riding."

"I can't, because I got to go home."

Alice was not part of the crowd. She was short with long black hair and very good looking. She was an "A" student who stayed out of trouble. Alice thought for a moment. She was always the good girl who did what was expected of her but not tonight. She decided that she was going to have a little fun for a change.

"Move over, Gary. I'm coming with you."

Punky burned rubber in the first gear and a little squeak in the second gear as he headed north out of town. Gary played dumb.

"Punky, where are we going?"

"We're going for a wild ride in the country."

"Punky, if you don't slow this tin can down, I'm getting out."

"OK, Alice, I'll slow down just for you."

"Where are we going, Punky?" asked Alice.

"We are going for a ride in the country."

As Punky slowed down, the watermelon patch flew by. Punky stopped and pulled over to the side of the road.

"Hey, girls, let's get some watermelons and have a party at the park."

Before anyone could answer, Punky spun around in the middle of the road and smoked tires, heading back to the watermelon patch. There were woods on one side of the road and the watermelon patch on the other side. There was a full moon out, and you could see the watermelons from the road. Punky pulled over to the side of the road, leaving the car running.

"Everybody out! Nobody stays in the car. Everybody gets one watermelon and returns to the car. Be sure they are ripe, because we don't need any green watermelons."

"How do I know if it's ripe? They are all green," asked Alice.

"Get someone to show you."

"Aren't they heavy? I don't know if I can carry one."

"Just go with the group, and they will help you."

Mike and Leroy watched the group descend on the watermelon patch, then spread out to find a good watermelon. Mike raised his shotgun into the air.

"OK, Leroy, let's make some noise."

"You got it. Let's fire on the count of three."

On the count of three, they both fired at the same time, and in the still of the night, they sounded like a cannon.

All hell broke loose. The girls screamed, "We are going to get killed!"

Everyone ran for the car. Alice was closest to the car. She got in first, followed by Jan, who dove through the window and got under the steering wheel.

"Come on, everybody, we got to get out of here!"

Gary came running up, trying to keep from laughing, and got in front, on the passenger side.

"Let's get out of here!" screamed Jan.

Gary put his hand on the gearshift. "Wait until the rest of them get here."

Punky came running across the watermelon patch with Artis hot on his heels. Mike moved out of the bushes for another shot. He fired the gun and watched Punky fall to the ground. Artis ran over Punky and kept going.

She was yelling, "Wait for me! Please don't leave me!"

Artis, being a little on the plump side, was a sight to see, plowing across the watermelon patch in a full run.

Mike had seen Punky go down. Looking over at Leroy, he said, "Oh my god, I've shot Punky."

"You couldn't have. You were shooting in the air."

"But I saw him fall just as I shot the last time."

This was to be fun, but now it had turned into a nightmare. Mike and Leroy ran over to Punky. Artis had made it to the car and jumped into the backseat, screaming, "Let's get out of here! Punky has been shot!"

Jan hit the first gear and burned rubber down the road. She drove like the devil was after them. Punky was holding his chest and moaning as if he was in great pain. He looked up at Mike.

"Sorry, I'm not dead, just got stepped on by an elephant. Help me up, and let's get after them. They left me and took my car. So much for friends!"

Meanwhile, a few miles down the road, Gary started to worry about Punky. The shot part was not in the plan.

"Jan, stop the car, because it was all a joke."

"You are crazy if you think I'm going to stop the car."

Gary repeated three more times that it was all a joke before Jan finally pulled over and stopped the car. She sat there frozen to the steering wheel with a blank look on her face. Artis felt something wet on her hand.

"Oh my god, Alice is shot also!"

"No, I'm not shot. I wet my pants."

The shock finally started to wear off, and everybody started laughing. The joke was over and proved to be fun. Mike stopped alongside of Jan.

"I'm going to kill you and Leroy."

"My, my, you are such a spoiled sport!"

"Just wait. We'll get even with you guys."

"Boy, Leroy, I sure am glad we have the guns in our car!"

Punky took over as usual. "OK, gang, let's head for the park in town and have a watermelon party."

"We don't have any watermelons," said Jan.

"Sure we do. Mike and Leroy picked some before we got there."

Alice had to go home with her wet pants, but the rest of the gang went to the park for a watermelon party. They talked about how they had planned the joke and set the girls up. It had been a wild night, but everyone was full of watermelon.

Mike drove home from the party. His thoughts were about finding another job. He needed the extra money with his last year of high school coming up. He needed new clothes, and he wanted a watch. Mike had never owned a watch and planned to buy himself one for graduation from high school. Tomorrow he would go job hunting. He didn't have much hope of finding one.

The next day was a beautiful day with the sun shining brightly. It was a good day to go fishing, but as usual, work had to come first.

"What are you up so early for?" asked Mrs. Love.

Mike entered the kitchen and sat down at the kitchen table. He was going to eat a good breakfast for a change.

"I'm going job hunting."

"Good, you'll find one."

"I wish I could be as sure as you are about finding a job."

"Mike, you are a nice young man, and someone will hire you."

Mike ate a good breakfast of bacon, eggs, and toast before going to town. By noon he had made the rounds all over town for a job without any luck. He started singing an old song. *Some guys have all the luck. I know I don't have any luck.*

He started home for lunch when he came up with an idea. Since he had lived on a farm and ranch, maybe the local veterinary needed some help. He pulled in and parked at the veterinary clinic. Mike went in and approached the counter.

"Are you by chance hiring?"

"I'm sorry, I got the only position they were hiring."

"Thank you anyway." Mike turned to leave. This was his last shot.

Mike knew Betty from school and was glad she had a job. Betty watched as Mike was leaving and stopped him.

"Didn't you live on a ranch?"

"Yes, why do you ask?"

"I know where you might get a job if you don't mind working on a ranch."

At this time, Mike would take anything he could get. "I don't mind working on a ranch," he lied, but he needed a job.

"The LLB Ranch is looking for someone to help with their horses. Do you know anything about horses?"

"Yes, I had a horse most of my life, and we always had horses on the farm. I never heard of the LLB Ranch."

"That's because it has been renamed. It was the old Langford Ranch, east of town."

"I know where it is located. What happen to Langford?"

"They sold out to Mr. Carson. He is rich, rich, and you wouldn't know the old ranch. They got a new ranch house, barns, and fences. It is something to see."

"Where did they come from?"

"I heard they were from Oklahoma and had a lot of oil wells and also a small ranch."

"Why did they move to Texas?"

"Word has it. He sold the small ranch and moved to Texas to start a large horse ranch. He liked the area around here."

"Thanks for the tip. I'll check it out after lunch."

Mike went home and had lunch. He told his mother he didn't find a job yet but was going out to LLB Ranch and try there.

"Good luck, Son."

"Thanks, Mom. I'll need it."

The ranch was just like Betty had described it. A large sign over the entrance read "LLB Ranch." White iron pipe fences had replaced the old barbed wire fences. A paved road led up to the ranch house with pine trees on either side of the road. The place was beautiful.

Mike followed the road up to the ranch house. There was a circular driveway, and the house was located among the trees. There were several outline buildings and two big barns in back. Horses were grazing in several corrals.

The garage off to one side of the house held a large motor home, several cars, and pickups.

"Boy, what a spread! It must be nice to be rich."

Mike parked his car and got out. He went to the front door and rang the doorbell and then waited. A housekeeper opened the door, dressed in a black-and-white uniform. She had a look of authority about her.

He knew most of the people around Booneville, but he didn't know her. She probably came from Oklahoma with Mr. Carson.

"May I help you?"

"I came to see Mr. Carson about a job."

"He is out in the large barn directly behind the house. You can go through the garage and out the back."

*Nice friendly woman,* thought Mike. Mike entered the barn and took in a very dangerous scene. A beautiful palomino stallion had both front feet tangled in some bailing wire. He was turning and kicking while four men tried to get close enough to catch the horse. A fifth man stood back with much concern on his face while yelling to the men to do something.

Suddenly the palomino kicked and caught one of the men in the chest and sent him flying backward, hitting the floor hard. Another man rushed over to help him. Mike ran over in front of the fifth man. That was probably Mr. Carson.

"Sir, you're going to cause the palomino to break a leg. He is scared, and all of you are scaring him more."

"Who the hell are you?"

"I'm someone who likes and understands horses. Get everyone out, and I will take care of him."

After a slight hesitation, Mr. Carson yelled, "Everybody get out of the barn!"

Mr. Carson backed slowly up to the door and watched Mike slowly approach the palomino. Mike talked to the palomino in a low soothing tone.

"Well, you sure got yourself in a mess. I wonder who left this old bailing wire lying around for you to get tangled up in."

Mike put his hand on the horse's shoulder, stroking him gently, while still talking to him. "Easy, boy. Nobody's going to hurt you."

The palomino turned his head to get a good look at Mike. He had fear and hurt in his eyes. Mike looked him straight in the eyes and kept talking to him. He rubbed his shoulder and neck as he talked to him.

The horse was starting to calm down. Mike could feel the horse starting to relax. He wanted him completely calm before he started to work to free him.

"OK, old fellow, this isn't going to hurt. Just be still."

The palomino whinnied softly, like he understood what Mike said. Mr. Carson watched in amazement at Mike. He didn't understand what was going on. He had heard of what people called a horse whisperer, but he thought it was bullshit.

Mike stroked the palomino's upper leg and slowly moved down his left leg. "Easy, boy. Easy, boy. It'll be over soon."

Mike slowly unwound the wire from his leg. After the left leg was free, he stood up and put his hand on the horse's neck, stroking him gently, while crossing under his neck to the right leg. After the right leg was free, Mike put both arms around his neck.

"Good boy, good boy, it's all over."

Mike turned and headed back to the barn door. He looked back, and the palomino was following him like a puppy dog.

"Young man, how did you do that so easy?"

"The name is Mike Love, sir. I'm an old country boy, and old plow horses are always getting tangled up in their harness, so it just came natural to free him. I live in town, but I was raised on a farm."

"I can't thank you enough. That was a very valuable animal. What did you come to see me about?"

"Sir, I need a part-time job."

"Say no more. You got the job."

"Thank you very much, sir."

"No, it should be me thanking you for saving my palomino."

"Come with me and let me show you around."

Mr. Carson gave Mike a complete tour of the ranch. The ranch was big, and it took a while.

"I want you to work with the horses. I have never seen a horse take to a stranger the way that palomino did to you."

Mr. Carson lined out his duties of feeding, cleaning the barn, and helping with the breeding of the horses. If he could gentle the palomino, he would be a big help when trying to get the horses to mate.

"Mike, I have a feeling you are going to fit in real well here at the ranch."

"I hope so. I like horses and like to work with them."

Mike glanced around at all the corrals. Each corral held a different breed of horse. One corral held appaloosas, another held palominos, and still another held chestnuts. He saw one corral off by itself. It held a beautiful albino stallion.

"Stay away from that one," warned Mr. Carson.

"What's wrong with him?"

"He belongs to my little girl Linda. He won't let anyone near him. She raised him from a colt."

"We try to mate him with a chestnut from time to time, trying to get a perfect palomino. We sell them for show and parade horses. We also have a lot of quarter horses we sell to the other ranches for stock horses."

"I'm going to like working here with all the different horses. It should be very interesting."

"You can start tomorrow if you like. That large barn will be yours to keep clean and take care of the horses, when we have horses in it."

"I'll be here bright and early tomorrow."

"My wife Lucy and little girl Linda will be down from Oklahoma in a couple of days. Feed and water Linda's horse through the fence. She will take care of him herself when she gets down here."

"Yes, sir, I'll take care of him like he was my own."

"Good, I'll see you tomorrow."

Mike left the ranch happy to have found a new job. He was sure he wouldn't have any trouble doing the job. Mrs. Love was waiting supper for him.

"Did you get the job?"

"Yes, I did, just like you said I would. I'm back to being a country boy again, but I think I'm going to like it this time."

"What are you going to be doing?"

"I'll be working with the horses."

"Good, you were always good with horses."

First thing the next morning, Mike decided he was going to make friends with Linda's horse. He walked up to the fence, only to have the horse try to bite him.

"Well, good morning to you. Did you have a bad night? I think your problem is you don't like men. Am I right?" Mike tried his most soothing tone as he continued to talk to the albino.

The albino stared at him like he was crazy talking to a horse. Mike just kept on talking like it was the natural thing to do. "You sure are pretty and white. I bet all the young fillies flip over you. How would you like me to fix you up with a young filly?"

The albino rotated his ears in Mike's direction and let out a low whinny. "Well, I guess I finally got your attention."

Mike watched as the albino glanced over to another corral, where a young chestnut filly was watching them.

"Oh, so that's the one? Well, if you are good, I'll put in a good word for you."

Mr. Carson found Mike feeding the horses after he had cleaned the barn. "I see you found the feed and know how much to give each horse."

"Yes, sir, Dad taught me years ago when I was small. He always had a good set of plow horses and a riding horse. I had a black-and-white paint that I raised from a colt. When I was twelve, I went hunting on horseback."

"You did what?" Mr. Carson was amazed at Mike's story.

"I shot squirrels from out of trees without getting off my horse. I also went bird hunting. I would run him across a field and jump the birds. When they took to flight, I would stop my horse and take a shot. It's a lot less tiring than walking and a lot more fun. I didn't hunt with a dog, only my horse."

"That's quite a story. How long did you live in the country?"

"We moved to town when I was sixteen."

"Do you still have your horse?"

"No, sir, we sold everything when we moved to town, including the other horses and livestock."

"I got to go to town on business. I'll see you this afternoon when I get back."

"Sir, the albino is ready to mate with one of the chestnuts."

Mr. Carson was amazed at Mike's ability with horses again, how he seemed to communicate to them, and they knew what he was talking about.

"Are you sure?"

"Yes, sir, I'm sure."

"OK, put the mare in with him and be careful."

"Yes, sir, I will."

"After they mate, take the mare back out if you can or wait until I get back to help you."

"I don't think I'll have any problems."

"Just be careful of the albino. I don't want you to get hurt. That horse can be real mean."

"No problem. I'll be all right."

Mr. Carson got in a pickup and waved bye to Mike. Mike turned his attention back to the albino. He walked over to the gate to the corral, and immediately the albino came over to nip at him.

"Well, I see you are still in a bad mood. I know just what you need to cure it."

Mike pointed toward the corral holding the chestnut. The chestnut was standing at the fence, watching them with big sad eyes.

"You want her, then come over here and let me pet you."

The albino walked back and forth in front of Mike, with her ears pointed straight ahead, unsure of what to do. Mike's dad had taught him to watch a horse's ears. A lot of the time you could tell the way a horse moved his ears what he was going to do.

The housekeeper looked out the window and saw Mike at the corral. *Didn't he know to stay away from that horse?*

"What is that fool kid up to? He's going to get hurt." She walked outside to watch. Two of the men working over at the other barn stopped to watch also.

"What is that crazy kid going to do?" asked one man.

"I don't have a clue, but he had better leave that albino alone."

"Now what's he doing?"

"He is talking to the albino."

"What's he saying?"

"I don't know. I can't hear him."

The albino continued to pace back and forth while Mike talked to him. Finally, he stopped and faced Mike.

"If you want her, come here."

The albino let out a whinny, and the chestnut answered him.

"See, she wants you. All you have to do is let me pet you and she is yours."

The albino slowly walked over to the fence and put his neck over the fence. Mike gently touched his nose and softly stroked his forehead. Then he put his arm around the albino's neck.

"See, that wasn't so bad. I think you like to be petted."

The two men watching couldn't believe what they saw. They had never been able to get near the horse.

"I'll be right back." Mike turned and walked toward the chestnut's corral.

"Now what's he up to?" asked one of the men.

"We'll wait and see what he's up to."

Mike wanted to call the albino by name, but he didn't know it. Horses usually work better when are called by name. They are probably a lot like people. They like to hear their name. The chestnut met Mike at the gate like she knew what was going to happen. She was as nervous as a woman, but she wanted that albino.

Mike forgot to go by the barn and get a halter. He took his belt off and put it around her neck.

"OK, girl, let's go. You don't want to keep your boyfriend waiting, do you?"

He led her out of her corral and down to the albino's corral. The albino was standing at the gate, waiting.

"Back up, boy, and let the lady in the gate."

The albino backed up a few feet. Mike opened the gate and let the chestnut in. He removed his belt from her neck while reaching over to pat the albino on the forehead.

"You be nice to the lady, you hear?"

He shut the gate and left them alone to let nature take its course. He went back to work. The housekeeper realized what was going to happen. She blushed red and went back into the house. The two men looked at one another.

"I'll be damn. Can you believe that?"

"No. But we had better get back to work, or the boss will fire us."

"He made it look so easy to get the horses to do what he wants them to do. It's like they understand him and does what he tells them to do."

Just before quitting time, Mike went back to the albino's corral. The two horses were standing very close together, like a couple of lovebirds. He opened the gate and went into the corral.

"Boy, you two look like you're in love."

He walked over and put his arms around each horse's neck. They both turned to him to try and nuzzle him.

"You sure look in bad shape."

The albino stared at him. He looked completely worn-out.

"What's the matter? Is the lady too much for you?"

The albino let out what sounded like a low moan. Mike laughed out loud.

"Next time take it easy."

The albino stared at him. Mike put his belt around the chestnut's neck and took her back to her own corral.

"Good girl. May you give birth to a beautiful palomino colt."

He petted her and found she was wet with sweat. "You two did have a good workout."

Mike started his car and was pulling out, when Mr. Carson pulled up beside him.

"How did you make out with the breeding today?"

"The chestnut over in that corral is mated." He pointed to the corral.

"Good. I've been trying to get that one to mate for a long time."

"Sir, I guess she was playing hard to get."

"I guess so." Laughed Mr. Carson.

"I'll see you tomorrow."

"Good job, Mike. Keep up the good work."

"Yes, sir."

Mike headed for home. He had to work at the drive-in tonight.

The next day about noon, he was cleaning out the barn and heard a lot of noise. He went outside to see what was going on. A fancy new car was coming up the driveway, and the albino was going crazy.

The car stopped, and a young woman jumped out. The housekeeper came out the front door with her arms open.

"Oh, it's good to see you, Ms Linda."

"I'm glad to see you too, Millie."

They hugged each other. Lucy got out of the car and hugged the housekeeper. Linda turned and ran to the albino's corral. The albino was waiting with his neck over the fence. Linda reached the fence and threw her arms around his neck.

"Lightning, I missed you so much!"

Linda climbed upon the fence, and Lightning turned so she could straddle his back. She loved Lightning.

Mike watched her and Lightning and thought that was the most beautiful sight he had ever seen.

Linda rode around the corral while stroking Lightning on the neck. Mrs. Carson called, "You're going to ruin that new dress!"

"Mom, I haven't seen Lightning in a long time."

"Get off that horse. Linda, you come in here this minute. Millie, what am I going to do with that girl?"

"Mrs. Carson, she is a tomboy and likes horses. It will blow over in time."

"When I was her age, I was going with young men. One was a freshman in college. All she wants to do is play with horses."

"Be thankful, Mrs. Lucy. You don't have to worry about her coming home nights late with some man or sex problems. You know what I mean."

"Yes, I'm afraid I do. When I had sex the first time, we didn't use anything, and I was scared to death until my period showed up."

They turned and went into the house. Linda stopped Lightning at the gate and turned sideways. She slid off his back and dropped to the ground, the air catching her dress and blowing it up past her waist. She pushed it back down with a strange feeling that she was being watched.

*That's some little girl,* thought Mike as he watched Linda walking toward the house. He looked her over and liked what he saw. She was about five feet six inches tall with long blond hair. She looked to be about 36-24-35. He wanted to check the measurements out to be sure. She was a beautiful young woman. He felt a tremendous desire to meet her.

Linda glanced toward the barn and saw a young man watching her. She blushed as she looked him over, wondering if he had seen her when her dress was around her waist. He would have got an eyeful, because she was wearing thin panties. For some reason, her body became warm.

She glanced at him again. He looked to be about five feet eleven inches tall, brown hair, and a medium build. He was probably a plain old country boy, but she looked his way again.

There was something about him that held her attention. He was still watching her, and she kind of liked the attention. She glanced toward him one more time before going into the house.

She had this strange feeling. Her body was warm, and her heart was beating a little faster. Her breasts felt heavy, and her nipples were hard. She had never felt this way before. She wondered what was wrong with her. It was probably the heat. *Yeah right!*

"I just had a sexual reaction to someone I don't know." That scared her.

Linda got a Coke out of the refrigerator and went over to the kitchen table. Lucy and Millie were catching up on all the news, also all the local gossip.

"Millie, who is that young man by the barn?" Linda asked.

Mrs. Carson looked surprised at Linda's question. She was never interested in boys before. She noticed the color on Linda's face.

"Did he say something to you?"

"No, it's just hot outside. Millie, who is he?"

"His name is Mike Love, and he lives in town. Your dad hired him to help with the horses."

"Dad hired a city boy to help with the horses. Has he lost his mind?"

"He lived in the country when he was growing up. His father was a sharecropper."

"But that doesn't explain why dad hired him."

"He has a way with horses."

"What do you mean, a way with horses?"

"They all like him, and when he tells them to do something, they obey him. I don't understand why. They seem to understand everything he says. It's very strange."

"When you say all, does that include Lightning?"

"Yes, dear, I'm afraid it does."

"Has he pet Lightning?"

"Yes, he has. I saw him myself." She didn't say what else she saw.

Linda was shocked. Nobody had ever pet Lightning but her, not even her father, and he was good with horses. She suddenly felt jealous of him and Lightning. She shook her head. What was wrong with her? She was a young woman, and it was silly to be jealous over a horse. She went to the window and looked out, but Mike had gone back into the barn.

"Linda, come away from the window. He might see you and think you are interested in him."

She turned to her mother. "You and Dad were poor country folk before they struck oil on our small ranch."

Mrs. Carson started to cry. She forgot how poor they had been and had to scrape to make ends meet.

"I'm sorry, Mom. I didn't mean to sound so hateful."

"That's all right because I had it coming. Sometimes I forget where we came from."

Later in her room, Linda wondered why she had taken up for a man she didn't know. She undressed and stood naked before the tall mirror on her closet door. She remembered him watching her, and her body became warm again. She touched her breasts, and the nipples became hard. What was wrong with her? She didn't even know him.

Linda put on red shorts and a long white shirt. She put her hair into a ponytail and applied a small amount of makeup. She wanted to look casual when she met him. Looking in the mirror, she decided she was ready to take the plunge.

She walked to the barn and stopped at the door, looking inside to spot Mike. She saw him working on a halter with a broken strap. The palomino stood close by like a guard dog. Mike stopped working on the halter and put his arm around the palomino's neck, petting him.

"You sure are a beautiful horse. I wish I had one like you. Let's practice the trick I taught you yesterday. Lie down, boy." Mike gently touched his left leg at the knee.

The palomino lay down on his side, and Mike slid his leg across his back.

"Stand up, boy."

The palomino stood up with Mike on his back. He slid off his back and put his arm around the palomino's neck, petting him again.

"Very good boy! You learn fast!"

Linda clapped her hands and smiled at Mike.

"That was a good show. Does Dad know you are turning his horses into trick horses?"

Mike turned and stared into the deepest green eyes he had ever seen. Linda stared back at him.

"No, but I guess he will know now."

"Not if you don't want me to tell him."

"That's all right. I don't think he would care if I teach them tricks. I think they would sell better when a customer can see how smart the horse is."

"Where did you learn to teach horses tricks?"

"I don't know."

"But horses understand you."

"I have never understood why, but I can read a horse by his actions."

"I heard people call a person like you a horse whisperer."

"I wouldn't go that far."

Linda walked over and petted the palomino on the forehead.

"You must be Daddy's little girl Linda?"

Linda laughed. "Dad always calls me his little girl. When I'm fifty years old, he will probably still call me his little girl."

"You sure don't look like a little girl to me."

"Thank you, I think."

They both petted the palomino and talked. Mike continued his repair job while Linda watched.

"Well, I'm finished. It's time for me to get off work."

"I'll walk you to your car."

"OK, I would like that."

As they walked side by side, Linda asked, "Did you pet Lightning?"

"Yes, I did."

She wasn't going to ask, but suddenly she wanted to know. It would tell her more about the man walking beside her. Linda was getting that warm feeling again. She could feel her nipples becoming rigid. "How did you do it? He won't let anyone touch him but me."

After a long hesitation, Mike decided he had to say something. "Maybe he liked my 'old country boy' look?"

Linda wasn't satisfied with his answer. "No, he is a very smart horse. How did you do it?"

"Well, if you must know, I gave him something he wanted."

"What did he want?"

Mike opened his car door and got in. Looking into her deep green eyes, he felt hot all over. Their eyes were locked.

"I let Lightning have the chestnut filly over in that corral."

Linda blushed and broke eye contact. She turned and headed for the house.

"See you tomorrow," said Mike.

"Don't count on it," replied Linda.

Walking back toward the house, Linda realized what a fool she had made of herself, but she had found out how he petted Lightning.

It was funny when she thought about it. Of all ways to pet a horse, that took the prize. Driving home, Mike realized he couldn't wait until tomorrow to return to work. All the way home he had Linda on his mind. She was going to be his girl. He didn't know when or how, but she would someday be his girl.

Mike lay in bed that night dreaming. He could picture Linda in his mind, kissing her and making love to her. It was a good dream, but could he make it happen?

Early the next morning, Mike was feeding the horses. Mr. Carson approached him.

"Mike, I want you to go to a private horse sale with me today. I'll get Joe to finish your work."

"Yes, sir."

"Drive the blue pickup and trailer around front."

"Yes, sir, right away."

"I'll meet you around front."

Mr. Carson went inside the house, and Mike went to get the pickup. Mike wondered why Mr. Carson was taking him with him to a horse sale.

"Millie, don't hold supper for me, because I will probably be late getting back."

"Where are you going, Daddy?" asked Linda.

"I'm taking Mike and going to a horse sale."

"May I go with you? I love to go to horse sales."

"OK, but hurry up. We are ready to leave."

Linda still had her robe on, but she had combed her hair and put it in a ponytail. She ran to her room and put on some tight-fitting jeans and a white shirt. She left the two top buttons open. She put a dab of perfume behind each ear and between her breasts. Lipstick was all the makeup she had time for.

For some reason, Linda wanted to look nice. Why was she fixing herself up for an old country boy? Millie came in just as she was on her way out.

"My! But don't you look nice this morning? Have you got a date?"

"No, Millie, I'm going to a horse sale with Daddy and Mike."

"So it's Mike, is it?"

"Millie, it's just a horse sale."

"Yeah right, just a horse sale."

Mike started to get out of the pickup, when Mr. Carson approached.

"Stay where you are. You drive."

Mr. Carson opened the door on the passenger side and waited. Linda came running out of the house and slid in beside Mike.

"I'm ready. Let's go."

Mr. Carson got in and closed the door. "Drive on, Mike. I'll give you directions as we go."

Linda's leg was resting against Mike's leg, and he could feel the heat from her body. The gearshift was on the floor, and he had to reach between her legs to shift gears. His hand would brush her leg every time he had to shift gears. Mike was having a hard time keeping his mind on his driving. He was trying to control his manhood from getting hard, but the heat from Linda's body was driving him crazy.

Linda could feel the heat from Mike's body, and her body reacted to it. Her nipples became hard, and she could feel her juices start to flow into her panties. She wondered if Mike was having the same problem with his body.

She glanced at his crotch and saw his manhood trying to rise. Mike stopped at a stop sign. He turned his head, and his tortured eyes gazed into hers. She smiled at Mike, knowing he was feeling the same as her, but she kept her leg pressed firm against his.

"Daddy, how much further is it to the horse sale?"

"About another hour and we will be there."

"Daddy, I'm hot. Could we stop for Cokes?"

"Mike, stop at the next service station."

Mike was hot too, but he didn't say so. Mike pulled in at the next gas station and parked. He needed to use the restroom. They finished their pit stop, and Mike pulled back out into traffic. Linda smiled at Mike and pressed her leg against his leg again. They drove for another hour before they got there.

"There's where we're going. Turn off at the sign."

There was a large "Horse Sale" sign beside the road. Mike pulled off under a sign that read "Lazy S Ranch." The area was crowded with pickups and trailers. Mike looked around for a place to park. He finally found a place big enough to park the pickup and trailer.

"Come on, kids. Let's see if they have some horses that we may want to buy."

Mike got out and helped Linda out on his side. When their hands touched, it was like a lightning jolt for both of them. They stared at each other. What was happening to them?

They followed Mr. Carson as he started to make the rounds, looking the horses over, before the auction began.

"What are you looking for, Dad?"

"I want to buy an appaloosa stallion and a couple of good quarter horse mares for breeding."

They stopped at a group of stalls. There were three appaloosa stallions. They had a choice.

"Oh, Dad, they are all so beautiful!"

"I know, but we only need one stallion."

Mike carefully looked each horse over. He saw one horse looking them over. Mr. Carson watched Mike as he inspected each horse. He had brought Mike along to help him buy horses. He had a gut feeling that Mike could pick out a good horse.

"Mike, which horse we would buy?"

"I'll let you know as soon as I inspect this one. Come here, boy."

The appaloosa came limping over. Mike opened the gate and went in. He petted the appaloosa on the neck and dropped his hand down his leg. The appaloosa let him pick up his foot and inspect it. He let his foot down.

"Stay, boy."

Mike walked around the horse and back out the gate. Mike watched the stallion, and the stallion stared back at him.

"Well, have you decided which one you would buy?"

"Yes, sir, I would buy this one."

"Why would you? He has a limp, probably a bad foot or leg. Why not buy the one in the next stall?"

"That one has been rode to death and abused."

"How can you tell?"

"Look very closely at him."

"I don't see anything wrong with him."

"He has sad eyes and doesn't pay attention to anything, not even the mares over in that corral. One of them is bound to be in heat." Mike glanced at Linda, and she blushed.

"Why not the horse in the stall on the other side?"

"He's too nervous for a stud. He keeps his ears constantly pricked forward."

"OK, but the one you picked has a limp."

"It's nothing but a simple bruise caused by improperly fitted shoes. All the horse needs is new shoes."

Mr. Carson still wasn't totally convinced. He looked at the stallion, and the stallion stared back at him.

"He is very smart. He answers to voice command. He is calm and very sure of himself. You can probably get him a lot cheaper because other buyers will shy away from him unless they have inspected him."

"OK, this is the one we will bid on to buy. Now let's hunt some mares."

By the time the auction started, they had picked out a couple of good quarter horse mares to bid on.

"You are going to pay good money for the mares."

"How can you tell?"

"Everybody can see there's nothing wrong with them."

The auction started, and as Mike had predicted, Mr. Carson bought the stallion for a steal. He had to bid high for the mares.

Driving home, Mr. Carson was well pleased with the horses in the horse trailer. He was glad he brought Mike with him. Linda's leg was resting next to Mike's leg. She glanced at him and smiled. He was not just a plain old country boy. He was a horseman. He didn't realize what a talent he had, but she knew by watching her dad that he knew and would use that talent. She couldn't remember when she had enjoyed a day so much. She liked a man that was good with horses.

Mike was as happy as a hog in a wallow. It had been fun, and he was getting paid for a day's work. He was setting next to his girl. At least he hoped she would be. The heat from her leg was driving him crazy, but he loved it and didn't want it to end. To test her, he moved his leg over, and she just moved her leg back against him. He knew she wanted the contact just as much as he did.

"Mike, we got a good deal on the horses."

"Yes, sir, you got the stallion for nothing. All we got to do is treat the bruise and put on a new pair of shoes."

"We will be going to more sales in the coming weeks."

"Daddy, I'm coming with you. The sales are fun."

The next few weeks, Mr. Carson, Linda, and Mike went to horse sales. Mr. Carson told Mike about his breeding schedule and wanted his help. Mike became totally involved with the ranch. Mike still worked at the movies at night and was dead tired most of the time. He would like to quit the movies, but he needed the money.

It was a couple of weeks before school was to start. Mike would have to quit his ranch job. He didn't want to, but what else could he do?

Mrs. and Mr. Carson decided to give a big housewarming party and dance. They wanted to get to know their neighbors and the business people in Booneville. All the prominent people were invited along with their young people so Linda would have someone her age to socialize with. Linda was helping her mother make out invitations.

"Mom, why isn't Mike's name on the guest list?"

After a slight hesitation, she replied, "He wouldn't fit in."

"Why wouldn't Mike fit in?"

"He's just a country boy and hired help."

"I want him to come. I like being around him, and I bet he is a good dancer."

"If you like him, don't ask him to come. You will hurt him."

"How will I hurt him?"

"Mike won't know how to act around upper-class people."

"I'll take that chance. If he isn't invited, then I won't come."

"OK, honey, but don't say I didn't warn you."

"Thanks, Mom." She made out an invitation for Mike. She looked up his address on the payroll records.

"Finish the invitations while I finish my shopping list."

"OK, Mom."

Linda wondered how Mike would dress. She decided not to put a dress code on his invitation. If she put formal, he probably wouldn't come. She sat and dreamed about Mike dancing with her and holding her tight.

Mrs. Carson watched her daughter and wasn't happy about what she saw. She knew she was thinking of him. She wanted Linda to date the upper-crust boys. She didn't want her to throw her life away on some old country boy.

"Linda, what are you thinking about?"

"Nothing, Mom," she lied.

Mike received his invitation to the party. It was for the coming Saturday night, and he worked at the drive-in that night. He would have to swap Friday for Saturday with the other movie operator if he decided to go to the party. He was undecided what to do until the next day when Linda walked by while he was mending fence.

She smiled at him. "Are you going to our party?"

He replied, "Yes." He couldn't say no to her.

"Great! I hoped you would come."

"I'm not sure about coming."

She changed the subject. "Are you a good dancer?"

"Fair I guess," he lied. He was a good dancer, but he didn't want to brag.

"I like to dance."

Saturday night rolled around, and Mike dressed for the party. He had bought a new pair of jeans and a black Western shirt. He shined his old boots. He wished he had a new Western belt buckle, but his old belt would have to do.

The party started at eight, but Mike waited until nine to show up. Linda had watched the door for Mike to arrive, but it looked like he wasn't coming to the party. Linda was dancing with the banker's son, when she glanced at the door and saw Mike come in. She finished the dance and then went looking for Mike.

Mike stepped through the door and knew he should have stayed home. The crowd was dressed formal. He was out of place. Even if he came in formal dress, he would still be out of place. He was just a country boy.

Linda couldn't find Mike. She looked everywhere but couldn't find him. Millie came through the door with a tray of food.

"Millie, have you seen Mike?"

"He went out the back door and headed toward Lightning's corral."

"Why didn't he stay at the party?"

"Honey, he wasn't dressed for it, and he knew it."

"I don't care how he was dressed."

"I know that, but people are cruel. They would have made fun of him."

"Thanks, Millie."

Linda ran to her room and quickly pulled off her dress. She put on jeans and her long white shirt. She went back down through the kitchen.

"Where are you going dressed like that? Your mother will have a fit."

"Where the fun is, with Mike." Linda went out the back door. She approached the corral and saw Lightning with his neck over the gate. Mike had his arm around his neck. She approached from the opposite side and put her arm around Lightning's neck.

"I think he likes you more than he does me now."

"That's because I'm his pimp. I bring him all the good-looking fillies to make love to."

Linda giggled. "I guess that would be a good reason."

Mike glanced across Lightning's neck at Linda. He noticed she had changed her clothes. He wondered why. She was so pretty in her dress.

"Why did you change clothes?"

"You couldn't come to my world, so I came to yours."

Mike came around Lightning's neck and stood facing Linda. She leaned back against the gate. Their eyes locked. Lightning backed up and watched. They stood face-to-face, not moving. *Stupid people. What's wrong with them?* Lightning put his nose to Linda's back and pushed her into Mike's arms.

"I think Lightning is trying to act as your pimp now." Giggled Linda.

Linda put her arms around Mike's neck and molded her body to his, inviting further intimacies. Mike put his arms around her waist and slid his hands down to cup her buttocks, then pulled her closer.

He lowered his head and brushed her lips with the tip of his tongue. She opened her mouth for him, and he slid his tongue into her mouth to explore her softness. She whimpered and arched her body against him. She could feel his erection peak between them. She had never felt so wanted.

"Oh, Mike!" she moaned.

She saw love and desire in Mike's eyes. She was swept by a reckless desire to make love to him right then.

"Linda, you're missing your party. You should be in there dancing."

"I don't care. I had rather be out here with you and Lightning."

Mike covered her mouth with his. She shyly slid her tongue into Mike's mouth and explored. She moved back from him. With their eyes locked, she took his hand and led him toward the barn. They walked in silence.

They were very nervous about what they were going to do. When they entered the barn, Linda led Mike up the stairs to the hayloft. When they entered the loft, she turned and faced him.

Mike gazed into her eyes and saw desire, but he saw something more. He saw a woman in love. He could feel the electricity between them. It was just like his mother had described it. He knew he was in love. He knew he had found the right girl. Mike reached for the top button on Linda's shirt and slowly unbuttoned her shirt. She turned her back to him, and he pulled her shirt off, letting it drop to the hay. He reached for the clasp on her bra and let the bra drop to the hay. She turned back around to face him.

"Are you sure you want to do this?"

"Yes, Mike, I'm sure. I want you to make love to me."

He gazed at her breasts. She felt her nipples become hard. Her body was hot.

"Touch them."

Mike cupped a breast in each hand and lowered his head to take a nipple in his mouth. He nibbled and sucked on each nipple while Linda quivered and moaned. She knew there was no turning back now. She didn't want him to quit, or she would die. While sucking on her nipple, he reached down, unbuckled her belt, and unzipped her jeans.

Linda felt an evocative sensation as Mike ran his fingers inside her jeans and then into her panties. He eased one finger in part of the way into her place of desire. She was throbbing and clamoring for release.

Mike slid her jeans down to the floor while slowly running his finger in and out. He lowered her to the floor. She was burning up with passion. She was arching to meet his finger. He slid one more finger in. She hunched his fingers and moaned. Mike knew she was close to a climax. He would let her have the first climax. He pulled her panties off and kept running his fingers in and out.

"Oh, don't stop! It feels so good!"

Mike picked up the pace and felt her squeeze his fingers and throbbing around them. She bucked and twisted and tossed her head from side to side.

"Oh, Mike, I'm coming, I'm coming!" When her breathing became normal, she said, "Mike, I'm sorry. You didn't have any fun."

"It is fun just watching you have a climax."

Linda unbuttoned his shirt and reached for his belt.

"Time out. I'll do it."

He jumped to his feet and quickly removed his clothes. His erection stood straight out, and Linda stared at it. It was big, and she wondered if she could take all of it, but she was going to try. She wanted Mike inside her.

After removing his clothes, Mike lowered himself over her. She spread her legs to receive him. His erection slowly entered the folds to the center of her passion, and she tensed up.

Shyly she said, "There's something I have to tell you. I'm a virgin."

After hearing her confession, it only made Mike love her more. He was the first. She had chosen him to be her first. He hoped he would be her last also.

"That's not a problem. We just have to take it slow."

"But doesn't it hurt?"

"Relax and it will only hurt for a moment. Then it will feel good."

Mike kissed her gently, sucking her tongue into his mouth. He lay on her breasts, with them flat against his chest. He didn't go any deeper while he waited for her to relax. She slowly relaxed and arched against him, taking his erection a little deeper.

"Do it now. Give me all of it."

"This may hurt a little."

With one brutal stab, he went all the way home. Mike lay there, not moving for a moment until the pain on Linda's face stopped. He could feel her muscles tightening around him and see the sensuous pleasure in her eyes, and then she arched against him. He moved slowly in and out as she rotated her hips, picking up the rhythm. Linda was bucking and moaning, tossing her head from side to side.

"Oh, Mike, I never knew anything could feel so good!"

"Does it hurt anymore?"

"No, it just feels so good. Don't stop, don't ever stop!"

Mike knew by experience, all good things come to an end. He slowed down, trying to make it last as long as possible. He wanted Linda's first time to be a good experience. Too many guys only thought about themselves and didn't worry if a girl was satisfied or not as long as they got what they wanted.

Linda's heart hammered against her ribs until she thought it would burst. Her hot center throbbed around Mike's manhood, and she had her very first orgasm.

"I'm coming! I'm coming! Oh, give it to me hard!"

"Keep going. Enjoy it to the fullest."

"I am! Oh, I am!"

She whimpered with pleasure and squeezed his manhood with her inner muscles. He started pounding home with each thrust. Linda arched and rotated her hips to meet each thrust. It seemed so natural to her. She couldn't get enough of Mike. She could feel another spasm coming on. Mike felt her throbbing around his erection and her juices flowing. She was so slick. He slammed deep into her hot passion and exploded. Linda could feel his hot come as it went deep into her body.

"Linda, you feel so good. You are so tight."

"You're not so bad yourself," she teased.

"I wish we could do this all night."

"Me too. It was so good."

"I wanted your first to be good."

"It was fantastic."

Mike lay on top, still in her, while gently kissing her swollen lips. Finally exhausted, he rolled off and lay beside her. She turned her back to him, and he cuddled up to her, spoon fashion. Mike put his arm around her and cupped one of her breasts. After a few minutes, his manhood started to rise again. He eased his erection into the folds of her passion and let it push its way deeper as he reached a full erection.

"You're hard again."

"I'm going to lie here and rest with it all the way in you."

"Oh, Mike, it feels so good!"

Linda didn't just want to lie there passive. She tightened her inner muscles around his erection and tried to squeeze it off. Mike couldn't stand it any longer and started slamming deeper with each thrust. When he felt her close to a climax, he would slow down and almost stop, then start again. After several times, Linda said, "I can't take it anymore. Give it to me fast and hard."

Mike controlled his climax until he felt her throbbing around him and knew Linda was having another climax. He gave her one final thrust. She squeezed him, and he shot another stream of come deep into her body. She moaned and went limp. He felt their juices flowing out around him, but he was too tired to move.

They lay still connected and dozed off to sleep. Mike was waked up by cars leaving the ranch.

"Linda, wake up. The party is over."

"Not now," she moaned. "Let me sleep. I'm so tired."

"Come on, sleepyhead, your mother will be out looking for you."

Linda sat up suddenly. "Oh my god, she will!"

She jumped up and started dressing. Mike stood up and dressed also. After they were dressed, Mike peeked out the barn door.

"Mike, will you wait until I get in the house before you come out of the barn?"

Linda kissed Mike good night and ran out of the barn toward the house. He watched her until she was in the house. Before he left the barn, he gazed up at the hayloft. It had been the most wonderful night of his young life.

Linda slipped in the back door. Her mother was standing there, waiting for her. She didn't look happy.

"Where have you been, young lady?"

"I was at the corral with Lightning."

Her mother reached and plucked some straw from her hair. "Come in the kitchen. We have to talk."

"Mom, can't it wait until tomorrow?"

"No, it can't. I should have had a talk with you sooner."

"But, Mom, it's so late."

"Come in here now."

"Yes, ma'am."

They sat facing each other while Mrs. Carson planned what she would say. She was shocked to see Linda come in like that.

"I didn't pay you much attention, because I thought all you wanted to do was play with horses. I guess I was wrong."

Linda dropped her head and stared at her hands in her lap. "Mom, I don't."

"Did you go all the way?"

"Mom, I couldn't stop."

"Did you go all the way?"

"Yes yes, I love him."

"That's what I thought the first time, and I was a lot younger than you."

Linda glanced at her mother. "You did it a lot younger than me?"

"Yes, and I thought I would go crazy waiting to see if I had my next period."

Linda was more at ease listening to her mother's story. She told about her first love. She told the first time she made love.

"Did you use protection?"

"No, Mom, we didn't. It just felt so right at the time."

"Well, young lady, in the future, if you have sex again, be sure you use protection."

"Yes, ma'am."

"I can't tell you not to do it again, because I know if the time is right, you will do it again. I did. Telling you all of this doesn't mean I approve of your conduct, but I do understand. I have been there. I won't ask who it was, but I could probably guess who it was."

"Thanks, Mom, for understanding."

"Now get to bed, young lady."

"Good night, Mom."

The next day, Mike came by to pick up his last paycheck before school started. He saw Linda down by Lightning's corral. He walked down to see her. They were silent as they petted Lightning.

"Mike, I don't know what came over me last night. I shouldn't have . . . have—"

"We made love. It was wonderful. I love you, Linda. I sensed it the first time we met. I knew for sure when we made love."

"Mother said it was puppy love, because it was my first time."

"Your mother is wrong. You love me too, but you haven't realized it yet. I saw it in your eyes, and the eyes don't lie."

"I couldn't fall in love with you. You're just an old—"

"Country boy and a sharecropper's son, not much of a catch." Mike turned and went up to the house.

"I don't love him," she said to Lightning. "I'm too young to be in love. I got another year of high school, and then I want to go to college. He could mess up everything. Mom was right. I probably think I'm in love with him, because he was the first one to make love to me." Linda stroked Lightning's neck. "I just can't be in love with Mike."

A few minutes later, Mike came out of the house. Lightning let out a loud whinny. Mike looked toward the corral and waved. He got in his car and drove off.

"I'll forget him in a few days." But she didn't.

Every time she went to ride Lightning or feed him, he was standing at the corral gate looking down the driveway toward the highway.

"You miss him, don't you?"

Lightning moved his head up and down and let out a low whinny.

"I guess I do too, but I just don't want to admit it. He was hurting when he left. I could see it in his eyes. I hurt him bad."

# Chapter 6

School started on Monday. As usual, all the boys watched the girls as they arrived. They could look them over and check out any new girl. Mike sat on the front steps with Punky talking over what happened during the summer break.

Linda pulled in and parked her little red sports car. Mike glanced her way and guessed Mr Carson bought it for her to drive to school. He thought to himself, *It must be nice to be rich.*

Linda gazed over the crowd, finally locating Mike. He didn't look too happy, and her heart went out to him. She didn't like the first day of a new school. As she got out of her car, Mike got up and started over toward her, but two of the football team got there first and walked her into school.

Mike sat back down, remembering he was just a country boy in her eyes and didn't have enough class to be seen with her. She would fit in the upper-crust crowd. That's the way in a small town.

He only had one class with Linda, and she sat up front. He sat at the back where he should be. He was sure by the end of the day that she had been informed who she should socialize with and whom not to. He was sure he was on the not-to list.

*God, I hate small towns and how people are classed! Why couldn't people just be people and not divided by how much money they had?* He decided Linda was a rich girl and out of his class.

Mike hurt inside because he loved her, but he realized it was a one-sided affair. She didn't love him the way he loved her. He would just have to try and forget her. He knew he would never forget her. She had stolen his heart. Next summer he would have to find somewhere else to work. He couldn't stand to work on the ranch and see her every day, but he loved his work there. What was a guy to do?

Punky saw Mike outside fixing to leave school and went over to talk. Mike looked so sad, and he wanted to know what was wrong.

"OK, old buddy, spill it."

"What are you talking about?"

"I don't think you told me everything that happened this summer."

"Well, maybe not all."

"I saw you looking at the new girl like a lovesick puppy. Do you know her?"

"She is the daughter of the man I worked for this summer."

"And what happened?"

"I made a fool of myself. I forgot I was out of her class."

"I'm sorry, old buddy."

"I'll get over her I hope."

Mike settled into the same old routine of going to school and working nights at the movies. He had Linda on his mind all the time but kept his distance from her. He didn't want to embarrass her in front of her rich friends.

Punky and the others guys were back doing their crazy things, but Mike just worked and went home. He didn't even want to go to the Chicken Ranch. Punky thought he was sick with something. Punky thought he had been kicked in the head by a horse that summer while working. Mike just wasn't himself anymore.

Linda tried out for cheerleader and got it. That was the final straw to separate them. He knew the code that the football players claimed the cheerleaders for themselves, and they were off-limits to the other students.

Mr. Carson missed Mike around the ranch. He was always his sounding board for new ideas, and also he was very good with the horses and his work. He called the drive-in on Thursday night and invited Mike to come out for supper on Friday night, on his night off. Mrs. Carson was mad at her husband for inviting Mike out.

"We just got rid of that country boy and you invite him back into our home!"

"I thought you liked Mike."

"I did, but Linda was just starting to socialize with her own kind, and I don't want him to mess it up."

"Well, you had better start liking him again, because when he gets older, I plan on him being foreman of this ranch. I'm going to start grooming him for the job now. That's why I invited him to supper to offer him a full-time job, with enough pay so he won't have to work at the movies."

"But he is just a country boy."

"He may be a country boy, so what?"

"Linda may start up with him again."

"That young man is going places, and I plan to help him."

"I hope you know what you are doing."

"I think one day he will be a great horse trainer."

"Well, I think you are making a mistake."

"He is the best I have ever seen with horses and doesn't realize what a talent he possesses. I will teach him the rest of the ranching business, and you will teach him the books. I want us to be able to leave the ranch and travel when Linda goes to college. What good is money if we can't enjoy life with it?"

"OK, I'll teach him the books. I hope you know what you're doing, putting so much trust in that young man."

"He is a proud young man, and all he needs is someone to give him a chance. Hasn't Linda told you that he stays clear of her?"

"Yes, why do you ask?"

"Don't you know why he stays clear of her?"

"No, not really. I was just glad he does, so she can meet some nice young men."

"What you mean is *rich* young men. By the way, the reason he stays clear of Linda is because he thinks he isn't good enough for her, as we are rich."

"I never thought of that."

"I think Linda likes him but is confused by his actions. One of these days she will understand, if she cares that much for him, but only time will tell. You and I need to stay out of their lives and let them make their own choice. Do we have a deal, Mrs. Carson?"

"Yes, Mr. Carson, we do. How would you like a cup of coffee to seal our deal?"

"I love you, Mrs. Carson."

"I love you too, Mr. Carson." She giggled.

Mike arrived at the ranch for supper. As he got out of the car, Lightning let out a loud whinny and paced back and forth in his corral. Mike went straight to the corral and put his arms around Lightning's neck.

"I sure missed you, old fellow."

Linda heard Lightning whinny, and she ran to the door. She saw Mike heading for the corral, and she followed him.

"Did you miss me too?" asked Linda.

Mike turned to face her. "You will never know how much."

Their eyes locked, and they stared at each other. They missed each other, and it was in their eyes.

"Then why did you stay away from me at school?"

"You know why."

"Then you don't know me at all. I pick my own friends, rich or poor. Nobody tells me who I can talk to."

Linda was mad. She turned and headed back into the house. Mike watched her cute backside move on the way into the house. He realized he was still in love with her. Mike petted Lightning on the forehead and then followed Linda into the house.

"Good evening, Mike," said Mr. Carson. "It was good of you to come."

"Thank you, sir."

They shook hands and then went into the dining room. Mrs. and Mr. Carson carried the conversation at the supper table. Linda and Mike glanced at one another from time to time but talked very little.

Mike wished he hadn't come tonight. He couldn't stand being near Linda and not be able to touch her. Linda left the table first, saying she had to study for a test. Mike thought to himself, *Nobody studies on Friday night.*

Mike decided it was time for him to leave. "Thank you, Mrs. Carson, for having me over for supper, but I got a test to study for also."

"Mike, would you come into the study for a few minutes?"

"Yes, sir." He followed Mr. Carson into the study.

"Mike, I'll get right to the point. I want you to work full-time at the ranch and quit your job at the movies."

"Sir, meaning no disrespect, but I couldn't take the job."

"Is it because of Linda?"

After a short hesitation, he replied, "Yes, sir."

"Do you like working at the ranch?"

"Yes, sir, very much."

"Then it's settled. You will start at two hundred a week and work when I need you, day or night when you aren't in school, if we have a problem at the ranch."

Mike thought he had a hearing problem. He thought Mr. Carson said two hundred a week. It took two months to make that much at the movies.

"Did you say two hundred a week, sir?"

"Yes, I did. You will get pay raises as you progress with your ranch training and duties. Your problem with Linda will work itself out."

Mike's father only made fifty a week at the sawmill. Mike had a hard time with the two hundred a week. He just couldn't believe it. It was too good to be true.

"Mike, I said two hundred a week, and don't worry. You will earn every penny of it. Do we have a deal?"

"Yes, sir, I guess we do." They shook hands on it.

"Give your boss a week's notice and start here next week."

"Yes, sir, and thank you."

"You're going to have to stop this 'sir' bit, because you're making me feel like an old man."

"Yes, sir, I mean—"

They both laughed. Mike said good night and headed for home. He couldn't believe his dreams were slowly coming true. Maybe things were looking up for a change. Maybe he could make something of himself. Then he thought about Linda. After a time, maybe he would have something to offer her. He would work hard and save his money. Time would tell with Linda.

Mike knew she planned to go to college, and he wouldn't stand in her way. He was afraid when she went to college, his worst nightmare would begin. She would probably find a college boy and get married.

Mr. Carson found his wife getting ready for bed. He looked at his wife and thought she was still beautiful for her age.

"Well, I did it. He starts in a week. I want you to teach Mike the books one evening each week, and by summer we should be able to leave the ranch when we want."

"You got two problems, you know?"

"And what would that be?"

"The first one is Linda."

"I think Mike and Linda will work that one out."

"The second one is the men."

"And why is that?"

"He will be the youngest man on the ranch, and do you think the other men will take orders from an eighteen-year-old?"

"He will be nineteen shortly after school is out."

"He is still very young."

"I think the men will follow Mike. They respect his skill with horses, and this is a horse ranch."

"You really think he can do it?"

"Yes, fence repair and feeding. The men know what has to be done, so all he has to give orders on is the horses. He knows more about horses than I do."

"What about Linda?"

"I think she likes the young man more than she wants to admit to herself. They can work it out. Right, Mrs. Carson?"

"If you say so, but why don't you come to bed, and we will talk about it?"

Mr. Carson closed the bedroom door and turned around. Mrs. Carson slipped off her robe and lay down on her back, bending her knees, spreading her legs, and giving her husband a slow coaxing smile.

"Lady, I like the way you talk." He quickly removed his clothes, turned out the lights, jumped in bed between her legs, and made a perfect coupling. Lucy giggled like a schoolgirl. They were a little loud in their lovemaking.

Linda was not asleep and heard her mom and dad making love. She smiled and dreamed of Mike and the time they made love in the hayloft. It made her nipples become hard and her body hot. She drifted off to sleep in a dreamworld.

Mike gave Mr. Jones a week's notice that he was quitting. He thanked him for giving him a job when he needed one.

"Mike, I'm glad you got the job at the ranch. You deserved it."

"Thank you, and I'll still be coming to the movies. If you get in a bind, just call me, and I will help you out."

"I wish you all the luck in your new job."

"Thanks, I will need it."

"I heard talk from some of my customers that you are a natural with horses."

"I do enjoy working with them."

"They say you talk to horses, and they do what you want them to do."

"It's because I was raised with horses."

"Well, good luck again."

The following week, Mike started full-time at the ranch. Mrs. Carson told Mike that every Friday evening they would do the books for the week.

Mike was to help her and learn the ranch operation. He learned fast and soon was doing them without her help. Mr. Carson was letting Mike make more and more decisions about running the ranch. Mr. Carson referred to Mike as his ranch adviser. The men liked Mike and came to him with their problems.

Mike loved his work and worked hard. He stayed clear of Linda and decided if she wanted anything to happen between them, it would be up to her to start it. Linda stayed clear of Mike as much as possible, but when she saw him working the horses, or doing the books with her mother, and working with the ranch hands, it always had the same effect on her. Her body became hot and her nipples hard. What was she going to do about that darn country boy? Was it possible she was in love with him?

Linda decided to go out with other boys. Her mother told her it was because he was the first to make love with her. She decided it was time to find out if her mother knew what she was talking about.

Mike spent a lot of time with Lightning since it made him feel close to Linda. He knew she loved the horse very much. He wished she loved him as much as the horse. He was a little jealous of Lightning. Linda watched Mike spending time with Lightning and wondered what he talked to the horse about. Was it about her?

He started teaching Lightning tricks. Lightning was learning voice command. Mike could talk to him like a person. He opened the gate and gave a command.

"Lightning, come over here." He came to Mike.

"Now stay, Lightning," and he did.

"Go back to the corral," and he did.

"Lightning, come back," and he did.

Mike touched his knee. "Now bow to the lady."

He couldn't believe how easy it was to teach Lightning, what he wanted him to do. He was one smart horse. "Pay close attention. You are going to play dead." Mike lay on the ground and played dead. Lightning stared at him.

"Now it's your turn. Play dead." Believe it or not, Lightning fell over dead.

"Good boy. Now we need a grand exit. Up, up on your hind legs."

Mike made a new latch for the corral and taught Lightning how to go in and out without any help. He couldn't come out until Mike gave the command.

Mr. Carson called Mike into his study one evening to talk. He had an idea, and he wanted to run it by Mike.

"Mike, what do you think about starting a full-time stud service?"

"It sounds good to me. We could pick up some extra income from the local ranchers."

Mr. Carson watched Mike for a reaction. He could tell when Mike had something on his mind. "OK, but what else are you thinking? Out with it."

"Sir, we could set up half the barn with stalls and an exercise corral next to the barn. We could board the mares all the time until the foal comes. Some people would probably like that and pay money for the service. We could keep the mare until we are sure she is with fold or longer."

Mr. Carson paced the floor, thinking. "OK, we'll do it. I'll also get a vet we can depend on when we need him."

"Yes, sir, we'll need a good vet. Some of our horses will be very valuable."

"I want you to go to horse sales and buy us two more studs. I want to be able for us to service any breed of mare."

"I'll get started on the drawings for the barn and corral tomorrow as soon as I finish with the horses."

"I think I'm going to like this project," said Mr. Carson.

Linda was getting out of her car as Mike came out the front door. "Hi," said Linda. "Hi, Mike. How have you been?"

"Just working, but I like working on the ranch."

"Dad told me you were full-time now."

Linda started toward Lightning's corral. She missed him and wanted to put her arms around his neck.

"You don't have to go to his corral. Just call him, and he will come to you."

Linda stared at Mike with a frown on her face. "Just call him?"

"Yes, call him."

"Come here, Lightning. Come here, boy."

She watched Lightning unlatch the corral gate and come running up to her. She petted him and stared at Mike.

"I suppose he can put himself back into his corral?"

"As a matter of fact, he can."

Lightning nibbled at Mike's shirtsleeve, trying to get his attention. Mike put his arm around his neck and petted him.

"Good boy." He whispered something in Lightning's ear and moved away.

Lightning suddenly started to stagger and fell over on his side. He moaned as if in great pain and rolled big sad eyes up at Linda. She screamed and fell down beside him.

"What's wrong, boy? What's wrong?"

Linda looked up at Mike, and he had a big grin on his face. She knew she had been had. She slowly got up and turned back to Lightning.

"Get up, you big fake, and go to your corral!"

Lightning got up and ran back to his corral, pulling the gate closed behind him. Linda turned back to Mike, but he was already in his car and waving bye to her.

"You come back here, you hear? Just you wait! I'll get even!"

Mike drove off, and Linda smiled. It had been funny, but she would still get even with him. At least she wouldn't have to go to the corral to see Lightning. All she had to do was call, and he would come to her. She liked that, and he did it for her.

She knew he still cared for her. Her body was getting warm, and her nipples became hard. He still had an effect on her.

Linda looked down at the corral. "Lightning, come here."

Lightning unlatched his gate and ran back to her. She would like to know what else Mike had taught him.

Linda stared at Lightning. "What else did Mike teach you?"

It was like he couldn't wait to show off for Linda. Lightning bowed with his head down like a gentleman. Linda giggled.

"What else has he taught you?"

Lightning lay down on his side and looked at her. He let out a loud whinny. He was trying to tell her something.

"I'm thinking, I'm thinking. Now I remember." She had seen Mike with another horse, the palomino. She went over and put her leg across Lightning's back. Lightning stood up to his feet.

"Good boy. You are one smart horse." He tossed his head up and down.

Linda petted him. "Now go back to your corral."

By the end of the week, Mike and the men had half of the large barn set up for stud service and boarding service for the mares. They also built an exercise corral beside the barn. Mike was in charge of the construction.

Mr. Carson came by and picked Mike up to help him with the signs. They put a large sign at the entrance to the ranch and a couple more along the road. They also put signs on the ranch trucks. When they finished, Mr. Carson handed Mike a set of keys.

"Those are the keys to the blue pickup. It will be your pickup to drive from now on."

"Mr. Carson, I couldn't take your pickup."

"Sure you can, and you will be advertising for the ranch."

"Yes, sir, I guess if you put it that way."

"Put your car in one of the garage spaces and drive the pickup."

Mike drove his car into the garage. "Thank you again."

"There is a key to the gas pump on your key ring."

Mike didn't know what to say. He wouldn't have to buy gas anymore. That was a big bonus. He had a new Ford pickup to drive. He thanked Mr. Carson again.

"Don't worry. You will earn it when we start rolling."

It didn't take long for word to get around. And start rolling they did. It wasn't long before almost all the stalls were full of mares with foals.

At first kids at school ribbed Mike about the "Stud Service" sign on his truck, but later on, the ranch kids wanted to know about the stud service, because some of them had mares of their own and wanted to breed them. He signed up several of the kids to have their mares bred.

The FFA wanted Mike to give a lecture on raising horses. He also told them about the stud service. Word had got around how good he was with horses. The boys and girls hung on to every word he said. They wanted to train their horses. Mike was asked to visit some of the ranches and give them pointers. They couldn't believe how easy their horses took to Mike and soon did what he wanted them to do.

Linda decided to date other boys. Her first date was with the banker's son. All he talked about was his daddy's money and his new sports car, trying to impress her. By the time he brought her home and tried to kiss her good night, she was ready to scream. They didn't have anything in common.

Next, Linda went out with the captain of the football team. All he talked about was football and tried to impress her with his body. She was the envy of all the girls at school. So why didn't she feel happy? When he kissed her, nothing happened. Her body didn't respond to him at all.

Finally, Linda went out with a very rich one. He was good looking and rich, a good combination in any standards. Her mother was as happy as a cat with a warm bowl of milk. She helped Linda dress for her date.

"You are lucky to go out with a boy like Jerry."

Linda went out with Jerry, and it didn't take long for her to realize how repulsive he could be. He thought he was God's gift to women and expected her to fall all over him. She fought off Jerry's roving hands all night. When he brought her home, he stopped a long distance from the house. She had a feeling she was going to have trouble with him.

"I always get what I want, and right now I want you."

Jerry pinned her against the car door and ran his hand up her dress, trying to get his hand inside her panties.

"I like a girl with fight in her. It makes it better when I stick it to her."

"Let go of me, Jerry! You are disgusting!"

"You won't feel that way when I get it in you."

He pulled one of her hands down to feel his manhood through his pants. Suddenly the car was rocked by something. Linda looked up at Lightning standing beside the car.

"Help me, Lightning, help me!"

Lightning let out a loud whinny. He stood up on his hind legs and brought his hoofs crashing down on the hood of Jerry's car.

"What the hell is going on?" screamed Jerry.

"My protector is here to save me."

Linda opened her door and jumped out as Lightning came crashing down on the hood of the car again.

"Thanks for a lovely date!" Linda giggled.

"You'll pay for this, you bitch!"

"I don't think so. Slam him again, Lightning."

Jerry spun out before Lightning could tag his car again. Lightning chased the car down the driveway like a guard dog. Then he turned around and came back to Linda.

Linda petted Lightning and walked him back to his corral. "Thank you, boy, for your help. I'm not sure I could have fought him off."

Lightning had done a real job on Jerry's car. She could see him trying to explain the hoofprints on the hood of his car tomorrow at school. Linda was sure he would bad-mouth her. He would probably put out word that she was a cold fish or a cold bitch. She didn't care. She went into the house to find her mother waiting for a report.

"Well, dear, how was your date with Jerry?"

"Please don't ask."

"Was it that bad, dear?"

"Yes, Mom, he was disgusting."

"Well, from now on I will stay out of your social life. I'm sorry if I caused you any trouble or pain."

"Now I know for sure who I want to be with, but he doesn't give me the time of day. All he does is work on the ranch and stay clear of me."

"Honey, your dad said he stays clear because he doesn't think he is good enough for you with us being rich."

"Mom, I think I care for him very much, but I want to go to college. What can I do?"

"Have both."

"But how can I have both?"

"I'm sure if you want him and college bad enough, you will find a way to work it out."

"It's so hard. I want to go to college, but I don't want to leave Mike. What if he finds another girl while I'm away?"

"What if you find a boy?"

"I don't want one."

"I don't think Mike wants another one either. I'm going to bed and let you think about it. I'm beginning to like Mike myself."

"But you said he was just a country boy."

"I think your father is changing my mind. He thinks he will make a great rancher and horse trainer. I'm beginning to believe him. Mike is very smart."

"But he is still a poor country boy."

"He is saving every penny he makes, and I think Mike is trying to amount to something."

Linda lay in bed thinking about Mike and college. Her mother said she could have both. She was determined to have both. She was afraid if she went to college, Mike would get tired of waiting and find someone else. She finally drifted off to sleep.

Mike lay in bed thinking about Linda. She had been dating other men, but he hoped someday she would see how much he loved her and feel the same way about him. He couldn't offer her any of the things they could. He could only offer her his love. He had to face the facts. He was just an old country boy.

He realized he loved Linda very much, but it looks like it was a one-way street. He didn't sleep well that night with Linda on his mind.

The next day, Linda had formed a plan to trap Mike. She would start off by teasing him until the right moment came along to express her love for him.

Her dad had been right about Mike. He wasn't just an old country boy. Her body trembled when she remembered the time they had made love in the hayloft. She was glad she had gone out with other men, and now she knew that she was in love with Mike.

"I'm in love with Mike. There, I said it, and it feels so good."

She wanted to go to college, but she had her priorities straight. Mike would come first, and then she would solve her college problem.

Linda came home from school and decided to start her plan for teasing Mike. She changed into a pair of shorts and a long white shirt. She tied the tail of the shirt in a knot, resting just below her breasts. She started not to wear a bra but changed her mind and put on a skimpy uplift bra. She looked in the mirror and saw a lot of skin. Was she asking for it? Yes, she was, she realized. She was hot all over.

She brushed her hair for a long time until it hung in waves. She watched herself in the mirror as the hair flowed around her face. She touched her nipples, and they became hard just thinking about Mike. Was she ready for this?

Her mother came into the room. "I see you have been thinking about what I said. What are you going to do?"

"Flirt with him until he can't stand it."

"What if he wants to do more than flirt?"

"I don't know. I haven't thought that far ahead."

"You better, young lady. You may catch a tiger by the tail and not know what to do with it."

Her mother left the room, and she decided to go all the way. She unbuttoned her shirt down to the knot and applied some fresh makeup.

Linda parked her car next to where Mike usually parked when he came to work at the ranch. She broke out the things needed to clean and wash her car. Then she hooked up the water hose. She started to work on her car while she waited for Mike to arrive.

When Mike arrived for work, Linda was busy cleaning the inside of her car. She had her rear end in the air, and her shorts were stretched tight across her bottom. Her shorts were riding up and showing a lot of skin. Mike got out of the pickup, watching the most breathtaking view. He wanted to just stand there and watch her, but that would be impolite to stare.

Linda could feel Mike's eyes on her as she turned to face him. Her body knew he was staring at her, and it became hot.

"Hi, Mike, did you like the view?"

"Yes, very much." His face turned red, and he headed for the barn.

"What's your hurry? You can help me wash my car," she teased.

"I got to check on a mare that is due and having trouble. The vet checked her and told us to keep a close eye on her."

Linda followed Mike into the barn and watched from a distance while he checked the mare with the foal. She could see concern in his eyes as he continued to check the mare.

"What's wrong with her?"

"I'm not sure, but I think she is about to have it. She seems to be in great pain."

"What can we do?"

"I don't know yet, but something is wrong."

Linda stroked the mare's neck. "What's wrong with you?"

"She doesn't talk, but I wish she could tell us what is wrong."

"Mike, you talk to the horses all the time and seem to know what they are saying."

"Well, this time I don't know."

"She isn't too steady on her feet. Shouldn't she lie down?"

"Probably, if I can get her to."

"Linda, call the vet quick. I think she is going to have problems having it."

"I'll be right back."

Linda ran for the phone. Mike watched her run away. He still liked the view.

"Come on, girl, lie down."

When Linda returned, the mare was lying down, and Mike had his arm inside the mare. Linda couldn't believe what Mike was doing.

"Hold her head and talk to her."

"I couldn't get the vet. He hasn't got home from his office yet. Now what do we do?"

"We can't wait. You have got to help me."

"What's wrong with her?"

"The colt's leg is twisted, and I can't get it straight. Talk to the mare and keep her calm."

Linda talked to the mare, while Mike worked frantically to get the colt's leg straight. Sweat ran down Mike's face as he glanced at Linda. He must be dreaming, because he thought he saw desire and love in her eyes. Mike had always watched a person's eyes, because the mouth may lie, but the eyes don't lie.

Finally, he got the leg straight, and he sat back to watch while the mare had her colt. She would have a normal birth now that the leg was straight.

"Oh, Mike, it is pure white like Lightning. Isn't it darling?"

"Yes, but your father will be furious, because it was to be a palomino colt. He already had it sold for a show horse."

"I'm going to get Daddy so he can see it. I'll be right back."

They returned just as Mike had the colt on his feet. It fell a couple times, but finally it could stand on his feet. Mr. Carson looked the colt over.

"Well, that's not what I wanted, but it is a fine-looking colt, and I can sell it."

"Sir, could I buy him? I would like to have my own horse again. You can take some out of my paycheck each week until he is paid for."

"Mike, you can have him as a gift from me."

"Sir, I had rather pay for him."

"I understand. I'll sell him to you at a fair price."

"Dad, now Lightning will have another horse just like him."

"They may not get along since they are both studs."

"I think they will."

"I hope you are right, or we will always have to keep them apart."

"Mike, we have a matched pair now." She gave him a sweet smile.

"They will look beautiful running together."

Linda was impressed that Mike wouldn't take the colt without paying for it, but she already knew he wouldn't. She liked a man who stood on his own two feet, and someday she would stand beside him. He just didn't know it yet.

She turned to him and smiled.

"What?"

She pecked him on the cheek. "We worked as a team together. Didn't we, Dad?"

"Yes, you did. If you hadn't known what to do, the mare would have died taking the colt with her. Linda told me how you helped the mare. I still wish you would take the colt, but I know you won't."

"Thank you for selling me the colt."

Linda put her hand on Mike's arm. "What are you going to name him?"

"I don't know. I didn't know I was going to get another horse."

"Why don't you name him Thunder? It would be a match for Lightning."

"Sounds good to me. Thunder it is."

Mike glanced at Linda. Could it be she did care for him? Did he see desire and love in her eyes? It was too much to hope for, but he always thought he could read a person's eyes. Maybe he was seeing what he wanted to see, not what was really there, like his mother liked to tell things the way she wanted to hear them. Just maybe he was doing the same thing.

"The mother and her colt are doing fine, so how about staying for supper?"

"Yes, sir, I would like to."

"Good, you two get washed up so my wife will let you come to the table."

Taking Mike's hand, Linda said, "Come on, I'll show you where the bathroom is."

Mr. Carson watched in amusement as Linda led Mike inside the house. He wanted the two of them to get together. Maybe this was a start.

Linda led Mike into the bathroom and stood beside him at the sink. Their legs were touching, and the sparks were flying.

"I'm going to watch you wash your hands to be sure they are clean," teased Linda.

"And who is going to watch you?"

Linda smiled at him. "You can if you want to."

"Are you flirting with me?"

"Yes, I am."

Mr. Carson followed them into the house. He could hear them talking and hoped they would get together. He had big plans for Mike when the ranch became larger. He wanted him to have a part of the ranch when he was older. He wanted Linda married to him and for them to live on the ranch or close by. Then there would be grandchildren for him to spoil. He went into the dining room.

Mrs. Carson had fixed a good supper. Supper was fried chicken, corn on a cob, mashed potatoes, gravy, English peas, corn bread, and cherry pie with ice cream on top for dessert. Mike ate so much he thought he would pop a button.

"Mike, would you like some more pie?" asked Mrs. Carson.

"No, ma'am, I'm full. I couldn't eat another bite."

"Linda, you didn't eat much."

"Mom, I don't want to get fat."

Mike glanced at Linda. She didn't look fat to him. She was beautiful. "You don't look fat to me."

"That's because I watch what I eat."

Linda had to tell her mother about how they had helped the mare deliver the colt. Mike blushed when she told how she found him when she returned from trying to phone the vet.

"He had his arms up in the mare and tells me to talk to the horse. What do you say to a horse?"

Linda giggled, and her mother burst out laughing. Linda didn't want Mike to leave so soon after supper.

"Mike, do you want to watch television?"

It surprised him. He had never been invited to hang around in the house. He was hired help.

"Yes, that would be great. We don't own a television. The only time I have ever seen one was at a friend's house."

They went into the living room to watch television. Mike sat on the couch, and Linda sat close to him. She could feel the heat from his body, and her body responded by becoming hot. Her nipples became hard. No other man had that effect on her. She was amazed how Mike affected her. Mike couldn't remember what they watched on television. He hated to leave, but it was getting late.

Linda walked Mike to his pickup. She could feel her body respond to being close to him. She wanted him to kiss her, but it was too soon. She didn't want to throw herself at him. Linda wished he wasn't so shy and would make the first move. Mike slid into the driver's seat. He turned and looked into Linda's eyes.

They were staring at each other. She was just out of reach for Mike to touch her. Linda didn't want him to leave without kissing her. Mike looked deep into her eyes. He couldn't be wrong. He saw love and desire in her eyes. If he were wrong, he would make a big fool of himself.

Linda parted her lips and wet them with her tongue. She held her breath. He was going to kiss her. She shouldn't let him, but her body wanted it, and she wouldn't stop him.

Suddenly, Mike pulled her into the car with him. She fell into his arms, and he kissed her until her body melted against him. She opened her mouth to touch his tongue with hers. Her body was on fire, but finally, she pulled away. When she pulled away, it felt like part of her was missing. Why had she pulled away?

"Why did you kiss me?"

"Your eyes said you wanted to be kissed."

"Don't be silly. How could my eyes say anything?"

"Believe me they did. Now tell me the truth. Didn't you want me to kiss you?"

After a long hesitation, she decided to tell the truth. "Yes, I wanted you to kiss me."

"Why did you want me to kiss you?"

"I wanted to see if the old zing was still there like the last time we . . . we—" she blushed, "made love."

"And was the zing still there?"

"Well, sort of," she hedged.

"What do you mean sort of?"

"Yes, it was, but don't get any ideas."

"I won't," said Mike as he pulled her into his arms again and kissed her lightly.

"Good night and sweet dreams." He eased her out of the truck, closed the door, and drove off.

It weren't to go down that way. *Why did I let him do what he wanted to do?*

She stared at the taillights on his pickup. She had lost control of the situation. She thought she would be in control. *What had happened?*

Linda stood there mad but couldn't figure out why. She was kissed and lost control. Maybe that was the reason she was mad. She wanted to take things slow and be in control, or just maybe she didn't want him to stop. The thought made her body clamoring for release. She slowly made her way back into the house. She decided she would have to take a cold shower to cool down.

Mike lay in bed staring at the ceiling. He was going over in his mind what had happened. He had seen love and desire in Linda's eyes, so why was she holding back? He guessed because he was still just an old country boy. He didn't have anything but love to offer her. He had to get his life on track so he could ask Linda to share his life with him.

Then he remembered a small plot of land next to the Carson Ranch for sale. He decided he would look at it tomorrow. He had to start someplace. With that on his mind, he dozed off to sleep.

The next day after school, Mike stopped to look at the land on his way to the ranch. It was only ten acres, but he had to start someplace.

School would be out soon, and most of the kids would move off, or go to college. The rest would find jobs. Most of them would soon be married and start a family. There just weren't many jobs in a small town. Some would take over the family business. He had to get something started. He didn't want to be a ranch hand all his life.

The land had a spring-fed creek running through the middle of it, with flat land next to the road, high land on the other side of the creek.

There was a perfect place for a house on the high side from the creek, and there was also a small waterfall in front of the house. It just needed the brush cleared away, and it would be perfect.

Mike walked down to the waterfall and watched the clear water flow over the waterfall. It looked inviting to him, and he decided to take a quick dip. He removed his clothes and went skinny-dipping. The water was cold, and he didn't swim very long. It wasn't very big, but it was still nice. The place was beautiful, and he fell in love with it.

He started to daydream. He could see a house with a woman coming out the front door. It was Linda wearing her red shorts and white shirt. She must like that outfit because she wore it so much. He knew she had plenty of clothes to pick from. Her hair was loose and flowing down her back. She saw him and came running over to where he was. Then she was in his arms, and they were kissing.

Mike shook his head and got back in his truck. It was time to go to work. Linda was riding Lightning when Mike arrived for work, and would you believe? She was wearing red short shorts with a white shirt! Her hair was flowing down her back. She stopped next to him.

"Hi, what's going on?"

"I'm giving Lightning a good workout. I just left little Thunder. He is growing like a weed and will be grown before we know it."

"I guess I'll go look in on him before I check the horses."

"By the way, Dad wants you to eat with us tonight. He has something he wants you to do, but I don't know what it is."

"OK, guess I had better get to work. I'll see you at supper."

Mike walked into the stall with little Thunder and petted him while talking to him in a soft low voice.

"You're going to be something when you grow up. Well, I got to get to work."

Mike worked hard to get all his work done. Linda watched him complete each task and couldn't get enough of him. She would like to throw herself in his arms and demand he kiss her now. It was a good dream anyway. She was at the door watching him coming to the house for supper. He looked tired.

"Mike, wash your hands. Millie will be serving supper in a few minutes."

Mike stared at her, and she blushed. She was so beautiful he couldn't keep his eyes off her.

"Now go get washed up."

"Yes, ma'am."

Linda giggled at his good manners. "Hurry up."

When Mike returned to the dining room, everyone was seated. He took the chair across from Linda. She smiled at him.

"Everybody, dig in, and you men can talk business later," said Mrs. Carson.

Linda and Mike glanced at each other all through supper. The conversation was light through the meal. Linda glanced at Mike. *Darn Mike,* thought Linda, *for having such an effect on me!* She wanted to be in control. But every time he was near, her body had a mind of its own. It made her mad that she couldn't control her own body. She was hot all over, and her nipples were hard, straining at her bra to be free.

Their legs touched under the table, and she thought she would go up in flames. She looked at Mike, and he blushed. She smiled and realized he was having the same problem. She ran her foot up his leg close to his manhood, which was hard.

Mike was nervous and afraid he would knock something over or drop something. He would be glad when supper was finished. Linda was driving him crazy. He thought he could feel the heat from her, from across the table, but that was stupid, or was it? Then why was he burning up with the air condition running?

A couple of minutes later, Linda knocked over her tea. She looked at Mike and turned red. She felt so stupid. Millie came and cleaned up the mess.

She looked at Linda and laughed. "You haven't done that since you were five years old."

She was embarrassed and wouldn't look at Mike. Mrs. Carson watched Linda and smiled. The girl was trying to make an impression on Mike. Well, she did.

After supper was over, Mr. Carson turned to Mike. "I want you to take a trip to Oklahoma this weekend and deliver the new palomino colt and his mother. Mr. Wilder can't make it down to pick them up, and I told him we would deliver them. Saturday is his son's birthday, and the colt is his birthday present. We want to get them there in time for his birthday."

"No problem, sir. I would be glad to go."

"Are you sure about it? Because if you have something planned for this weekend, I can send one of the other men."

"It's just fine. I'll go for you. I have never been to Oklahoma, and it would be fun to go."

"Good. I wanted to send you because the horses won't be any trouble with you handling them."

"Where in Oklahoma will I be taking them?"

"It is on the south side of Oklahoma City."

"Will it be hard to find?"

"No, it is a huge ranch. Anybody can tell you where it is."

"Great."

"They said you could spend the night and look the ranch over. I think you will enjoy the trip."

"It sounds like fun."

"The ranch you are taking the horses to is called the Triple W Ranch. William Wayne Wilder owns a whole valley, and the ranch is in the middle of it. He owns the land as far as the eye can see. They shoot Western movies on the ranch from time to time. The movie company built a small Western town on the ranch for shooting movies."

Linda had been eavesdropping. "Dad, may I go to Oklahoma with Mike?"

He raised an eyebrow. "What for?"

"I want to see the ranch and then go to Oklahoma City to see Grandma."

"I don't know."

"We can spend the night there and start back Sunday morning. Please, Daddy, let me go. I want to see Grandma." What she didn't tell him was she wanted to be alone with Mike.

Mr. Carson looked at Linda and then at Mike. "OK, only if Mike doesn't mind putting up with you."

Linda gave Mike a sweet smile. "It's OK by me if she wants to come, and she can help with the horses."

How could he refuse with her looking at him like that? Not that he wanted to anyway. Mike was overjoyed that she wanted to come.

"OK, you can go with Mike."

"Thank you, Daddy." She tried to hide her excitement about going.

"Take the large blue-covered trailer. I want the horses to have plenty of room. It's a long trip. If you leave at six, you should arrive in plenty of time. The birthday party is at four."

"We will be there on time, sir."

Mr. Carson gave him a gas card and some money for the trip. He gave him a map with the ranch circled on it.

"I'm going to pack. See you in the morning, Mike."

"Is there anything you need for the trip?"

"I can't think of anything."

"Good, I'll see you in the morning."

"Good night, sir."

That night, Mike tossed and turned in his bed. All he could think about was being alone with Linda on the long trip. He didn't want to make a fool of himself, but with Linda around, it was easy to do. He asked himself, *Was she just going to see the ranch and her grandmother?*

# Chapter 7

Mike hoped she wanted to be alone with him. *Did she or didn't she?* That was the sixty-four-thousand-dollar question.

By six the next morning, Mike had the trailer connected to his pickup, the horses loaded, some feed and water in the trailer, and the rig parked in front of the house waiting for Linda.

At ten past six, Linda came running out the front door with a small traveling bag. She was dressed in jeans, boots, and a Western shirt. Her hair was flowing down her back. Mike loved her long hair and wanted to run his fingers through it.

"Well, am I on time?"

"Close enough."

Mike got out and went around and opened the door for her. She got in, and he closed the door.

"Thank you, kind sir." Linda giggled. This was going to be fun.

Mike turned the key, and the pickup engine roared to life. He put it in the gear, and away they went.

"Do you know how to read a map?" asked Mike as he pulled out onto the highway and headed north.

"Some, but I'm not very good at it. I would probably get lost if I didn't have you with me."

Linda smiled at him, and his heart did a flip. He handed her the map to keep them on the right course.

"I have the trip marked all the way, so just follow the line I have marked beside each highway."

She studied the map. "I think I can keep us on the right highway."

She gave Mike another heart-stopping smile. His heart was skipping a beat now and then after that.

"Do you think we will make it there on time?"

"I don't see any problem."

"We sure left early."

Linda looked like she was sleepy, but she still looked beautiful to him. He couldn't get enough of watching her.

"We're making good time. You don't even know the trailer is back there."

Linda was silent for a long time. Finally, she stirred and said in a rather low voice, "Do you mind if I doze off? I didn't get my nap out."

"Sure, go ahead. I won't need you for until later to read the map."

She lay her head back against the seat and in a couple of minutes was fast asleep. Apparently, she wasn't an early riser. Mike tried to keep his eyes on the road, but with a beautiful girl next to him, how could he? Mike watched her breasts rise and fall, while here nipples strained at the material on her front. He thought he would go crazy.

Later on, Linda slowly slipped down in the seat until her head was resting on his lap. She lay her hand on his inner thigh. She was still asleep.

Mike tried to remain calm, but with her head resting on his private, how could he? His heart was beating out of control, and something else was out of control.

"What am I doing like this?" murmured Linda.

She slowly woke up. Her head was resting on something hard, and when she realized what it was, a shock wave went through her body. She sat up quickly, turning her head to look out her side window.

"You fell asleep and slid down in the seat."

"Why didn't you wake me?"

"You looked so contented lying there I didn't want to disturb you."

"Well, you should have."

"I will next time."

*I just fell asleep and slid my head down on his . . . Oh, how could I have done such a thing? But I did.* She was dreaming about Mike making love to her and no wonder with her head resting where it was. She wondered if she had talked in her sleep. *Oh god, I hope not!*

"Did I say anything while I was sleeping? I mean, did I talk in my sleep?"

"You said you loved me."

"I did not."

"How do you know? You were asleep with your head resting on—"

"Mike, you are making this up."

"Now would I do that?"

"Yes, I don't trust you."

"I was teasing you. You moved around a little."

"I didn't do anything else?"

"Why? Were you dreaming?"

"Yes."

"What were you dreaming about?"

Linda turned and faced him. She gave him her best smile. "I can't tell you, or it won't come true."

Mike knew she wasn't going to tell him what she was dreaming, but he hoped she was dreaming about him. Linda was having a wonderful dream about her and Mike making love.

"Are you hungry?" asked Mike.

"Just a little. I didn't have time to eat before we left."

Pulling into a Dairy Queen in Athens, Mike asked, "Would you like to eat here or take it to a roadside park?"

"We can get some food and take it with us. That way we can stop and eat while we feed the horses. Then we can walk them around."

"Good idea. I'll get the food. What do you want to eat?"

"No, you won't. Dad gave us expense money to pay for everything."

Linda was out of the truck and gone. A few minutes, she returned with a large paper bag.

"Did you get enough to feed an army?"

"Almost, drive on. I want to find a park in a hurry because I'm so hungry after smelling the food that I could eat a bear, raw."

A few miles out of Athens, they found a roadside park. "This is nice," said Linda.

Mike parked the pickup, and Linda bailed out with the food. She carried it over to a table. Mike hurried over to the table. Linda opened the sack of food between them.

"Why? Hamburgers and hot dogs?"

"I told you I was hungry."

"You said a little hungry. What do you get if you are hungry?"

"I get two hamburgers, one hot dog, one large order of fries, and a large Coke later. Now I'm so full I can't move," complained Linda.

"Sit still while I walk the horses."

"You got it. I don't think I can walk anyway."

Linda decided to get out and watch. Mike opened the tailgate to the trailer. "OK, girl, come on out."

The mother backed out and came to stand in front of Mike. The colt hesitated a moment before coming out to join his mother. After he was out, he ran around Mike and his mother, kicking up his heels, playful like a child.

Mike pointed beside himself and said, "Come on, girl, let's go for a walk."

The mother walked up until her head was at Mike's side and walked with him. Linda watched, and she was amazed at Mike's ability with horses. The mare had only been at the ranch to have her colt, and she did what Mike wanted her to do. He made everything to do with horses look easy.

After the walk, Mike stopped in back of the trailer and petted the mother. He put some feed in a bag and hung it in front of the trailer. He pointed into the trailer.

"OK, girl, back into the trailer."

The mother stepped up into the trailer, and Mike stepped back to allow the colt to follow his mother. He closed the trailer gate and went back to the truck.

"That was easy. She is a smart horse."

"How long does it take to train a horse to follow your instructions?"

"It depends on the horse."

"How is that?"

"Each horse is different just like people."

"Like people?"

"Some are smart and catch on fast while others are slow to catch on. Some it takes a long time to train."

"You make it look so easy."

"Horses like to be loved and given praise. In turn, they will try to please you."

"You mean like a dog?"

"Yes, the same thing. Dogs try to please their master."

"How about cats? Is it the same way?"

"No, people pick dogs for their friend while cats pick people."

"What do you mean?"

"A cat picks his own master. If he doesn't like the home he is in, he will hunt a new home and master."

"Have you ever thought about training horses for a living?"

"Yes, I have, but it takes money and land. I don't have either one."

"You will come up with the money somehow."

"I am saving for a down payment on a small piece of land next to your ranch. I hope to get it when we get back home. I need one more week's pay, and I can swing it, but I'll need someone to cosign for me."

"I'll take Dad into signing for you."

"Thank you. He won't be sorry. I'll make my payments somehow."

"I see Dallas in the distance," said Linda.

"So do I. I guess we didn't get lost so far."

"Where do we pick up the highway to Oklahoma?"

"Would you get the map out and find where we pick up Highway 77 to Denton? I think we pick it up somewhere downtown."

"Here it is. I see it on the map."

"OK, here we go. Navigate us through Dallas."

An hour later, they were through Dallas and on their way to Denton. Mike was sure glad to be out of Dallas. It was too much traffic for an old country boy.

"I got us through Dallas without getting lost. Can you believe it? This is the first time I have had to use a map," explained Linda.

"You were great. I think we'll drive until we cross the Red River before we stop again."

"That sounds good to me."

The Red River lived up to its name, because it was blood red. They crossed the bridge into Oklahoma. After stopping for a few minutes to watch the river, they continued on their trip.

Linda watched Mike as he drove and realized one thing. She would always be by his side. He just didn't know it yet. She would let him chase her until she caught him. She smiled and couldn't help but giggle.

Mike wondered what she was thinking. He could read horses, but when it came to women, he didn't have a clue.

"Linda, I'll give you a penny for your thoughts."

"Sorry, I was daydreaming."

"It must have been good, since you were giggling."

"It was good."

"But you won't tell me?"

"Right, you are. Where are we now?"

"We aren't too far from Turner Falls. I thought we would stop there and sightsee. They say it is real pretty, with mountains and a waterfall. I haven't been there, but I saw it in a travel guide on what to see in Oklahoma."

Linda watched as Mike drove. He made her body have hot flashes. She played back each moment of the time they made love in the hayloft. It was nice to daydream, because it was your dream and you could dream it the way you wanted it.

Right now she wished they could pull over and make love, so she dreamed it that way. Her nipples became hard as rocks and strained to get free of her bra. She decided to try to control her thoughts, or she would be a basket case.

"Are you feeling all right? Your face is flushed."

"No, I'm just tired of traveling," she lied.

"You look like you might have fever."

"Well, I don't. How much further to Turner Falls so we can stop?"

"Maybe a couple of miles, I think."

A sign read "One mile to Turner Falls," letting them know they were close. The highway was narrow with a lot of curves as it descended down into the valley. They could see the falls in the distance. At the bottom they stopped at a small paved area for travelers to see the falls up close.

As they got out of the truck, Linda grabbed Mike's hand and pulled him toward the waterfall.

"Let's get closer to the waterfall."

They ran closer to the waterfall like a couple kids. They pulled off their shoes and waded in the water. It was cold, and they came out putting their shoes back on.

"That water sure is cold," said Linda.

"Do you want to go swimming?"

"You got to be out of your mind."

"It wouldn't be the first time."

They faced each other. "Mike, this is beautiful and so romantic. Wouldn't it be fun to explore?"

"Yes, explore." He was staring at her.

"I don't think we are talking about the same thing."

Slowly as if drifting, she felt Mike's arms around her waist. He was going to kiss her. He pulled her hard against him, molding their bodies together as one, letting her feel his needs. He covered her mouth with his own. Her mouth was sweet and giving as she parted her lips, inviting him in to explore. Clinging together, their passion grew. It felt like they were feeding on each other.

Suddenly a car pulled in beside them and broke the spell. Linda pulled back. Her pulse was beating fast. Her legs felt like rubber, and she wondered if she was going to fall. Mike kept an arm around her waist and walked her around to her side of the truck, helping her into the truck.

"Thanks, I needed that."

"Now who is going to help me back around to the other side of the truck? My legs are about to give out on me."

Linda giggled. "You can fend for yourself."

Back in the driver's seat, Mike looked at his old watch. "We had better get back on the road if we are going to make it on time."

"Mike, how much further until we turn off?"

"Check the map and see."

"We still have a pretty good way to go. Do you want me to drive awhile?"

"I'm OK. Just watch the map so we don't drive past our turnoff."

Clipping along at sixty, they were making good time. They both were lost in their thoughts, glancing at each other from time to time. Linda thought to herself that she was becoming too vulnerable and had to watch her control. Her skin was covered in perspiration, and her stomach was tied in knots. She wanted to tell Mike she loved him, but the words wouldn't come. She wanted him to say it first, so she would wait for it now. Then she remembered that Mike had already told her he loved her, and she had rejected him. She had thought at the time he was just an old country boy, but now she had changed her mind. The old saying was that a girl could always change her mind about anything she wanted to.

"I have changed my mind." Linda didn't realize she had said it out loud.

"What are you talking about?"

"Nothing, honey." She giggled.

"I think I have heard that phrase before."

The closer they got to Oklahoma City, the more crowded the traffic became. Mike had to concentrate on his driving. Maybe for somehow, he could get Linda out of his every thought.

"There's your turnoff."

Linda pointed to a sign on the left side of the road, and Mike made a left turn down a small paved road. They were now on the Triple W Ranch. They followed the road down into a large valley.

"Oh, Mike, isn't it beautiful?"

"Yes, it is. This man must be rich. I mean really rich."

In the middle of the valley stood a huge ranch house, with several large barns and small buildings behind it. Off to the right was a large lake with a dock extending out into the lake, and a boat was tied to the dock. Cattle and horses grazed everywhere.

Off to the left they could see the small Western town constructed for shooting movies. It really got their attention.

"Mike, the town is so cool."

"Looking at it, I wish I lived back in those days."

"Not me. I like my modern things too much."

Mike pulled the rig up in front of the house and killed the engine. Mr. Wilder came out of the house to greet them when they got out of the truck. They exchanged greetings and then turned to walk up to the steps leading to the porch.

"My son is with his friends that came to the birthday party. We have a small problem. He is only ten years old, and I thought a boy on a ranch would want his own horse, but I guess I was wrong. He wanted a scooter. Do you have any suggestions?"

Mike could see the hurt in Mr. Wilder's eyes. He wished he could make it go away. He had to try.

"Maybe I can change his mind about wanting a horse."

"I thought the colt was a perfect gift for him."

"It is. He just doesn't know it yet. If you will give me permission to try something, I'm not sure I can change his mind, but I'm willing to try."

"I'm willing to try anything at this point."

"It may be a little drastic."

"Do it. I'll bring him and his friends outside."

"Linda, I think I just stuck my foot in my mouth."

"Have you been teaching the mare and colt tricks? I know you do that with all the horses."

"Yes, the mare loves to do tricks, but the colt is too young."

"Show the kids some tricks that the mare can do, and maybe he will want the colt."

"OK, what have I got to lose?"

While they waited for Mr. Wilder and the kids to return, they looked around. Mike and Linda watched a group of men and women seated around a table on the porch.

"There sure is a crowd of people on the ranch," remarked Linda.

"Yes, and I wonder who they are."

Mr. Wilder came out the front door with a group of kids. The kids looked like they would rather be someplace else.

"Mike, this is my son William Wayne Jr."

"I'm glad to meet you," replied Mike, extending his hand.

The kid didn't take it.

"Your dad said you don't like horses."

"It's not that I don't like them, but what good is a dumb old horse?"

This kid was a hard nut to crack, but he had to try. He walked to the back of the trailer and opened the tailgate.

"Come on out, girl." The mare backed out of the trailer, and he closed the gate to keep the colt inside.

"Follow me, girl."

He walked out in front of the boy and stopped. The mare stopped beside him. She stood staring at the boy.

"So she followed you. Big deal. She probably wants something to eat."

"Young man, you don't know anything about horses. They are smart when somebody takes time to train them."

"I still had rather have a scooter."

"Wouldn't you like your own horse to ride and train?"

"No, I had rather have a scooter."

The people around the table turned their attention toward what Mike was doing. He was up to something.

Mike looked at Linda, and she shrugged. She didn't want him to give up.

Mike thought, *What's wrong with that kid?* When he was that age, he would have done anything for a palomino colt like that. It was time for something drastic.

"So you think the horse is good for nothing? I guess there is only one thing to do." Mike spoke softly to the mare so nobody else would hear.

"Dead, horse."

Mike looked at her. He thought to himself, *Trixie, don't make a fool out of me.* He walked back over to the truck. The director of the movie group suddenly said, "Everyone shut up and watch. Something exciting is going to happen. I can feel it."

Mike turned around from the truck with a gun in his hand. He pointed it at Trixie and fired twice. She stumbled and fell. She lay on her side, not moving.

"Dad, he shot your horse!" cried Wayne Jr.

Everyone stared at Mike and the horse, too stunned to move. While the film group stared at Mike, the director smiled.

"You don't like the horse or the colt, so I guess you won't care if I shoot the colt also." Mike started toward the back of the trailer.

"Don't you shoot my colt!" screamed Wayne Jr.

"OK, I won't shoot the colt."

He put the gun in his belt and walked briskly over to Trixie. He nudged her with his foot.

"Time to get up, you ham actor."

Trixie raised her head and looked at him, as if to say, "Do I have to?"

She started to rise. Mike slid his leg across her back, and when she stood up, he was on her back.

Mike whispered softly, pulling back on her mane, "Up, Trixie." She stood up on her hind legs and pawed the air.

The crowd went wild clapping for them. Mike was controlling the mare by voice command that nobody could here. The director was watching Mike very closely. He had never seen anything like it. He had many horses trained for his movies, but they usually had trouble with them while shooting the movies. The horse made the scene so real that at first he thought Mike had really shot the horse. Then he looked for blood and didn't see any.

"Drop down, Trixie." Mike walked her over in front of Wayne Jr. He touched her on the left shoulder.

"Take a bow."

Trixie took a bow, and Mike slid off her back and took a bow with her. Everyone clapped and cheered for them. Mike and Trixie took another bow. Mr. Wilder looked at Mike and smiled. His horse didn't do tricks when he left the ranch.

"Could my colt do tricks like that?"

"Yes, you can teach him many tricks. You can ride him, go swimming together, hunting together, or just be your friend."

"Oh boy! Will you teach me how to train him?"

"I'll get you started off on the right foot, but you have to trust him, love him, and have a lot of patience while training him."

"I will, I promise."

"That's good enough for me. Let me fetch your colt."

Mike walked back to the trailer while Trixie followed him. Linda held the gate while Mike went into the trailer. He snapped a short rope with a snap on both ends to the colt's halter and led him out of the trailer next to his mother. He snapped the other snap to his mother's halter.

"Trixie, take your colt to his new master."

The mother led her colt over to Wayne Jr. and stopped. They stared at him, and he stared back at them.

"Wayne, raise your hand slowly and pet him. Start to make friends. Good, now slowly unsnap him from his mother."

"Like this?"

"That's good. Trixie, back slowly out and come over here."

She came and stood by Mike, watching her colt.

"OK, Wayne, you can take the colt to the barn and feed him."

Wayne looked at his dad. "Thank you. It's the best gift I have ever received."

Wayne took his colt and led him toward one of the many barns, followed by his friends. They would want a horse now.

Mike put his arms around Trixie's neck and hugged her. "I'm going to miss you, girl. You have been fun to work with."

Linda put her arms around Trixie also. She saw Trixie's big sad eyes. *This horse loves Mike like I do.* She looked at Mike, and he was sad also.

"OK, on your way. Follow your colt."

That was the last command Mike ever gave her. Mr. Wilder rushed over to Mike. "How can I ever thank you enough for what you have done? You have made my son and me very happy."

"I'm just glad that I could do it, but the thanks went to Trixie. She is one smart horse."

"She sure is."

"She loves attention. Please don't let her talent go to waste."

"It won't, because from now on, she will be my horse to ride."

"She is also trained to obey grounded reins. You want have to tether her each time you stop and want to leave her. Drop the reins on the ground and say stay. She will stay as if you tied her."

"Good, I guess I should ask, is there anything she doesn't do?"

"Like I said, she is one smart horse."

"You two come on in and get something to eat while I introduce you to my wife."

Mike and Linda followed Mr. Wilder up the steps and into the house. Mr. Wilder's wife was white and Indian. Linda loved her long black hair. She was shy, but she and Linda hit it off from the start.

Mr. Wilder and Mike talked horses. They talked about the movie company using his land to shoot films. They were starting another movie production. His land was perfect for shooting a Western. Linda and Mrs. Wilder eased off into the kitchen for some girl talk.

"Would you like something to drink?"

"Iced tea would be fine, if you have some already made."

Mrs. Wilder fixed two large glasses, and they sat at a large wooden table. Linda told her about the ranch she lived on and about her family and friends. She told her about Lightning and little Thunder. Linda even told her about her and Mike helping the mare to deliver her colt. She told her Mike worked on the ranch.

Mrs. Wilder told Linda how she met Mr. Wilder. They played together when they were kids. She was still living with her tribe. Mr. Wilder was a blood brother to her brother. They spent a lot of time together. He didn't notice her until she was sixteen. They were married when she turned eighteen.

"You are in love with the young man."

"Is it that obvious?"

"I see it in your eyes, and if you look closely, you will see that the young man loves you too. The eyes don't lie."

"I think I heard that before. He told me that one time."

"Have you told him how much you love him?"

"No, but—"

"Don't wait too long to tell him, or you might lose him to someone else."

Mr. Wilder and Mike came in and joined them at the table. "I was telling Mike that you should spend the night and go on to the city in the morning. We are having a big feed and dance tonight. How about it? Would you like to stay for the dance?"

Linda glanced at Mike. "Would you like to stay? It sounds like fun."

"I'm for it if you are, but what about your folks?"

"I'll call Dad and tell him about our change in plans."

"Linda, there's a phone on the wall you can use."

"Honey, then show these young people to their rooms. They will probably want to rest and freshen up before tonight."

"Yes, dear."

After Linda phoned her dad, Mr. Wilder showed them to their rooms. The house was as big as a hotel. Mike's room was across the hall from Linda.

"Why don't you take a shower and then take a nap?" suggested Mike. "I'll wake you later."

"I am tired from the trip. What are you going to do?"

"I'm going down to the barn with Wayne Jr. I promised to teach him how to get started training his colt. I'll wake you in time for the shindig."

Linda stood on tiptoes and kissed Mike lightly on the lips. She stepped back and looked into his eyes. She saw surprise and love.

"What was that for?"

"That was for this afternoon, for making two people very happy."

"If it hadn't worked, I would have felt stupid."

"Mike, it was so real it looked like a movie."

"I wish it was. Then you and I would be the stars."

"It would be fun." Linda opened her door and slid inside, closing the door.

Mike could still feel the touch of her lips on his own. *God, how I love that woman!* He walked on toward the barn. *Why was I born poor and she from a rich family?* If they were of the same class, poor or rich, he would confess his love to her right now. Mike found Wayne Jr. with his colt, and he started the lessons. He could teach him the basics, and Wayne could take it from there. Mike could see he loved the colt, and the colt was at his side. The colt liked all the attention he was getting.

Linda removed her clothes and took a long hot shower. She dried off and then brushed her hair. Pulling down the covers, she slipped between the cool white sheets, in the nude. She woke to the sound of Mike closing his door. She slipped out of bed and began to get ready for the party. She looked at herself in the mirror. She touched her nipples, and they became hard. She wished Mike were touching them. The thought made her hot all over, and she wanted to love him. Linda could see her straddle Mike and riding him until they were both exhausted. She could feel her juices flowing.

Mike's room had a large four-poster bed with a heavy solid oak dresser and a couple of chairs. Every guest room had a bathroom with a shower. Mike took a hot shower and shaved. He put on a clean pair of jeans and a Western shirt. His old boots and belt would have to make do. He splashed some old spice on his face for good luck. He needed all the help he could get. He would feel out of place with all the rich people at the party. He knew he would be the only poor one at the party, except the servants. He looked in the mirror and wished he had a fancy Western suit to wear. Even if he had the clothes, he would still be an old country boy.

Tapping lightly on Linda's door, Mike called, "Are you awake?"

"Yes, come on in."

Linda was in bed with a sheet pulled up to her neck. "I got a small problem and need your help."

Smiling, Mike said, "Your wish is my command."

"Wipe that silly smile off your face and close your eyes."

He obeyed.

She got out of bed and walked over to Mike, turning her back to him. She was a little embarrassed.

"Now open your eyes and fix the catch on my bra."

"For a moment I thought you had something else in mind."

"Don't you wish!" Linda giggled.

She couldn't help herself from teasing him. She was wearing her panties and a half-slip, while holding her bra in front of her breasts. Her body became hot, anxious for his fingers to touch her. Mike took a deep breath, sliding his left hand under her long hair to hold it up so he could see to fix her bra strap.

"Oh, I forgot to slip the straps over my shoulders."

She raised her arms to slip into the bra. That was the wrong move, or right move, depending on how you look at it. Mike couldn't control his hands any longer.

He slipped his arms around her waist and pulled her against him. Linda knew she should try to pull away, but she couldn't move. It felt too good with their bodies touching. Mike ran a path of feather kisses on her shoulder and neck. His hands burned another path up her body to cup her breast. She let the bra drop to the floor.

Linda moaned as Mike touched her nipples, causing them to become hard. She wiggled her butt against Mike and could feel his hard erection pressing against her butt. She was about to go up in flames.

"Linda, I want to make love to you."

"No, we can't."

"Why not? I know you want to."

She was honest. "Yes, I do want to, but we shouldn't."

Linda turned and faced Mike. He pulled her tight against him. His erection was now pressing into her belly. She couldn't take much more, or she would rip Mike's clothes off and have her way with him. He kissed her. She opened her mouth to take his tongue, and he explored her mouth with his tongue. She sucked his tongue, and their tongues mated together. Mike slid his hand down and into her panties. He stroked her folds with his finger and set her on fire.

Suddenly there was a knock on the door. The shock was like a cold shower. Linda tried to find her voice.

"Yes."

"It's Pam Wilder. May I come in?"

"One moment please."

Linda pointed toward the bathroom as she picked up her bra and headed for the door. Linda opened the door for Pam.

Mike closed the bathroom door just as Pam came through the door. Pam was a duplicate of her mother, with long black hair. She was, Linda decided, a very beautiful young woman.

"I'm Linda Carson," she finally managed. Pam looked at Linda with a curious stare. Linda was nude from the waist up and still holding her bra in her hand. She held the bra out.

"I'm having trouble with the catch on my bra."

"Oh." Smiled Pam. "May I ask you something personal?"

"I guess so."

"Why are your nipples so hard and standing out?"

Linda was so embarrassed. Her face turned a flaming red. "I . . . I . . . don't know," she lied.

"I'm sorry. I didn't mean to embarrass you."

Linda slipped into her bra. "Would you fix the catch for me, please?"

She turned her back to Pam. After her bra was fixed, Linda pulled a sweater over her head and stepped into her full skirt. Pam looked her over from head to toe.

"Boy, you're going to turn some heads tonight! Are you ready to go to the party?"

"Yes, I guess so."

"Good, I'm here to escort you and your friend to the party. I'll go knock on his door and see if he is ready."

It finally dawned on Linda that Mike was still in her bathroom. She started to giggle as she followed Pam across the hall.

"What's so funny?" asked Pam.

"I guess I did look kind of stupid when I opened the door holding my top in my hand."

Linda was thinking of Mike still in her bathroom. Pam knocked on the door to Mike's room, but there wasn't any answer.

"Well, I guess he will have to find his own way to the party. Come on, let's go on to the party and get a table."

Linda followed Pam down the hall. She was still thinking how funny it was with Mike hiding in the bathroom.

"Will there be other young people at the party?"

"Yes, there will be other young people our age at the party."

"Good, then the party should be fun."

Linda giggled again. Pam thought she was strange, because she couldn't keep from laughing. She didn't see anything funny.

Mike waited about five minutes and then followed them. It was easy to follow the flow of people toward the back of the house into a large closed area. There was a swimming pool on one side, and the other side was set up for the party. There was a large dance floor, and a platform for the band, tables, and chairs was set around the dance floor. There were tables in one corner loaded with food and drinks.

At one table, Mike saw several young people around his age. Linda waved for him to come on over.

"I see you found us," said Linda.

"It wasn't hard with a party this size. All you had to do was follow the crowd."

Linda whispered, "Did you get lost?"

"You know where I was. Do you want me to tell everybody where I was?"

"Don't you dare tell!"

Pam introduced her friends to Mike and Linda. Their names went in one ear and out the other. Mike had always had a hard time remembering names. After a short time, Mike started to relax. He liked the group. There wasn't a stuck-up one in the bunch. Everyone was talking, laughing, and having a good time.

Pam stood up. "Let's eat before the band starts playing. The food is in that corner."

Everyone stood up and followed Pam. Mike had never seen so much food. If you wanted it, it was on the table. Linda loaded her plate and grinned at Mike.

"I'm hungry."

Mike got about half what Linda did. He didn't understand how she could eat so much and not be fat.

A short time later, the band started to play. Mike was sitting between Pam and Linda.

"Do you two dance?" asked Pam.

"Not very good," they replied in unison.

"We all like to dance," said Shirley, a cute little blond sitting across the table from them. "I'll be more than glad to teach you," her eyes locked on Mike, "if you would like to learn."

"Maybe," Mike replied.

Linda wondered if that was that all she wanted to teach him. *I don't like the girl or trust her.* She looked like a cat on the prowl, and Mike was the mouse she was after. Linda didn't like it at all.

The band's first song played was a Western two-step, and Shirley asked Mike to dance. Mike went around the table and escorted Shirley out onto the dance floor. They followed the large group around the dance floor. *For someone who didn't know how to dance,* thought Linda, *he is as smooth as silk on the dance floor.* At least it was a dance where they didn't dance close. The next dance was a slow one. Linda kicked Mike under the table.

"Would you like to dance?"

Linda smiled sweetly. "Yes, thank you."

Linda slid into Mike's arms, and they moved as one around the dance floor. It was a belt-shining song. He pulled her tighter against him, and she could feel him come alive. She moved against him and felt something hard against her belly. She was hot. She was sure that she would catch fire any minute and burn up. She had two out of three things needed to start a fire. She was fuel, and her body was at ignition temperature, but she had lost her breath, so there was no oxygen to start the fire.

Her nipples were hard. Mike could feel them through her bra. If this song lasted any longer, he would be a nutcase. He tried to control his manhood, or he would be embarrassed going back to the table.

Linda whispered in his ear, "You better get rid of that hard-on before the dance is over."

"Don't I know it? See what you do to me."

She liked teasing Mike. Rubbing against him, her juices were starting to flow. She knew her panties were wet, and she was ready for Mike. Too bad they weren't back in her room.

"Don't you wish we were back in my room?"

"You know the answer to that."

Finally the song ended, and they staggered back to their table like two drunks. "Why did you kick me under the table?"

"I wanted to dance."

"Why didn't you just ask me?"

Linda smiled that sweet thing smile again. "The gentleman should always ask the lady to dance."

"Do me a favor. Just touch me on the leg next time, and I will get the message."

"Would you get me a large glass of punch?" requested Linda.

Mike got up and made his way across the floor toward the huge punch bowl located in the corner.

"Do you mind if all of us dance with Mike?" asked Pam.

"No, go ahead. He is his own man. He can do what he wants to do."

"He is a good dancer, and most of the guys here are not too good at dancing."

"I didn't know he could dance so well."

"I saw how you two danced. If someone had struck a match close to you two, we would have had a fire." Pam giggled.

Linda's face flushed red, and she wished Mike would hurry with the punch. She needed something to cool her off. A large glass of punch was set down in front of her. Linda looked up and smiled. Then she started to drink.

"The punch sure is good. I needed that." She set down her empty glass.

Mike glanced at Linda. "Would you like another glass of punch?"

"That's all right. I'll get it this time."

When she returned, Mike wasn't at the table. She scanned the dance floor and saw he was dancing with Pam. She could tell Pam was having trouble following Mike's lead. There was only two people left at the table—she and Bob. He asked her to dance, and she danced with him.

Bob was a girl's dream. He was good looking. He was six feet tall and had cold black hair, a face like a Greek god, and a hard lean body to match. So why did she feel like she was dancing with her brother? He didn't set her on fire, and her nipples weren't hard. She relaxed and enjoyed dancing with him.

"Bob, where are you from?"

"I live in Oklahoma City. Where are you from?"

"I live in Booneville, a small town in east Texas. We just moved there from Oklahoma."

"Why did you go to Texas?"

"Dad bought a large ranch and is raising horses. Mike works for him."

When they returned to the table, Mike was trying to explain to Pam how to follow his lead.

"I'll never get it right!" complained Pam.

"Sure you will," said Linda. She sat down and started drinking her second large punch.

Linda watched Pam and Mike as he tried to teach her again. They were doing a lot better with this dance. Linda didn't mind Mike dancing with Pam, but she didn't like it when he danced with Shirley. She didn't like the way Shirley teased Mike, but was she teasing? She finished her second punch and headed for the punch bowl. That sure was a good punch.

Linda was on her third punch when Pam and Mike returned to the table. Mike couldn't believe how much punch she had consumed.

"Would you like to dance the next dance?"

"Yes, thank you." Linda smiled a lopsided smile at him.

The next dance was a sweetheart waltz. Mike led her out on the dance floor. It wasn't a real close-together dance, but Linda could still feel the heat where his hands touched her. She could see burning desire in Mike's eyes. She thought she would melt and become a puddle at his feet. When the danced ended, Linda started on her punch again, trying to cool down.

The band took a break, and Linda watched Shirley head for the bandstand. She wondered what Shirley was up to. No good that was for sure. Mike came back to the table with more food.

"Are you trying to make me fat?" asked Linda.

"No, I just thought we would eat, drink, and have fun tonight. We can fast tomorrow."

"I'll drink to that!" Linda giggled.

She started to giggle about anything said, and her words were starting to slur. She took another drink of punch.

"You had better slow down on that punch," warned Bob.

"Why would I do that?"

"It's highly spiked with vodka and will slip up on you."

"Now you tell me." Linda was getting a little tipsy.

"Are you all right?" inquired Mike.

"I don't know. I don't drink, and you better not laugh at me, or I'll slug you."

"I would never do that."

"I got to go pee," she whispered to Mike. She made for the bathroom.

When she returned to the table, she said, "I needed that, and now I feel better."

Pam started to tell Linda how her father let sailors from the navy school in Norman come out to the ranch, but he wouldn't let her go out with any of them. After a while, Linda had a hard time keeping up with the conversation and just nodded her head. She glanced at Mike, and he was watching her with a broad grin on his face. *I would like to slap that grin off his face.* She hoped she didn't make too big a fool of herself.

Linda decided to go to the bathroom and wash her face. *Maybe that would help.* She asked Pam to go with her. She washed her face and tried to get back in control of herself. Pam watched her. "You like Mike, don't you?"

With a slight hesitation, Linda decided to tell Pam how she felt about Mike. "Yes, I do, very much, and one day I'm going to marry him. He just doesn't know it yet."

"Does he love you?"

"Yes, I'm sure he loves me."

"Has he told you?"

"Yes, and I can see it in his eyes every time he looks at me."

"Then what's the problem?"

"Mike is a little shy. He is a country boy, and we have a lot of money. It causes a lot of trouble. He thinks he isn't good enough for me."

"I have had the same problem. I liked one of the cowboys that worked for Dad."

"What happened?"

"He gave up and left the ranch."

"I'm sorry."

"So am I, because I liked him very much. Dad says I should stay in my own class."

"My dad likes Mike, and Mother is starting to like him. Maybe we got a chance of making it."

"I wish you all the luck, because you will need it."

"Are you feeling better?"

"A little, but I'm still a little dizzy."

"Come on, Linda. Let's go back to the party."

When they returned to the table, it was empty. Everyone was out on the floor, dancing. It was a fast one for all the young people. Linda scanned the dance floor, looking for Mike. If she were a betting person, she would bet Mike was dancing with Shirley. Linda could have guessed who asked the band to play the fast dance.

She watched as Shirley slid across Mike's back with her legs high in the air, dress up, and showing her panties. After a couple more fast turns and spins, Mike caught her waist and lifted her in the air, tossing her upon one hip, then the other, back in the air, and coming down, going between his legs, then catching her and pulling her back to her feet. After that little show, they went back to spins and fast turns. They looked real good together. Linda wished she could dance like that.

Linda sat at the table and didn't like what she saw. Was she jealous? Damn right she was, but she was trying to control herself and not do anything foolish.

When the song ended, Shirley and Mike returned to the table. He glanced at Linda, and if looks could kill, he and Shirley would be dead. He didn't think Linda was jealous of him, but if she was, he was happy about the fact. It meant she cared for him.

Mike wanted to ask Linda to dance a slow dance with him again, but he wasn't sure he could take the heat from her body again.

Shirley was watching Mike like a cat watching a mouse. She wanted to see if the story was true about everything being bigger in Texas. She started to get hot, and her nipples became hard. She wanted Mike.

Linda was keeping an eye on Shirley, and she could read her like a book. She knew she wanted Mike. She would have to dance the next slow dance with Mike and find some way to get him to leave the party before Shirley made her move. She wasn't going to let Shirley get her hooks in Mike.

"Are you having fun?" asked Mike.

"I'm a little tired, but it has been fun. I see you had fun dancing with Shirley."

"She is a good dancer, and we danced fine together."

Linda couldn't help but put in a jib, "I think dancing isn't all she wants to do."

"Are you jealous?" He couldn't help asking.

"No, you can do what you want to do."

"Then you wouldn't care if we hooked up for the night."

"Don't you dare! We are guests in this house. It wouldn't be right."

The band took a break, and Linda asked Mike if he would get her some more punch. He went and got her punch. He set her glass down in front of her.

"You had better lie off the punch."

"I'll lie off when I'm good and ready."

The thought came to Linda, and she started drinking her punch, because if she had too much to drink, Mike would have to help her back to her room. She would make sure he didn't return to the party.

"Linda, you're going to be drunk."

"So what? You said eat, drink, and have fun. I quote you."

The band started to play again, a slow, slow song. Linda knew she had to act fast. She reached to touch Mike's leg to let him know to ask her to dance, but she touched something else and couldn't keep from giggling. Mike blushed red, but he asked her to dance.

They left the table, and Linda glanced back at Shirley. If looks could kill, she would be dead. She smiled at her and thought, *This time you don't. This is my man, and you can keep your hands off.*

She slid into Mike's arms, and they moved to the music. She felt his arousal pressing against her abdomen. She felt his throbbing heat through her clothes, and a growing ache started in the lower part of her body. She felt his hands go up and down her back while his fingers caressed her.

Mike wanted to curve his hands on her buttocks and fit her tighter against him, but he thought he had better not out on the dance floor. Linda wiggled against him, rubbing his crouch with her hot spot. She wanted more but couldn't get it on the dance floor. She pulled his body closer to her and let out a low moan.

"I think I'm a little drunk. Do you mind if we leave and go back to our rooms?"

"No, not at all. I'm ready to leave if you are."

"I'm ready. Let's go."

"Don't you want to finish the dance?"

"Not really. I've had enough of this party." *And Shirley*, she almost said.

Mike put his arm around her waist, and they left the dance floor. Linda was swaying back and forth as they walked back to the table.

He thought he must be crazy to leave a hot number like Shirley sitting at the table. He knew she wanted his body. *Oh well, such is life!*

"We enjoyed the party, but we have to get up early in the morning. Thanks for having us come to your party."

"You'll have to come back again," said Pam.

Mike had to help Linda as they left the party. He put his arm around her waist and supported her while they walked back to their rooms. The vodka from the punch was starting to have its effect on her.

He opened her door and helped her into her room. He sat her on the bed and sat down beside her.

"Are you all right?"

"No, my head is spinning. I think I had too much punch."

"You had better lie down and get some sleep."

"But my head spins when I lie down."

Mike stood up and started to leave. "Good night, Linda."

"No, don't go." She stood up. "Help me get undressed, because I don't think I can by myself."

"Are you sure you want me to?"

"Yes, I do." She stood up with her arms at her side, smiling at Mike. She wanted him to take her in his arms. *Why is he so shy?*

"OK, hold up your arms."

Linda held her arms over her head as Mike caught the bottom of her sweater and worked it up over her head. He hung it on a chair and turned back to Linda. She had lowered her arms and was staring at him.

"I guess we take off the skirt next," he said, expelling a sharp breath.

"Yes, I guess we do."

She was having fun teasing him. Mike shut his eyes for a second, trying to imagine how she would look completely naked.

"Well, are you going to finish undressing me or not?"

"Yes, I am."

With trembling hands Mike unbuttoned the button on her skirt and pulled down the zipper. He let it fall to the floor. Next he pulled her slip down, letting it fall to the floor. She stepped out of them and turned her back to him. He bent down and helped her out of her shoes and bobby socks. He stood back up and admired her cute little buttocks. He was trying not to get a hard-on while watching her undress, but his manhood had a mind of its own. Having her back to Mike, she didn't see his physical need. He was trying to control his body but with very little results.

"Is this all you want me to take off?" said Mike hoarsely.

"Take it all off. I want to sleep in the nude. I feel reckless tonight."

Mike was trembling so much, he wasn't sure he could unfasten her bra. He touched her skin, and Linda felt a physical hunger building in her lower body. Her nipples tightened painfully in need to be touched. Mike finally got the bra unfasten and let it fall to the floor. He hooked his fingers in her panties and started pulling them down as she let out a moan. When her panties fell to the floor, she stepped out of them.

"You finally got me undressed."

"Yes, I guess I did."

"You wanted to see me naked, didn't you?"

"Yes, I wanted to see you naked."

Linda hesitated a few seconds more before turning around to face Mike. She could see the desire in his eyes, and glancing down she could see his physical need. She raised her eyes and locked with his.

"My god, you are so beautiful!" he said in a hoarse voice.

"You like what you see?"

"You don't know how much."

Mike extended his hand to her face, and she went to him without reservation. Linda put her arms around his neck and arched against him. She was burning up with desire. His hand slid up her body, burning a path along the way, and then cupped her breast. He caressed first one breast and then the other. His caress felt good, she thought she would cry out, but he covered her mouth with his. Their tongues met and twined together. He couldn't get enough of her.

Linda could feel his arousal pressing hard against her belly. She arched her back and rotated her hips against him. She wanted to make love to Mike, *now.*

"Mike, make love to me, please."

"Are you sure about this? You are a little drunk."

"I'm very sure. I want you inside me. I want you to put out the fire. I'm burning up."

He couldn't take it any longer. He picked her up and laid her on the bed. He quickly removed his clothes while Linda watched. She watched his manhood standing straight out and knew Mike wanted her very much. She was wet and waiting for him, but suddenly her eyes closed.

"Oh no, not now!"

She was fast asleep.

Mike bent down and sucked a nipple into his mouth. Linda didn't move, because she was out like a light. He put his clothes back on, pulled a sheet over her nude body, and kissed her on the forehead like a child.

"Good night, my love. Sleep tight."

He left and went back to his own room. Mike took a cold shower and went to bed, but he couldn't go to sleep. Staring up at the ceiling, he was mumbling to himself, "What a night!"

He was still trembling with desire. The cold shower didn't put out the fire, and it still raged out of control. The thought went through him. Maybe he should go back to the party and let Shirley put out the fire. She looked hot enough to set a forest on fire. He realized that Linda was the only one he wanted to put out his fire. He knew the night would have ended different if Linda hadn't passed out. He could still taste the punch from kissing her. *If only she hadn't drink so much!* He closed his eyes and dreamed how it would have been making love to her.

The next morning, Linda woke up to the sound of someone knocking on her door. "Who is it?"

"It's me. Mike."

She started to say come in but realized she was naked. She sat up in bed, and her head felt like it would fall off.

"I'm not dressed yet."

"OK, I'll meet you in the dining room."

After Mike left, she got up and stared at herself in the mirror. *Why am I naked? What had I done last night? Had I and Mike made love? If we had made love, why isn't he still in bed with me? Or did he leave after he got what he wanted?* She was confused to say the least. She decided to take a cold shower. *Maybe this will help.* She had a throbbing headache. *What happened last night?* She couldn't remember a thing.

She dressed in a Western shirt, jeans, and boots. After applying some light makeup and fixing her hair in a ponytail, she was ready to face the day.

Staring at the clothes on the floor, she was still confused about last night. It made her blush seeing her clothes on the floor. *What have I done?*

Linda tried hard to remember, but the last thing she remembered was coming in her room with Mike. *Did I pass out at that time?* She must have passed out, or she would remember. She picked up her clothes and packed them. She took her things to the truck and then found her way to the dining room.

The room was full of people. She sat down across from Mike and Pam. She was very nervous.

"Good morning," said Pam.

"It's morning, I guess."

"Did you get a good night's sleep?" She grinned at Linda.

She looked at Mike and blushed. "I don't know. The last thing I remember was going into my room last night, then nothing until I woke up this morning. Everything in between is a total blank."

Mike didn't say anything. He thought it would be better to tell her after they were back on the road.

"I also have a throbbing headache. I think my head is going to fall off."

"I'll get you an aspirin for your headache," said Pam.

"Thank you."

Pam returned shortly with the aspirin. She handed her the aspirin and a glass of water. Linda took them and hoped they would help.

"You had too much punch last night," said Mike.

"How well I know it. I'll never do it again."

After saying good-bye to the Wilders, Mike turned the truck in the direction of Oklahoma City to visit her grandmother. She was her grandmother on the Carson side of the family.

They rode in silence, each one with their own thoughts. Linda wanted to ask what happened last night, but she was afraid she had made a fool of herself. Mike glanced at her and was sure she was going to ask about last night. What should he tell her? That she wanted to make love to him, and he wanted to make love to her? Maybe it had been the vodka causing her to act that way.

"How much further do we have to go?" Linda asked.

"We just went through Norman, next we go through Moore, then Oklahoma City."

"Good, then we don't have much further to go."

Mike wanted her to come to him on her own free will, not because she was drinking. He wanted her sober when she came to him.

"Did you have a good time at the ranch?" asked Mike.

"Yes, I did. How about you?"

"Yes, I guess I did. I thought I would feel out of place, but they were nice people, and I had fun."

"I would say you had a real good time with that . . . that Shirley."

Did Linda sound jealous? It was too good to hope for. "All we did was dance, and I danced with you and Pam also."

"I'm sorry. I didn't have any right to snap at you. You are your own man."

Mike thought, *I wish I belonged to Linda.* He didn't want to be on his own, but did he dare hope there was a chance with Linda? She was high class, and he was low class. Small-town classes didn't mix.

"Where does your grandmother live?" They were going through Moore.

"We stay on Highway 77 until it turns into Shields. She lives in a little white frame house on the left, and it has a white picket fence around it."

"Down a little further. There it is. Pull into the driveway."

They got out of the truck as the front door opened, and a gray-haired old lady hurried out to greet them. Linda ran into her open arms.

"Oh, Grandma, it's so good to see you!"

They both had tears in their eyes. When Linda was back in control, she turned and introduced Mike to her grandmother.

"Grandma, this is Mike."

"Glad to meet you, ma'am."

"Glad to meet you, young man." She gave him the once-over.

"Why don't I find a service station and fill up? That will give you and your grandma time to visit."

"OK, but don't get lost and take all day."

"Yes, boss lady."

Linda gave him that "I'll get even" look and laughed. "Pick up something for us to smack on when we get back on the road."

"I shall return." Mike grinned at her.

Linda turned and went into the house with her grandmother. Mike drove down Shields until he found a service station. Two attendants came out to his pickup.

"Fill her up, sir."

"Yes, sir."

One attendant pumped the gas while the other one washed the windshield and checked under the hood. Mike checked the price on the pump. It was thirty-four cents a gallon. That was higher than in Texas.

"That will be five dollars and ten cents, sir."

Mike gave him six dollars and received his change. "Thank you, sir, come again."

He drove around until he found a grocery store and bought some junk food for the trip home. He drove downtown and looked around. He thought he would give Linda time to visit her grandma.

"Sit down at the kitchen table, and I'll fix us some tea. I have dinner cooking. Your father called, and I was expecting you."

Linda watched her grandmother fix the tea. She had always liked to visit her. Grandpa Carson had been dead for three years, but Grandma refused to live with anyone. She stayed on in the house Grandpa built for them when they were young. Linda's dad was born and raised in this house.

"So tell me about Texas. Do you like it? How is the ranch doing?"

"Slow down, Grandma. I like it OK, and the ranch is just great. The ranch is paying its own way, and we don't need the oil money to make the ranch work."

"Sounds like you like it there."

"Yes, it is exciting living on the big ranch. Mike has been a big part of why the ranch is doing so good. He is something else with horses."

Grandma Carson watched Linda as she talked about Mike. She smiled and let her rattle on.

"Dad likes Mike, and I think Mom is starting to like him."

"Sounds to me like you are hot for the young man."

Linda blushed red and got very nervous.

"I may be old, but I'm not blind or stupid. I tell it like it is."

"Mike is a hired hand that works on the ranch."

"Are you in love with him?"

Linda stared at her grandma. She knew she couldn't lie to her. "Yes, I am."

"Are you sure it's not puppy love?"

"Yes, I'm sure. I love Mike."

"Then what are you waiting for? If you want him, go get him."

"Grandma, you make it like going hunting."

"You could compare it to hunting. You hunt until you find the man you want to spend the rest of your life with and then you trap him."

"You did that to Grandpa Carson?"

"I sure did. I had him hog-tied before he knew what was going on."

"Grandma, you are something else."

"I know. I will come to Texas to your wedding, provided you don't give up the hunt and let him get away."

Mike pulled into the driveway. "I guess that ends our girl talk," said Grandma.

When Mike came in the house, he glanced at Linda and saw that she was red from blushing. He would have liked to know what they were talking about.

After lunch, Mike waited in the pickup while Linda said good-bye to her grandmother. He saw the Carsons were a close and loving family.

"It will probably be dark by the time we get home."

"That's all right, because I told Dad to expect us when he saw us coming. I didn't know long we would stay at Grandma's."

"I liked your grandma."

"She liked you too."

"How is your headache?"

"It has finally quit hurting, but I am tired."

"Take a nap, and I will wake you before we get to Dallas."

Mike put his arm on the back of the seat and turned toward her a little, giving her an invitation to lean on him. She paused, looking shocked at Mike's action, but she moved over next to him and rested her head on his shoulder, letting her hand rest on his thigh. She felt his body tremble.

She was right where she wanted to be and could stay there forever. Mike glanced down at Linda. He loved her more than life itself. If only he had money to keep her in the way she was used to living!

Linda felt Mike's body tremble again, and she smiled to herself. She liked the power she possessed over him. She liked to tease him, but she knew one day she would go too far, and he would lose control. Maybe that was what she wanted him to do.

She breathed in his male scent mixed with old spice. She liked it. She was tempted to let her hand roam higher up his thigh until it touched his manhood.

Mike tried to control his aroused manhood, but it strained down his leg, trying to meet Linda's hand. Linda moaned softly and fell asleep. Mike didn't know if he was relieved or mad.

Linda opened her eyes and looked around. Mike pulled into a service station in Lewisville.

"We can gas up here and make it the rest of the way home. The pickup is using a lot of gas pulling the trailer, and we are headed into a headwind."

Linda nodded. "I got to use the restroom."

After paying for the gas, Mike made a trip to the restroom. He came out while Linda was paying for Cokes and candy bars.

"I got us some more junk food, but if we get hungry later, we can stop."

"Sounds good to me. Let's get back on the road."

After they were through Dallas, Linda asked, "Would you like for me to relieve you and let you rest?"

"Sure, if you want to. Dallas traffic has me beat. I could use a rest."

Mike pulled over, and they swapped places. He wasn't used to all that traffic. He preferred driving in a small town.

"Look at all the beautiful flowers," remarked Linda.

"Yes, they are pretty, but not as pretty as what I'm looking at."

Linda glanced at Mike, and he was staring at her. She smiled at him but kept looking at the flowers. On both sides of the highway, bluebonnets, Indian paintbrushes, and many other wild flowers were in full bloom.

"I love this time of year when everything is bloom."

He glanced at Linda and said, "You are the most beautiful of all the flowers." He had better keep his mind on the road, or they could end up in a ditch. That would be very embarrassing.

"I'll change places in Athens with you and drive the rest of the way home."

In Athens, Mike changed places with Linda and drove the rest of the way home. They were starting to get tired. It was just getting dark when they pulled in at the ranch. They were glad to be home again.

They got out of the truck, and Lightning began to nicker. Linda ran to the corral and threw her arms around his neck.

"I missed you," she said softly.

Mike came over and petted Lightning on the forehead. "I guess I had better check on little Thunder."

Entering the barn, he found Thunder standing next to his mother getting supper. He looked like he had grown over the weekend. When Mike returned, Linda and Mike walked to the house together. They glanced at each other as they walked, very much aware of the electricity between them.

"I had a lovely time," said Linda.

"I did too," replied Mike.

Mrs. Carson burst out the door to greet them, with one question after another. "Did you have any trouble on the trip? What was the Wilder Ranch like? Did you see the movie people making movies? How was Grandma Carson?"

Linda answered each question for her. Mr. Carson came in the house and wanted to know everything also. She repeated everything for her father. Linda explained how Wilder Jr. didn't want a horse and how Mike saved the day.

"Have you kids had supper?" asked Mrs. Carson.

"Just some junk food," replied Linda.

"I'll go fix something for you."

She fixed ham sandwiches, chips, and Cokes. After they had eaten, Mike told them he had better hit the road. He decided to drive his car home and disconnect the trailer tomorrow. He was tired and would sleep well tonight—that is, if he could keep Linda out of his dreams.

"I'll walk you to your car." Linda followed Mike as he left.

When Mike got to his car, he turned and leaned against it. He wanted a good night kiss before he left.

*What the heck!* He opened his arms, and Linda walked into them.

"I'm going to kiss you."

On the way home, Mike decided to stop by the Dairy Queen and see if some of the guys were there. He didn't hang out much with his friends since he went to work at the ranch. Punky and Leroy were in a booth having hamburgers, fries, and malts. Mike ordered a Coke and went over to sit with them.

"Well, look what the cat dragged in," said Punky.

"Hi, guys."

"We don't see much of you since you went to work at the ranch."

"Yes, I know. I go to school and then out to work at the ranch."

"Where were you last night?" asked Punky.

"I was in Oklahoma taking a couple of horses to the Triple W Ranch."

"Well, you should have been with us. We made a trip to the Chicken Ranch, and guess who we took with us?"

"I give up. Who?"

"We took Jerry."

Mike was shocked. "You took that creep with you?"

"I didn't want to, but I guess Jerry was hard up and promised to fix me up with a date with his sister Connie. Boy, she is a knockout!" Punky put his hand over his heart. "I think I'm in love."

"I think you call it lust," teased Leroy.

"Not this time. I think I have found the girl of my dreams."

Leroy and Mike looked at each other and grinned. They had heard that song and dance before several times.

"Mike, who are you going with?" asked Punky.

"Nobody. I haven't had time to chase girls."

"Well, that just shows. You should've been with us last night. You are probably getting hard up by now."

Mike wanted to tell them how he felt about Linda but thought better of it. They would probably laugh at him for wanting to go with a rich girl. They would tell him he was crazy to cross the line.

They finished their food and drinks and went their separate ways. Mike headed for home and bed.

Mrs. Love met him at the door. "How was the trip?"

"I enjoyed it very much."

"Then Linda must have gone with you."

Mike smiled at his mother. She could read him like a book. "Yes, she went with me to visit her grandmother."

"Sure she did. Sometimes I think you are stupid."

"Mom, you are right."

"That girl went on the trip to be with you. The trip to visit Grandma was an excuse to be with you. Don't you see that?"

"I hope you are right. I would like to believe that."

"Have you told her how you feel about her?"

Mike's expression became sad. "How can I? It would be a big joke. Poor man loves rich woman. What do I have to offer her? She has anything she wants when she wants it."

"She doesn't have you and don't sell her short. She may not care about money that much. Don't wait too long to tell her how you feel. She may get tired and give up the chase."

"Mom, she's not chasing me."

"If you say so, go to bed. You have school tomorrow."

"Good night, Mom."

The next day, Mike skipped his English class to go see the owner of the piece of property he wanted to buy. Mr. Smith was very nice and understanding. He sold Mike the property for a small monthly payment, to increase in two years, with no down payment. He would make his payments to Mr. Smith. This had to be a sign his luck was changing for the better.

The coming weekend he planned to work on his property. *His property.* That sounded so good. He couldn't believe he was a property owner. It wasn't much land, but it was a start.

This evening he had a lot of work to do at the ranch. The main thing was to try and get Lightning to breed a very shy mare. He would have his work cut out for him trying to persuade the mare to mate.

Mike arrived at the ranch and went straight to see Lightning. "I'm going to bring a shy little mare to see you. You be nice to her. It will be her first time." Lightning bobbed his head up and down, as if to say, "Yes, I understood."

Linda brought Connie home with her to spend the evening. She was Jerry's sister. They had become the best of friends ever since she turned Jerry down and Lightning did a number on Jerry's car.

Connie told her, "Any girl who could put Jerry in his place was a friend of hers."

They planned to go horseback riding. They walked out of the house and saw Mike leading a mare in the direction of Lightning's corral. Linda knew what was going to happen. She turned in the other direction.

"Come on, we need to get going before it is too late to ride."

Connie was full of curiosity. "Isn't that Mike leading the horse?"

"Yes."

"What is he doing?"

"You know."

"What?"

"You know, boy meets girl, stud meets mare, and—"

"Oh." Connie felt stupid, but she was a city girl. How was she to know?

"Can we watch?" She blushed.

"Connie."

"Well, I'm a city girl, and I have never seen it done before."

"OK, but we will miss our ride."

Mike opened the gate and turned the mare loose in the corral with Lightning. He followed her around the corral. She was trembling. She was young and scared. Mike called to the mare, and she came to him. Lightning stood and watched. Mike talked to her softly. Then he said something to Lightning.

"What is he doing now?" asked Connie.

"The mare is shy, probably her first time, so Mike is trying to get her ready for what is about to happen."

"You mean the mare is a virgin?"

"Yes." Linda giggled.

Suddenly, Lightning mounted the mare and rode her. The mare trembled as he entered her, but after they were coupled, she stood still and let Lightning have his way with her. Lightning had a big tool to work with, and he was giving her a good ride. Mike stood over to the side while they mated.

"Oh my god, how can the poor horse take all of that, that—"

"It's a mare, Connie, and they have a bigger . . . you know."

"No, I don't know anything."

Linda gave up on Connie. "Go ahead, enjoy and learn."

Lightning finished mating and got down. They both walked over to Mike. "Have you two had enough?"

Lightning raised his head and nickered. The mare and Lightning both looked exhausted and hot.

"OK, she can stay with you until I get ready to leave."

Mike turned and started to the barn to check on little Thunder. That was when he saw Linda and Connie. He wondered how long they had been watching. He turned and headed toward them.

"Oh no, he has seen us!" said Linda.

"That's all right, because I want to ask him what he said to the horses." Connie giggled.

*Oh boy, it is going to be one of those days,* thought Linda. One thing she had learned about Connie was, she was not shy.

"Hi, girls, what are you up to?"

"About five feet two inches." Connie giggled.

Linda started to say something but changed her mind. Connie was ready with questions, sink or swim. Connie had caught Mike off guard, and he stared at her, unable to come back with a sharp reply.

Connie stared back at Mike and blushed. Her body had nice curves and was sleek. She was a beautiful woman, but Mike preferred Linda.

"You don't seem like the same person at school," said Connie.

"I'm a country boy and try to keep a low profile."

"Oh."

"I don't like going to school but will stick it out to graduate."

"Why don't you like school?"

"I don't like the class thing. The rich are together, and the poor are together."

Connie thought it was time to change the subject. "By the way, what did you say to the horses?"

That broke the trance Mike was in. "Say what?"

"What did you tell the horses?"

Mike looked at Linda, and she couldn't keep from laughing any longer. "Tell her. She is a city girl."

Mike looked at Connie and turned red. "Are you certain you want to know?"

"Yes. What did you tell them?"

"OK, you asked for it. I told the mare to settle down and don't be nervous. To be still so Lightning could get on and couple with her. That she would like it after Lightning was in her."

Connie blushed and stood with her mouth open because she was embarrassed but still curious.

"Did you tell Lightning how to do it with the mare?"

Mike laughed. "I told him to get on with it or I was taking the mare out of the corral and he wouldn't get any."

"I can't believe you talk to horses like they were people."

"Believe him," said Linda.

"Horses are smarter than people give them credit for."

"Thanks for telling me about the horses."

Connie gave Mike a sweet smile. She stared at Mike below his belt as she ran her tongue around her lips to wet them.

"This was a new experience for me. Maybe sometime you can give me another new experience."

It was Mike's turn to be embarrassed. "I . . . I got to get back to work."

He made a hasty retreat to the barn. Connie watched Mike enter the barn. "I could have a lot of fun with a guy like that." Connie giggled.

She turned and faced Linda. She could tell Linda was mad as a wet hen. "What did I do?"

"It's too late to ride." Linda turned and stomped off back to the house with Connie right behind her.

"Talk to me, Linda. We are best friends. What did I do?"

"You didn't do anything."

Linda stopped and turned so fast that Connie bumped into her. They both laughed. "I'm sorry, Connie. You didn't know."

Connie stared at her. "Know what?"

"Come on, we'll get a couple of Cokes and go to my room. Then I will tell you all about it."

"Oh boy, I love good juicy gossip!"

Connie sat on the bed, and Linda began to pace back and forth in front of her. "I went to Oklahoma last weekend with Mike to deliver some horses. I told Mom and Dad I wanted to see Grandmother in Oklahoma City. I lied, sort of, because I wanted to be with Mike."

"Are you going with him?"

"No."

"Then what's the problem?"

"Do I have to spell it out to you?"

"Yes, you do. I'm stupid at times."

"OK, I'm in love with Mike." There, she had said it.

"You're not serious? He is only a hired hand."

"I don't care what he is. I love him. Please don't give him the come-on anymore."

"I'm sorry. It was just in fun. I'll find another man to have fun with."

"Thanks, Connie."

"No problem. And we are still best friends?"

Linda nodded. "Always."

"When did this all come about?"

Linda told her about the first time she saw Mike up until the present, carefully leaving out the hayloft and the time she was drunk.

"I go up in flames when he touches me."

"It sounds to me like you got it bad."

Connie watched Linda pace back and forth. She reminded her of a caged animal that couldn't get out of the cage.

"Are you sure you told me everything? We are best friends, and best friends tell each other everything."

"Well, maybe not quite everything." Linda giggled.

"I thought so. He has made love to you." It was a statement and not a question.

"I feel complete and content when I'm with Mike. The air is charged with electricity from us when we are close."

"Of all the guys you went with, you could have had your pick, but you want Mike. I can't believe you picked Mike."

"Well, believe it. You can have all the rest to pick from."

"By the way, how well do you know Punky?"

"He is a crazy friend of Mike's. Why do you ask?"

"Well, for some reason, my brother wants me to go out with Punky. He has been trying to talk to me at school. He opens doors for me and wants to carry my books for me. He has been nice, so far."

Linda stopped pacing and sat down beside Connie. "That doesn't sound like the Punky I know. Are you going to date him?"

"I haven't made up my mind yet. Maybe yes, maybe no. Time will tell."

"We sure killed the evening," said Linda.

"Yes, and I got to go home."

"Would you like to stay for supper?"

"Thanks for the offer, but we got company coming for supper, and Mother wants me to be there. I'll take a rain check."

"You got it." Linda drove Connie home.

Linda lay in bed staring at the ceiling. She was restless. School was almost out, and after summer break it would be time to go to college. She had originally wanted to go to the University of Oklahoma, but now she wasn't sure what she wanted to do. She was in love with Mike, but nothing was settled. Would it ever be? Maybe she should go to college closer to home. Maybe she should ask Mike what he thought about her going off to college. Finally, she drifted off to sleep, but her dreams were troubled, and she didn't sleep well that night. She could sleep late the next day being Saturday.

# Chapter 8

Mike was on his property by eight Saturday morning with his first load of pure white sand. He was going to turn the waterfall into a paradise. He wanted a place where he could come to dream.

After clearing the banks around the pool of mud, he spread the sand on the banks to make them look like a beach. Several loads of sand later, he finished the banks. He put two loads of sand on the bottom of the pool. He watched the spring-fed waterfall clear the water. Slowly he could see the bottom of the pool. The water was so clear it was like having your own swimming pool. The pool was four to five feet in places.

Mike stood back from the waterfall and gazed at his work. It still needed something. He wanted Linda to like it. Behind the waterfall he hoped someday to build a home for him and Linda. A woman would like plants and flowers. He made another trip to town, and when he returned, he was broke.

Working at a fast pace, Mike finally finished planting flowers, plants, and some bushes. He backed up and admired his work. Now it was complete, except for the house. That would have to wait until he came up with the money, but that may be never. The waterfall looked like a paradise. It was about four in the evening when Mike had finally finished his work. He was dirty, hot, and exhausted. He started to get in his truck and then looked back at the inviting waterfall.

Mike decided to take a bath.

Mike pulled off his clothes and dropped them on the sand. He climbed to the top of the waterfall and lay down, letting the cool water flow over his body. His head was resting on a large rock, and he fell asleep.

Linda was on her way home from town after she and Connie had taken in a movie, when she saw Mike's pickup. She pulled off the road on to Mike's property.

She shut off the engine and decided to walk the rest of the way to where Mike was. She followed the road Mike's truck had made his many trips in and out. She approached the waterfall but didn't see Mike. She stared in wonder at the waterfall. It was beautiful beyond belief.

Finally, she spotted Mike on top of the waterfall. Making her way to the top, she moved around behind him, her eyes studying him, her lips pursed in amusement. He was naked. She gazed at him, starting with his face. His lips were slightly parted as if waiting to be kissed.

Mike's face and the top part of his body were red from the sun. Looking lower she saw his shaft standing like a flagpole. She glanced back to his face. He had a lazy smile, and he arched his back while he mumbled something.

"He is having a dream," murmured Linda.

*Who is he dreaming about?* She thought about pushing him off the waterfall, but she was wearing her good dress.

Swept by reckless desire, she pulled off her flats, pulled her dress up high enough to clear the water, and waded into the stream.

Her heart hammered against her ribs as she slowly reached down to grab Mike. She was staring at the flagpole. He was on the edge of the waterfall, and it wouldn't take much to push him over.

Linda smiled, and with a surge of satisfaction, she pushed him over the waterfall. Mike was dreaming about Linda. They were in their new home, in a king-size bed, making slow marvelous love. It was wonderful.

His dream suddenly became a nightmare, and he was falling through space. He reached out to grab anything to stop the fall. Mike grabbed the bottom of Linda's dress, but it slipped through his fingers. He was still grabbing thin air when he plunged into the water.

Linda fought to keep her balance, but it was too late. She closed her eyes and held her breath. She knew she was going swimming. Mike broke the surface of the water and looked up, just in time to see legs and white panties falling on him. Linda's dress had blown up around her waist. She took Mike back under the water with her when she landed on him.

They both surfaced at the same time, with Linda's arms locked around Mike's neck. When she realized the water wasn't over her head, she let go and stood back.

"What were you trying to do? Drown me?"

"I should have. Look what you did to my dress."

Linda looked down. The flagpole had shrunk and fallen down. She started to laugh.

"What's so funny?"

"Nothing, honey." She giggled and brought her eyes back up Mike's face.

Mike was looking down her front. She looked down, realizing her dress had floated up around her waist. He was staring at slender legs, a small waist, and hair showing through her panties.

Linda glanced quickly back to Mike's face and down his front. The flagpole was back to full size and standing tall. She brought her eyes back up to meet his. She saw a desire so strong in Mike's eyes that it made her shiver all over with anxiety.

Mike slowly raised his hand and brushed some hair out of her face. Their eyes locked. His hand was slightly rough and warm touching her face, but it sent sensations rushing through her body. She leaned her head toward his hand. Slowly he brought his other hand up, and with both hands cupping her face, his lips lowered to cover hers. It was a slow, gentle kiss. He ran his tongue slowly over her lips. Linda opened her mouth to him, inviting further intimacies. He slid his tongue into her mouth, massaging her tongue. It sent tiny shivers of delight through her body. Closing her eyes, Linda tilted her head back, and Mike plunged his tongue deep into her mouth.

"Oh, Mike," she groaned.

He continued an assault on her body. Lowering his arms, never breaking the kiss, he put his arms around her waist and pulled her hard against his body. She could feel his throbbing arousal just above her hot spot on her panties. She could feel his heat through her panties. She put her arms around Mike's neck and pulled her body up until he touched her burning desire.

Mike let go of her waist and grabbed her by her buttocks, pulling her closer. She wrapped her legs around his waist and arched against him. They were burning up with passion and desire to make love to each other.

Placing her hands on his chest, she pushed back, breaking the kiss. "Put me down."

Mike took it that she wanted to stop. He lowered her until her feet touched the bottom of the pool.

Their eyes locked. She commanded softly, "Help me get out of my clothes. I want you to make love to me."

With trembling fingers, he unbuttoned the front of her dress. When he had finished, she raised her arms above her head.

"Take it off."

Mike pulled the dress off over her head and tossed it on the sand. She turned her back to him so he could unfasten her bra. She pulled the bra off and tossed it on the sand. With trembling hands, he hooked his thumbs in her panties, holding his breath while the water covered his head. He slid her panties down her legs to her feet.

When she stepped out of them, he stood back up and tossed them on the sand. Linda turned back around to face Mike. She was ready to make love.

"Mike, I want you to make love to me."

"I thought you would never ask."

Her arms went around his neck, and she kissed him. Starved for his lips on hers and the touch of his tongue, her tongue flirted with his until he filled her mouth with his tongue. She moaned in response. Mike slowly ran his hands up and down her back. He then grabbed her rump, pulling her tightly against his body, crushing her firm breasts and rigid nipples against his chest. She could feel his hard shaft on her belly. She wanted him inside her.

"I want you inside me."

"Take it easy. Let's go slow."

She pulled up with her arms, trying to make contact with his shaft against her hot center of passion.

With his hands on her buttocks, he raised her above his shaft. She locked her legs around his waist and murmured, "Now, Mike, please now."

Mike lowered her until the tip of his shaft entered her hot moist bed of passion. She was very tight, and he was afraid of hurting her.

"No, don't stop. I want all of you in me now. Please all the way home." She arched her back to take all of him.

Mike lowered her and thrust deep into her hot flesh. All the way in, he paused to give her an evocative sensation with his hot shaft throbbing wildly inside her.

"Oh, Mike! Oh, Mike! Oh, Mike!"

Linda drew in a deep breath and tightened the muscles of her passion around him. She was driving him crazy.

He started to thrust slowly and then ran wild. He had lost control. He wanted to make it last, but it was too late. He slammed into her hard.

"Oh yes, oh yes!" cried Linda.

He could feel her tighten and throbbing around him as she whimpered in passion. "I'm coming, I'm coming! Faster, faster, faster!"

He knew she was ready for a big explosion. "Hold on a little longer."

"I can't! Oh, it feels so good!"

"I'm coming too."

Then with a final thrust, they both quivered and exploded at the same time. For a long time, they were clinging to each other, waiting for their labored breathing to slow down.

"Oh, Mike, it was wonderful! You make me feel so good."

With a teasing smile, Mike replied, "You weren't so bad yourself."

"I thought the pool would be boiling by now from our heat." Linda laughed.

Mike was still holding her tightly against him with his manhood still inside her. "We can go again if you want to."

She felt him growing inside her. "We can do it again so soon?"

"Yes, so soon. I've been dreaming of nothing but this for so long. But let's go out on the sand. I have a blanket behind the truck seat."

"Oh yes, let's do it again!"

Linda unwound her legs from around his waist, and he lowered her until her feet touched the bottom of the pool. The water came up just above her nipples.

"I'll get the blanket." He waded out of the water.

He streaked up the bank to the pickup on the side facing away from the road. He removed the blanket from behind the seat and on impulse, took a spare shirt he kept in the pickup for when he got dirty working.

Linda watched Mike spread the blanket on the sand. She nervously fingered the ends of her long hair. She was a little embarrassed, standing in the pool nude. She didn't want to come out of the water.

She gazed at the male body standing in the middle of the blanket. His arousal was waiting for her.

Mike smiled and opened his arms for her to come to him. She hedged, trying to stay in the pool.

"What if someone comes by and sees us?"

"They will get a good show."

"But it's in the daylight."

"Are you chicken to come out of the water?"

"Yes. No, I don't know."

"Are you having second thoughts about doing it again?"

"Yes. I mean no, I don't know."

"It's just different out there in the open."

"Yes, it is different, in front of God and everything. I don't care, because I love you," said Mike quietly.

Linda stared at Mike. Had he said he loved her? "What did you say?"

"I said I love you!" he yelled.

She slowly waded out of the pool and went into Mike's open arms. Her arms went around his neck. "I love you too."

Hastily his arms went around her waist and pulled her against his body. Mike kissed her mouth, neck, and lower to her throbbing nipples. He ran his tongue over and around each nipple in turn, then gently sucking each one. Mike touched the bottom of her breast with his tongue, descending lower to her navel and across her flat belly. Linda ran her fingers through his hair, arching her back and moaning softly.

Mike cupped her buttocks with his hands and touched his final destination with his tongue. With her fingers in his hair, she pulled his head against her and arched her back. All she could do was moan. It felt so good. She felt wild and free. Mike looked up at her.

"I want to love you, taste you, touch you, hold you, and make you mine."

"Do it. Make me yours forever."

Mike lowered her gently down onto the blanket beside him. With a sigh, Linda leaned her head back on the blanket and gazed at the blue sky. Mike continued caressing her body, making her skin tingle. He ran his tongue around a rigid nipple before gently sucking on it.

Linda could lay forever with Mike doing wonderful things to her body. She couldn't get enough. She wanted more. He ran a hand up her inner thigh, caressing as he moved higher, finally touching the delicate part of her womanhood.

"I'm going to take it slow this time and make it last."

"Don't go too slow. I can't take it." She moaned and rocked her head from side to side, arching her hips to receive the fingers that probed gently in her moist opening.

"Oh yes, oh yes!" She bucked against his hand.

"You like that?"

"Yes yes, keep doing it."

Moving between her thighs, bracing his hands on each side of her head, their passion filled eyes locked on each other, Mike thrust deep, sheathing his shaft completely in her hot body. Locked together, she arched her back each time he thrust. Linda whimpered with hot passion, digging her nails in Mike's back, making him thrust deep and faster. They reached the top of the world at about the same time.

"Oh, Mike! Oh, Mike! Oh my god!"

Linda felt her hot liquid explosion first, and a split second later, she felt Mike throbbing. She felt him fill her with hot liquid deep inside her body.

"Oh yes yes!" cried Linda.

Mike lowered his chest over her breasts, and Linda wrapped her legs around his waist. She stroked his back while savoring his body pressing down on her. If only they could remain like this forever!

"I had better get off. I'm heavy," whispered Mike.

"No no, not yet. I love your body covering mine."

Her throbbing center drained the last drop of liquid from Mike and then slowly became passive. After a long time, Mike finally rolled off Linda and lay beside her.

"Can you stay awhile?" asked Mike.

"Yes, for a little while."

"Good. We can get a suntan before the sun goes down."

"We can get one all over." Linda giggled.

Exhausted, they lay on their backs, side by side, their hot bodies touching, in the middle of the blanket. Linda closed her eyes to keep the sun out and to dream about what just happened. She could still feel where Mike had touched her, and her body tingled. She went over their lovemaking in her mind over and over. Mike had made her his love.

"I belong to you now," she murmured.

She dozed off to sleep. Mike sat beside her and watched her sleep. Her long hair fanned out around her face, lips slightly swollen from their many kisses, nipples red from him sucking on them, and the center of her passion still moist. She looked like a woman thoroughly loved.

She had a smile on her face and looked contented. He liked to just sit and watch her sleep. He glanced over her naked body one more time.

"Wake up, lazybones. The sun is down, and it's time to go home."

"I want to sleep," murmured Linda.

*Now what?* thought Mike. His eyes had a wicked gleam as he spread Linda's legs and moved between them. Linda opened her eyes and felt his weight on her. She saw the raw hunger in Mike's eyes.

"Third time is the charm," whispered Mike.

"Oh yes yes," Linda replied.

Mike kissed her, and she arched her back to receive his first thrust. There was no restraint to their passion. She wound her legs around him, and they picked up a fast rhythm. Linda rolled her pelvis and thrust up each time Mike thrust down. She was driving him crazy.

"I can't hold back any longer!" he cried.

"Go for it. I'm ready too," she said. "I'm coming! I'm coming!"

"Linda, Linda," moaned Mike.

Mike gave her one final deep thrust. Their bodies quivered as they reached a climax together. Afterward, they took a dip in the pool, splashing each other with cool water.

"I hate to go, but I must. I should have been home hours ago."

They waded out of the pool, hand in hand. Linda put on her panties, and Mike handed her his shirt. It struck her about four inches above her knees.

"The shirt looks better on you than it does on me. Why don't you keep the shirt?" Every time you wear it, think of today and what we shared. Their eyes locked. "It was wonderful," said Mike.

"I know. I can't get enough of you." Linda sighed. "But I got to go."

She melted into his arms for a final kiss. Then she made her way up the bank with shoes, dress, and bra in her hands. She walked to where she had left her car. She didn't want to leave. Every part of her body was tuned to Mike. Never had she ever felt like she did right now.

*I belong to Mike, and he belongs to me.* It felt so good.

She waved at Mike before getting in her car and heading home. Mike watched her go and felt that part of him was missing. He felt complete with Linda with him. He wondered if Linda meant what she said. She had confessed her love for him, and he had told her he loved her.

"Linda, my love, how I love thee!" quoted Mike.

He dressed, picked up the blanket, and made his way up the bank to his pickup. He turned and took one last look at the place they had made love. This place was truly a paradise.

When Linda got home, she thought about trying to sneak in but changed her mind. She had just turned eighteen. She was a woman now. She walked in singing a Western love song and headed down the hall to her bedroom. Mrs. Carson got a glimpse of her as she walked by. She shook her head. *Where is the pretty dress she left in to go to the movie?* She wanted to ask but said, "Did you have a good time at the movies, dear?"

"Yes, it was a good movie. Connie and I had a good time."

She didn't lie. She just didn't tell her what happened after the movie. Linda smiled. That was when the good time began. Her mother would never know just how good a time she had.

Linda hung her dress and bra over the shower rod. She would have to tell her mother something sooner or later. Make that later. She was still high on love. She touched her fingers to her lips that were slightly swollen. She removed her shirt, Mike's shirt, and glanced at the mirror on the dresser. Her breasts and nipples were red and a little sore. She knew that would not be the only thing sore in the morning. She smiled, but it was well worth it.

Mike had confessed his love for her, and she had confessed her love for him. Now that it was out in the open, they could move on with their lives. She knew Mike had a problem with her being rich and him being poor, but somehow they would work it out. It would just take time.

Linda couldn't wait to see Mike at school tomorrow. Then it struck her about their class difference. She was shocked when she realized how little contact they had at school. Well, that was going to change tomorrow.

Mike was on cloud nine when he got home. His mother sat across the table while he ate. She watched him and saw the glow in his eyes.

"You look like a young man in love. Linda confessed her love for you." It was a statement, not a question.

"How did you know?"

"I saw the same glow in your father's eyes many years ago when I confessed I loved him. That was a long time ago."

Mike watched as his mother was caught up in the past. Then it struck Mike that nothing had changed—she was rich, and he was still poor. Mrs. Love watched her son turn from happy one minute and sad the next. Her heart went out to him.

"What is wrong, Son?"

"I guess I just woke up from an impossible dream."

"Nothing is impossible if there is enough love."

"I hope you are right."

"Trust me, everything will work out."

Parking her car in the school parking lot, Linda waited for Mike to arrive. Mike parked the ranch pickup next to Linda's car. She stuck her head inside the truck. "I have been waiting to walk you to class."

"Are you sure that's a good idea?"

"I'm going to show my love for you."

"What will your high-class friends think with you having something to do with a low class like me?"

"I don't give a damn what they think. Now get out of the truck before we are late for class."

Mike got out of the truck, and Linda took his hand. "Let's go."

They walked up the steps and down the hall. Punky, Leroy, Rex, and Gary spoke, but all her friends, except Connie, didn't know her.

"Did we just walk through an ice storm?" Linda giggled.

"I think we did. It sure got cold in the passageway."

"So I don't have any friends."

"I'm sorry, Linda."

"I'm not, and now I know who my true friends are."

Pecking Mike lightly on the lips, Linda turned and headed for her first class. "See you at the ranch," said Linda over her shoulder.

Standing in a daze, Mike watched Linda walk away. He realized she loved him and didn't care what people thought.

"That's our man," said Punky. They came at him from all sides.

"When did this happen?" asked Leroy.

"Boy, how did you do it?" asked Rex.

"Do what?"

"Land one of the best-looking girls in school while all the other guys couldn't get to first base."

"We are just good friends. I work for her dad at the ranch."

"Yes, and it just rained here in the hall," teased Punky.

"You're close, because we just had an ice storm in the hall."

Mike turned and headed for his first class. Punky, Leroy, Rex, and Gary stared at his retreating bask.

"Now what do you suppose he meant by that remark?" asked Punky.

The school handed out class rings that afternoon. Mike stared at the ring on his finger on his way to work at the ranch. It was a custom to give your ring to your girlfriend, and she would give you her ring. He wanted to give Linda his ring, but they had never been on a date. *After the cold shoulder by her friends at school, maybe she had second thoughts about our relationship.* Mike decided to wait. He couldn't stand it if she rejected him. He had a gold chain in his pocket if he changed his mind.

Checking on the horses, feeding, cleaning the stable, and brushing the horses, Mike couldn't get Linda off his mind. He had to snap out of it, or it would hurt his work, and a school test was coming up.

He finished his work and was on his way out when a new horse was led into the barn by one of the ranch hands.

"Where do you want me to put her?" asked Patrick.

"Put her in the end stall."

"Do you have a feeding schedule for her?"

"I'll get one for her."

Patrick handed Mike the mare's papers. He read them over. Mike put his arm around the mare's neck.

"Well, Duchess, you have a date with Lightning. He is going to like you."

Mike went into the tack room and returned with a feeding schedule. "Feed her a normal schedule for right now."

"Yes, sir."

"Patrick, you don't have to sir me. I'm just one of the hands. Besides, you are old enough to be my father. I should sir you."

Patrick gazed at Mike in disbelief. "You have been the boss for a long time and haven't even realized it. Haven't you noticed when you are on the ranch that all the hands come to you for help and what work needs to be done?"

"I just thought Mr. Carson was out of pocket."

"He is slowly working you into the full-time foreman position. He will probably promote you when you finish school, and with it comes a big pay raise."

Staring at Patrick with his mouth open, Mike was in shock. He didn't know about it and couldn't believe what Patrick was saying.

"Close your mouth, Mike, or you are going to catch a fly," teased Patrick.

"When did you know about this?"

"I knew when Mrs. Carson started teaching you the ranch books. The foreman is the only ranch hand to work on the books."

"Do you think I can handle the job?"

"Damn right. I know you can."

"All the hands are older than I am. Won't they be mad? And what about you, Patrick? You have been with Mr. Carson the longest, and you came with him from Oklahoma."

"We had a foreman in Oklahoma, but he didn't want to move to Texas. Since then, Mr. Carson has been looking for a new foreman."

"But I am too young for the job."

"Age has nothing to do with it. The other hands and I are followers, and you are a natural-born leader. It's as simple as that. You lead, and we will follow you."

"Thanks, Patrick."

"No sweat, and I didn't say anything." He turned and led the mare to her stall.

Mike finished his work and headed for his truck. Linda was waiting for him. She wore shorts, a white blouse, and had her hair in a ponytail. She looked so fresh and smelled of bubble bath.

"Do you want to stay for supper?"

"Sure if your mother doesn't object."

Linda let the remark slide. "You have to work for your supper by taking me to the store for a few things."

"I'll get the truck."

"Let's go in my car." She handed Mike the keys. "You drive."

Linda watched as Mike turned onto the highway and picked up speed. She slid over next to him and put her hand on his inner thigh. Instantly, she felt a hot flash go up her arm, through her body, and down to her toes. Mike's body had the same reaction to her touch. It was like touching a hot power line to ground and watching the fire fly.

"You had better move that hand, or we may be very late getting back to the ranch," whispered Mike.

"Oh," teased Linda.

She removed her hand but stayed close to him. She loved to tease Mike and watch him lose control.

"Are you going to the Sadie Hawkins dance?"

He frowned. "Probably. At least I won't feel out of place. I won't have to dress. I can come as myself."

Linda's temper flared. "You are not just a country boy!"

"I'm sorry, but I know my place. I have been put in it enough through high school."

"Don't pay any attention to them because they don't know you."

Mike started to say something else but changed his mind. They rode in silence the rest of the way to the store.

The store was on the edge of town. It was a small mom-and-pop store. Mike parked the car on the side of the store. He came around to open the car door for her. Linda liked it when Mike was a gentleman. They went around to the front of the store and went through the open door.

They walked in on a robbery in progress. A large man was standing at the counter with a gun trained on the cashier.

"OK, bitch, you have stalled long enough, and now you are dead meat."

"No!" screamed Mike. He slammed into the robber. A split second his pistol fired, the bullet missing Betty Pool's head by only a half inch and going through a window behind her.

Mike and the robber landed on the floor, with the robber dropping his pistol, and it went sailing across the floor toward where Linda was standing. Mike got to his feet first.

"Get out of here, Linda."

She couldn't move. It was like her feet were glued to the floor.

"Get out of here, Linda!"

The robber was slowly getting to his feet. The man was huge, six feet three inches, and two hundred and fifty pounds. Mike knew if he was going to have a chance, he would have to get in the first lick.

He slammed a fist into the robber's head, but it didn't faze him.

"Oh shit," Mike said weakly.

He slammed a fist into the robber's gut, and the same result. It didn't faze him.

"Now it's my turn, punk."

The robber grabbed Mike and threw him across the store, crashing into shelves of can goods. The robber came after him, slamming a fist into his gut and face. Mike went down. The robber turned to go after the pistol. Mike tripped him, and he went down.

"Linda, get out of here before it is too late!" screamed Mike.

"OK, punk, you haven't had enough. Now I'm mad." He jumped on Mike and started beating him.

Linda knew she had to do something. She ran over and grabbed the robber by the hair on his head. He tossed her back across the room like she was a rag doll. She got back on her feet and watched the fight. She knew Mike was losing the fight.

Mike could feel the darkness closing in on him. He didn't move anymore. The robber pulled out a large knife and started to open it. Linda watched in horror.

"Now, punk, I'm going to cut you."

"No!," screamed Linda.

He was going to kill Mike, her love and her life! She grabbed the pistol and charged the robber. She hit him behind the head as hard as she could. He fell forward on top of Mike, like he was poleaxed. The knife just missed Mike, sticking in the floor next to his left ear.

Linda dropped the gun while going to her knees, pushing and pulling on the robber. She was trying to get him off Mike. She looked up at Betty.

"Don't just stand there. Call the police and an ambulance."

Betty was in shock and just stood there.

"Snap out of it, Betty. Call the police and an ambulance."

Finally, she picked up the phone and called.

"Betty, help me get this monster off Mike."

Betty went back in shock and just stood there. "I can't."

Linda pushed and pulled until she got the big ape off Mike. She ran her fingers over his face. He had a busted lip, several small cuts, and some bruises on his face.

"Are you all right? Speak to me!" she begged.

Tears ran down her face. She loved him so much it hurt. The big ape was trying to kill him, and all the time he was trying to get her out of harm's way. Linda kissed him and got blood on her face, but she didn't care. Mike moaned and opened his eyes.

"Oh, Mike!" cried Linda, and she kissed him again. She backed off a little. "Are you all right? Where does it hurt?"

Mike tried to move, but it hurt, and he lay back down. It hurt all over, something like the flu. He tried to smile, but it hurt his busted lip.

The police arrived, lights flashing and siren wailing. The ambulance was right behind the police car. A policeman came through the door like a storm trooper, with his gun drown. After glancing around the store, picking up the gun and knife, he asked, "Betty, what happened here?"

She pointed to the robber on the floor. "He started to rob me, and when I wouldn't give him the money, he tried to kill me."

"Yes yes, and then what happened?"

"I don't know. I blanked out."

The policeman looked at Mike. "From the looks of you, maybe you can tell me what happened next."

"I charged the robber as he fired his gun at Betty, and then we had a fight."

"Then what happened?"

"He was beating me on the floor when I passed out.

"Great. Now someone tell me who put the robber on ice."

The policeman looked at Betty.

"Not me. I don't remember what happened."

"Then that just leaves you." He stared at Linda.

Linda gave the policeman a dazzling smile. He stared at her.

"Are you ready to tell me what happened?"

With a surge of satisfaction, she announced, "I put out his lights!"

"And how did you do that?"

"I hit him with his pistol."

"Where did you get the gun?"

"He dropped it on the floor when Mike charged him. He was beating Mike, and he pulled a knife. I had to do something, or he would have killed Mike. I picked up his gun and hit him as hard as I could."

"You did a good job because he is still out. How is he?" the policeman asked the ambulance driver.

"He will be all right, just a bad headache," explained the ambulance driver.

"Good. Let me get the handcuffs on him before he wakes up."

The robber started to come around. He looked at his handcuffed hands, around the room, and then at the policeman.

"Wait a minute," said the policeman.

"What are you looking at?" snarled the robber.

"This guy escaped from jail in Houston. He is wanted for murder, rape, robbery, and who knows what else. He is a bad one."

Linda and Betty both fainted.

"Just great. Now that is all over, and they faint." Laughed Mike.

The ambulance driver gave them both smelling salts. Mike kissed Linda when she came around.

"That sure is a good way to wake up." Linda giggled.

The ambulance driver looked at Mike. "Now let me take a look at you."

After a few minutes, he announced, "Nothing broken, but you will probably be sore for a couple of days."

The police had taken the robber to jail, and the store was back to normal, except for some can goods on the floor. Linda picked up the items for her mother. Mike managed to get up and stand by the checkout counter.

The police had taken a statement from Linda, Mike, and Betty. They wouldn't have to go down to the station.

"I guess you know we will be on the front page of the newspaper tomorrow and probably some of the large papers also. That was a big crook that we caught," said Betty.

"We did what?" asked Linda.

"OK, you caught the bad guy."

"Thank you."

Betty stared at Mike while she checked them out. After sacking Linda's groceries, she came around the counter and faced Mike. "You are my hero. You saved my life." She slid her arms around Mike's neck and put a lip-lock on him. Linda stormed out the door. Mike trailed Linda to her car. She got into her car and slammed the door. Mike got in slowly. It hurt just to move. Linda looked straight ahead.

They rode in silence. Linda thought to herself, *How silly of me! Betty was just thanking him. Why didn't she just say thank you?*

Linda turned and kissed Mike on his cheek. "You are my hero," she teased.

He slammed on the brakes and turned down a dirt road leading into the woods. He stopped the car in the woods and turned to face her. "You can do better than that."

She leaned forward to touch her lips to Mike's, slowly tracing his lips with her tongue until she touched the place where his lip was busted. Linda ran her tongue deep into his mouth, and her hands dropped to his lap to caress him through his pants. Mike had an instant erection.

Mike shuddered and raised his buttocks off the seat, pushing against her hands. It pleased her she could make him shudder with pleasure. She wanted to do wonderful things to him.

Linda began with the hollow at the base of his throat. Unbuttoning his shirt, she left a trail of blazing kisses down his chest, stopping at his belt. Her brain told her to go home. But her body had a mind of her own. Heat, when she touched him, brought her excitement to a level where she had to have more. Her breasts were swollen, the nipples as hard as marbles, and she had an aching between her legs that only Mike could cure.

"Mike, make love to me."

"That might be a little hard in this small car."

"I guess we should have driven the pickup."

"It's too late to cry over spilled milk."

"Oh well, where there is a will, there is a way."

Linda reached for his belt. He grabbed her hands and put them around his waist. It was like an electric shock going up her arms and through her body.

Touching his bare skin made her quiver. She was burning up and wanted more. She wanted Mike inside her.

"Wait a minute. Now it's my turn." Mike started to unbutton the front of her blouse, his eyes locked with hers. She leaned forward kissing him, while he reached around behind her to unfasten her bra. He slowly and lovingly removed her blouse and bra.

"You are beautiful," he said, smoothing his palms over her breasts, teasing her nipples with his thumbs, leaning forward to kiss and suck each nipple in turn. She ran her fingers through his hair and embraced him against her.

"I love you."

"I love you more."

"Damn this small car. Why do you drive something this small?"

"Simple. I have never done things like this before in my car." She giggled.

"That's not all our problem."

"What is our problem?"

"My condoms are in the pickup."

Linda looked at Mike with love and desire in her eyes. "I don't want you to use one. I want you inside me without any barrier. I think it is the safe time of the month, but I'll take a chance anytime with you, because I love you."

She pushed her seat back, removing her shorts and panties. She placed them on them on the console between them. Turning in her seat, she lay on her back, throwing one leg over the seat and one on the dash, spreading wide for further intimacies.

She whispered impatiently, "Are you going to make love to me, or shall I start without you?" She got the giggles.

"Wait for me." He pushed the seat back, removing his pants and shorts. She helped him with his shirt.

It was a slow process because he was still in pain. The robber had done a number on his body. Do or die trying, he was going to make love to Linda. He turned in his seat and positioned himself between her legs.

Mike lowered himself until his erection touched the opening to her womanhood. She quivered at the lightly tickling touch. "Are you ready to make love?"

"Yes, do it now."

Her hand closed around his erection to guide him home. She arched her body to meet him as he plunged deep inside her body. Mike set the rhythm, and she followed his lead. Linda thought she would die from the sensation and pleasure. She locked her legs tightly around his back as stars burst before her eyes. She shuddered and climaxed. She released him, and he started a slow deep thrust. Her muscles contracted around his manhood. Mike called her name over and over again. He gave her one final deep thrust, and they both shuddered and climaxed together. Mike was still inside her and lay on top of her until his organ began to soften, and then reluctantly he sat up.

Linda sat up and giggled. "When are we going to make love in a bed?"

"Someday soon I hope," teased Mike.

"Well, it won't be too soon for me."

"Me neither. A bed would be nice."

"Mike, you can love me anywhere."

"Oh really? Is that a fact?"

"That didn't come out right."

"It sounded good to me."

It was almost dark when they pulled in front of the ranch house. Mrs. and Mr. Carson ran out of the front door to meet them.

"We just heard the news on the radio. Are you two all right?"

"We are fine, Mom."

"Mike, you don't look so good," said Mr. Carson.

"I'm just a little sore. I'll be fine in a couple of days."

"You were so late getting back, I went ahead and fixed supper. Come on to the supper table."

"OK, let's eat."

Mike had trouble eating and drinking with a busted lip. His jaw hurt when he tried to eat, but he did manage to eat some. After a quick meal, Mike went home. He was worried in case his parents heard the news on the radio.

They both met him at the door, wanting to know what happened. Mike took his time telling them what happened at the store but leaving out what happened on the way back to the ranch.

"Well, I hope they lock the robber up and throw away the key," said Mrs. Love.

After taking a long hot bath, Mike took inventory of the cuts and bruises over his body. His body still hurt. He finally lay down to rest his hurting body.

"I wonder what tomorrow will bring."

Linda was waiting beside her car when Mike pulled into the parking lot at school. He pulled in beside her and parked. He was slow getting out of his truck.

"What's the matter? Getting old?" teased Linda.

"To tell the truth, I sure could have used some help getting out of bed this morning."

Linda put her arm around his waist. "Lean on me," she teased.

"Every bone in my body feels like it is broken."

"Poor baby. Would you like me to kiss where it hurts and make it better?"

He pointed to his lips. "It hurts right here."

She surprised him when she kissed him on the lips right there in the parking lot. "Does it feel better now?"

"Yes, I think I might live now." He laughed.

Betty was waiting at the top of the stairs for them, along with a pack of kids, all waiting to hear the story from the horse's mouth. Mike thought, *How stupid!* He had to get beat half to death for some of the kids in the crowd to speak to him and recognize him. Linda glanced at him and knew what he was thinking.

"Count to ten," she whispered.

He glanced back at her and smiled. "I can't count that high."

"Count as high as you can and start over." She grinned at him.

The next few days were very hectic. Mike and Linda had test after test at school and trouble at the ranch. Two mares were close to the time of having their colts and were having trouble. Mike stayed late hours at the ranch, watching over them. Linda would bring food and drink while they watched over the mares. They would study for tests at the same time.

Friday evening, Linda asked, "Mike, are you taking me to the dance?"

He seemed reluctant to pull his gaze from the mares. One of the things she learned about Mike was that he took his work very seriously. As much as she wanted him to take her to the dance, she knew he would stay with the mares if they needed him.

"Mike, are you taking me to the dance? I know if you need to be with the horses, it will be all right."

Seeing her head lower in disappointment, Mike smiled. "Go on to the dance, and I will join you there."

"Are you sure?"

"Yes, your dad said he would watch the mares tonight. He didn't want us to miss the dance. I think he wants us to be together."

"Mother seems to like you now. I think she knows that I love you."

"I have to go home and get cleaned up so I don't smell like a horse. Then everybody would call me a country boy." Laughed Mike.

Linda put her arms around his neck and kissed him. "See you later, country boy."

He put his arm around her and his hand on her buttocks as they left the barn. She swatted his hand away.

"Country boys don't do that." She giggled.

Being rich had its problems, Linda found out when she was going to get dressed. She didn't have any old clothes to wear. She took a new pair of jeans and sewed patches on them. She took a nice shirt and cut some holes in it. She did her hair in pigtails. She didn't use any makeup, only some perfume behind her ears and between her breasts. Her thoughts went back to the last time she and Mike made love. Her face flushed, and her body became hot.

*That country boy sure has an effect on me.* She smiled.

Linda put her class ring on a chain and put it in her pocket. She filled out two nametags and put them in her pocket. She was ready to go.

"Don't stay out too late," Mrs. Carson instructed.

"I won't," said Linda over her shoulder on the way out.

Being poor didn't have any problems. Mike pulled out one of his old faded shirts and a threadbare pair of jeans from the closet that he had worn while working on the farm.

After a hot bath, he got dressed. He didn't have any problem looking the part of an old country boy. He put on an old pair of shoes and finished off his dress with a piece of rope for a belt.

He took off his class ring and put it on a chain, just in case Linda wanted to swap class rings. He took a good look at himself in the mirror.

*Not too bad. I am just an old country boy.*

Linda arrived a little late at the dance. A few couples were already dancing. She spotted Connie and Punky at a table and went over to join them.

"What? No date?" Connie asked Linda.

"No."

"Do you want a date? I think my brother still wants to go out with you."

"No, I want to pick my own."

It was a traditional dance. The boys ask the girls to dance the first half. The last half the girls chose the one they wanted to dance with. The boy that wanted a date with a girl would ask her to dance and try to impress her, hoping she would pick him the last half. Since a lot of the boys or girls didn't how to dance or were shy, it gave the girl a chance to make the first move and show a shy boy she liked him.

Linda was constantly asked to dance. She liked to dance but wished Mike was there and would ask her to dance. She watched the door for him. The dance was almost half-over, and Mike still hadn't shown up.

"I'll kill him," mumbled Linda.

"What did you say?" asked Connie.

"I didn't say anything."

One of the football hunks asked her to dance and started coming on to her. He didn't want to take no for an answer.

"You're not my type," said Linda.

"And just what is your type?" he wanted to know.

"Stick around until half-time, and you will see."

Mike came in late and stood against the wall, watching Linda while she danced. She hadn't seen him come in. She looked right at home on the dance floor with the hunk and her other rich friends. He didn't want to embarrass her by asking her to dance.

Linda spotted him and was wondering why he hadn't come over to ask her to dance. His head was slightly drooped, and he looked like he had lost his best friend or girl. Maybe one of the mares was real sick.

Then it struck her what was wrong with Mike. She knew he didn't want to embarrass her in front of her friends.

"There is Mike standing by himself against the wall."

"I see him."

"Why doesn't he come and join us?" asked Connie.

"He needs an attitude adjustment, and I'll take care of that in a few minutes."

"What did you say?" asked Connie.

"Not a thing."

"Do you have a problem, Linda? I'm your best friend. Talk to me."

"Not anymore. I don't."

"What are you up to?"

"I'm going to stake my claim."

"What on earth are you talking about?"

"In a few minutes, you will find out." Linda smiled.

The band stopped playing, and the bandleader made the announcement. "Girls, the next dance is for you. Pick the mate of your choice."

Mike started to leave, but he had to see whom Linda picked. *No, I can't take that.* With his head down, he turned and walked slowly toward the door.

Linda was waiting at the door with her hands on her hips. Mike looked up as he reached the door.

"And just where do you think you are going?" asked Linda.

"I'm leaving because I don't belong here."

"You belong anywhere you want to be, but right now you belong to me."

Linda pulled out the nametags and pinned one on Mike. She handed the other one to Mike to pin on her.

"Read them."

The one Linda pinned on Mike read "I belong to Linda," and the one he pinned on her read "I belong to Mike."

She pulled her class ring from her pocket and placed it around Mike's neck. He pulled his class ring and placed around Linda's neck.

With a slow coaxing smile, she said, "Now kiss me."

"Here, in front of everyone?"

"Here and now."

"Won't we get in trouble?"

"Who cares? Kiss me."

She went into his arms, and he kissed her, causing a lot of heads to turn. From across the dance floor, there was a loud yell.

"Attaboy! What a way to go, Mike!" yelled Punky.

"Now dance with me." Linda pulled Mike out onto the dance floor. It was a slow dance, and Linda molded her body to Mike's body. They moved around the dance floor as one. When a fast dance started, Linda wanted him to dance with her like he danced with Shirley in Oklahoma.

"Pull out all the stops. Let's fly."

Mike took charge, and Linda followed. They were burning the dance floor up. Before the dance number was over, the couples around them stopped dancing and formed a circle around them. They were clapping them on. They were one hot couple on the dance floor, and the crowd loved it.

When the dance was over, Linda wanted to know how he learned to dance. "Living in the country, folks got together at someone's house and have a big dance. I learned by watching when I was small, but the most fun was sitting on the floor and looking up the girls' dresses while they danced."

"Why you little devil!" Linda giggled.

"You wouldn't believe how many different-colored panties there are."

"I think you are making that up."

"No, I'm not. Scout's honor."

"You never were a scout."

"Yes, but I wanted to be one."

While dancing the last dance, Mike asked, "What do you want to do after the dance?"

Linda pressed her body closer. "What do you think?"

"Are we going in my truck or your car?" They both laughed, remembering the last time they made love in her car. They left in the pickup to find a place to park.

"You realize we may have a hard time finding a place to park with the dance over and all the other couples also looking for a place to park," remarked Mike.

"Where can we go?"

Mike thought hard for a moment. "I know the perfect place."

He made a U-turn in the middle of the road and headed back to school. Linda was puzzled at where he was going.

"Where are you going?"

"We are going to pick up your car."

"Then where are we going?"

"Just follow me, and let it be a surprise."

"OK, country boy, but it had better be good," teased Linda.

Mike parked the truck overlooking the waterfall on his land. He got out of his truck and stood looking at the waterfall. Linda pulled in beside his truck and got out to join him.

"God, how I love this place!" said Mike.

Linda leaned with her back to him and against his chest. Mike put his arms around her waist, pulling her closer. She could feel his arousal against her buttocks.

"I have this dream," said Mike.

"Tell me about it."

"In my dream, there is a beautiful home overlooking the waterfall."

He let go of her waist and started to undo her pigtails, letting her long hair fall down her back. Linda's body started to quiver while her passion heated up.

"In the dream, I approach the house, and a girl with long hair, wearing red shorts and a long white shirt, comes out to meet me. She rushes into my arms, and we kiss. What do think about my dream?"

"I love it," responded Linda.

Linda turned around to face him, placing her arms around his neck and pulling his head down.

"Are you going to kiss me?" She now felt his arousal growing more demanding against her belly. She took him by surprise when she reached for the zipper on his jeans.

"It wants out," she teased.

Mike brought his mouth crushing down on hers, thrusting his tongue deep into her sweetness.

Arching her body against him, she moaned, "Make love to me now."

Mike picked Linda up and sat her on the hood of the truck. She took off her shirt, and Mike watched the swell of her full breasts as she removed her bra. He rushed to capture a nipple in his mouth.

It was cool outside, but Linda was going up in flames of passion. "Oh, please I want you inside me! I'm burning up!"

Linda unzipped her jeans while Mike watched, sliding them down over her hips, followed by her panties. He pulled her shoes and socks off. She slid further back on the hood of the truck and spread her legs so Mike could see her throbbing center of passion.

Once more she had taken him by surprise. "You are a wanton woman, Linda Carson."

"Yes, I know. What are you going to do about it?"

Mike quickly removed his clothes, letting them fall to the ground. Then he jumped on the hood. He slid between her spread legs, with a slight hesitation, a quick thrust, and his hard manhood hit bottom in her throbbing passion. With an exasperated breath, she threw her arms around him and held him to her for a moment. It hurt a little since she was tight. Slowly she relaxed her grip, and Mike started to move slowly at first, and Linda arched to meet each thrust. He increased his speed until Linda threw her legs around him and locked them. Pure unadulterated pleasure rocked Linda as her throbbing passion tightened around his hard organ.

"Oh god, oh god, I'm coming! I'm coming!"

Linda had her climax and relaxed her death grip on him. Mike started to move again but only a few good thrusts before one deep thrust, and he exploded deep into her body. He fell forward, crushing her swollen breasts with his chest.

"Linda, that was great! You were so tight."

"I loved it too, but I will probably be sore tomorrow."

"I'm sorry."

"Don't be. I loved every minute of it."

Then the cool night air hit their sweaty bodies, and they started to shiver. Quickly they dressed and got into the truck.

Mike opened his arms and she went into them. "I love you," he said quietly.

"I love you too," she responded.

"Someday, I'm going to make that dream come true."

"I know you will."

They both looked at the waterfall and dreamed.

Linda giggled, and Mike glanced at her. "What?"

"When are we going to make love in our own bed or any bed for that matter?"

"Very soon I hope." He laughed.

"Well, I hope it's soon."

"But think how good it will be when we finally make love in bed."

"I don't know if it can get any better than tonight." She giggled.

"It will. I promise."

Mike and Linda went on their first real date to the senior prom. He had picked her up and pinned a flower on her dress. Linda was on cloud nine. They enjoyed the prom as young lovers. A lot of the girls were still cherry, but most of them lost it that night. Graduation followed, and then school was out.

Mike worked full-time on the ranch while Linda helped him. They were always together. They talked about her going off to college. She wanted to go to Oklahoma and be a sooner. When they lived in Oklahoma while she was growing up, that was her dream. Now she wasn't so sure. She still wanted to go, but she didn't want to leave Mike.

"Linda, you want to go to Oklahoma to college?"

"Yes, but I don't want to leave you. You are my other half now."

"You go the first year there and see how you like it. I'll work hard and save for us a small house over the waterfall."

"Are you sure you want me to go?"

"No, but a year won't be too bad. You can come home and visit. After the first year, we can play it by ear."

"I don't care how small the house is as long as we are together."

"Linda, I love you. Don't you go and find a boyfriend while in college."

"Buster, that goes for you too! No girlfriend while I'm gone."

The day after Linda left for college, Mr. Carson called Mike up to the house and made him foreman. He gave him a large pay raise to go with the job.

Two months before Linda finished her spring semester, a big fancy car pulled into the driveway at the ranch. A short fat man wanted to speak to Mr. Love. Mike was out at Lightning's corral. He missed Linda, and being around Lightning made him feel closer to her.

"That's a mighty nice horse you got there."

Mike turned to see who was talking to him. "The horse belongs to Mr. Carson's daughter."

"My name is George Watson."

"Mike Love, sir." They shook hands. "What can I do for you?"

"I work for a movie company that is making Western movies. We film a lot of movies on the Wilder Ranch in Oklahoma. You were up there delivering a horse, weren't you?"

"Yes, sir, I was."

"My job is getting things ready to shoot the movie, and right now I need a good horse trainer. I saw you when you delivered the horses to the ranch. I was highly impressed with your ability with horses. You are the best I have ever seen."

Mike stared at Mr. Watson with his mouth open. He didn't know what to say. He had lost his ability to talk.

Mr. Watson smiled at Mike. "Do you want the job?"

"Yes, sir," stuttered Mike.

"Do you have a place to train?"

"I have a piece of land with nothing on it."

"No problem. I'll send our construction crew down. I'll mail you a contract. I'm sure you will be satisfied with all it offers."

Mr. Watson made some notes and checked off "horse trainer" on his list of what he had to do. They shook hands again. He left with Mike staring after him. He was in shock.

Linda pulled into the driveway at the ranch where Mike was waiting for her. Her blood ran hot at the sight of him. She harried out of the car and ran into his arms.

"God, how I missed you!" said Linda.

"I missed you too."

"I feel it too." She giggled.

She glanced down between them. His arousal was pressing against her belly. "I think you want my body." She giggled.

"You are so right."

Mr. Carson glanced out the window and smiled. Everything was coming together, and he loved it. They were kissing. They walked up the walk, hand in hand.

"I have a surprise for you."

"What is it?"

"I want you to put on your red shorts and white shirt."

Linda's heart slammed against her ribs and went into overdrive. Did that mean what she thought? Was Mike's dream coming true? She stopped.

"You wait right here. I'll only be a minute."

"I'll time you."

Linda was back in only three minutes. She was in a hurry to see what Mike was up to. She was so excited she couldn't wait.

Mike stopped, overlooking the waterfall. Linda screamed in delight at the sight before her. Above the waterfall was a huge brick home, the house covering what looked like a city block. There was a large barn off to the side with several corrals around it.

There was a beautiful black stallion in one of the corrals. In another corral was Lightning and Thunder.

"But how did you do all of this? Did you strike oil on your land?"

"No, but you remember the movie crew in Oklahoma at the Wilder Ranch? I train their horses for the movies. The black stallion is my first one. This was a package deal. When I have a horse almost trained, they send an actor down to work with the horse. The back part of the house is for the actors. The rest of the house is ours."

"Oh, Mike, it's too good to be true!"

Mike grinned at her. "The house is ready to move into."

"It is."

"There is a large four-poster bed in the master bedroom."

Linda grabbed Mike by his arm. "Then what are you waiting for? Start this truck moving!"

# Epilogue

The sign above the cattle guard—Double L Ranch—stood for Linda and Mike Love. It was a nice size ranch since Mike started with only ten acres. For a wedding gift, Mr. Carson gave them one hundred acres next to his ranch. Mike bought ninety acres on the other side.

Linda drove across the cattle guard and stopped. She watched Thunder and Lightning racing to meet her. She gazed at their home above the waterfall. It was breathtaking. Linda thought, *How lucky I am!* She was only twenty-three years old. She had the man she loved, had finished college early, had a good job, and a beautiful home.

She touched her belly and smiled. She was carrying Mike's child. The doctor had given her the news today. She was three months gone and six more to go.

Linda had told Mike last night after they had made love that he may become a father. He was so happy that she thought he would squeeze her to death. Then they made slow love until two in the morning.

She was replaying each moment of lovemaking from last night when Thunder and Lightning ran up beside the car. Both of them were trying to stick their heads inside the car.

After petting Thunder and Lightning, she continued on to the house. Both horses raced along beside the car. They liked to escort her to the house every day when she came home from work.

Parking her car, she walked over to the corral. Mike, a young man, and a young woman were training a horse. They weren't doing too well.

Linda was dressed in a dress. It wasn't ladylike, but she climbed up on the top railing of the fence. Thunder and Lightning stuck a head over the fence on either side of her. Linda put her arms around their necks.

Linda glanced back and forth between the two horses. "Looks like Mike is having a little trouble with his training lesson."

Both horses bobbed their heads up and down to agree with Linda. Linda giggled at their reaction.

The horse in training was to play dead, but he had to turn his head and look at Linda and the two horses.

Mike counted to ten, trying to keep his cool. "OK, let's take a break and start over later. Maybe we can get it right the next time."

All three came over to the fence, looking very curious. Linda guessed Mike had told them about her visit to the doctor.

"Having trouble with your training lesson?" teased Linda.

"Yes, I think the only way to get that horse to play dead is to shoot him."

"What's the trouble with him?"

"He is so curious he is afraid he will miss something."

"Why don't you let Lightning show him how it's done?"

"Good idea. It might work."

The horse walked up behind Mike and nudged him for attention. Mike turned around and put his arm around the horse's neck.

Suddenly, a car was flying across the cattle guard, heading for them. Linda and Mike looked at each other.

"Punky."

He stopped the car beside Linda's car. Punky was out of the car first. Leroy, Gary, and Rex were close behind him. They were all carrying a six-pack of beer.

"What are you clowns up to now?" asked Mike.

"It's party time," announced Punky.

"Why is it party time?"

"We are all leaving to find our destiny. Mike, you have already found your destiny."

Punky and Leroy passed around the beer. Everyone, including the two actors, had a beer. Punky held up his beer.

"Rules of the game after each toast, we drink. I propose a toast to Rex, the best electronics engineer to go to work for Texas Instruments in Dallas. To Leroy, who has joined Dallas's finest. He is studying law. To Gary, who hasn't decided what he will do yet, but he will be the best in what he decides to do. To Mike and Linda, they have it all."

Punky glanced at the young couple standing beside Mike. "A toast to Mike's friends. Just what do you do for a living?"

"They are movie stars," replied Mike.

Punky looked at Mike like he was pulling his leg. Then he remembered that Mike trained horses for the movies.

Mike held up his beer. "A toast to Punky, our very best town banker!"

"Cancel that last toast," said Punky.

He walked over to his car and unlocked the trunk. He pulled out a hat and put it on. He was wearing a US Navy Officer's hat. Everyone stared at him.

"I report to Pensacola, Florida, for the rest of my flight training next week."

"What about you and Connie?" asked Linda.

"It's over. We broke up." Linda could see the pain in his eyes.

"I couldn't work as a bank flunky, and Connie wouldn't go with me when I joined the navy. She said I would always be where the action or adventure was. I guess she is right."

"Why did you join the navy?"

"To see the world and ride the waves!" Laughed Punky.

"Same old Punky," mumbled Mike.

"Which waves, Punky?" asked Linda.

"Guess."

Everyone laughed.

"OK, everyone up to the house for food and drinks. We will make this a night to remember," said Mike.

From the top railing, Linda held up her hands. "Before we go to the house, I would like to propose a toast. Mike, my loving husband and soon-to-be father of my baby!"

Mike stared at Linda for a moment before he fainted and fell over backwards.

"Well, I'll be damned! He fainted!" Laughed Punky.

The horse in training took it for his cue and fell over playing dead.

"Well, I'll be damned again," said Punky.

Everyone laughed when Linda jumped off the fence to check on Mike. The dead horse raised his head to see what was happening.